For all his chivalrous a... yesterday and his han... Grant Rathmore was a stranger.

She narrowed her eyes to regard him and was taken aback when he laughed suddenly.

"You would very much like to tell me to go to the devil, would you not? I confess I would like to do the same to you! I do not know when I have ever met such a stubborn lass and one so determined to have her own way. But you hired me to escort you and I cannot, will not, allow you to ride into danger."

Still she hesitated, and after a moment he exhaled, looking up at the sky before turning to address her again.

"You are not in Inverness now, Miss d'Evremont. You are a stranger to this country, but I am a Highlander. I understand this land and its people. I know how best to keep you safe. Trust me in this."

Could she trust him? Madeleine looked into his eyes. Instinct said she could do so, but her head urged caution. True, he had saved her honor, perhaps even her life, yesterday, but she knew nothing of him. But what choice did she have, other than to turn him away and proceed alone?

"Very well, sir, we will go your way."

Author Note

Even before I finished writing my first Highland romance, *Forbidden to the Highland Laird*, I knew that I wanted to revisit the Rathmore family. Logan and Ailsa's son, Grant, came of age at a very turbulent time in Scottish history. By his twenty-third birthday he is already a seasoned—if reluctant—soldier, having followed Bonnie Prince Charlie into England and back to Culloden, where the Jacobites suffered their overwhelming defeat on Drumossie Moor. It was the end of the Jacobite dream.

Grant survives Culloden, but he knows he cannot go home, nor can he stay in the Highlands, where the rebels are paying a terrible price for the uprising. However, rescuing Madeleine d'Evremont from attack gives him a purpose, to see the lady safely out of the country, but as they try to find their way to the coast, he discovers that Madeleine is far from a helpless damsel in distress; she has skills and courage that make her a perfect match for a Highlander.

Taking Grant and Madeleine on a perilous journey through the Highlands of Scotland was a challenge. Based on actual history, the story could have been unremittingly grim, but hidden among the bare facts, there are cheering tales of heroism and even laughter, which allowed me to give Madeleine and Grant the happy ending they deserve.

I do hope you enjoy their story.

SARAH MALLORY

—

Rescued by Her Highland Soldier

HARLEQUIN®
HISTORICAL™

Recycling programs
for this product may
not exist in your area.

ISBN-13: 978-1-335-50618-4

Rescued by Her Highland Soldier

Harlequin Enterprises ULC
22 Adelaide St. West, 40th Floor
Toronto, Ontario M5H 4E3, Canada
www.Harlequin.com

Printed in U.S.A.

Sarah Mallory grew up in the West Country, England, telling stories. She moved to Yorkshire with her young family, but after nearly thirty years living in a farmhouse on the Pennines, she has now moved to live by the sea in Scotland. Sarah is an award-winning novelist with more than twenty books published by Harlequin Historical. She loves to hear from readers; you can reach her via her website at sarahmallory.com.

Books by Sarah Mallory

Harlequin Historical

The Scarlet Gown
Never Trust a Rebel
The Duke's Secret Heir
Pursued for the Viscount's Vengeance
His Countess for a Week
The Mysterious Miss Fairchild

Lairds of Ardvarrick

Forbidden to the Highland Laird
Rescued by Her Highland Soldier

Saved from Disgrace

The Ton's Most Notorious Rake
Beauty and the Brooding Lord

Visit the Author Profile page
at Harlequin.com for more titles.

To my writer friends everywhere, for helping
me stay sane and motivated in 2020,
when I was writing this book.

Chapter One

May 1746

The night sky was a gruesome mix of black and red. Behind him, the darkness was black as pitch, but from his hiding place beneath the gorse Grant could see the village, or what was left of it. He watched the angry flames leaping from the roofs and windows, and listened to the cries of the cottars, men, women and children, their screams cut short as the redcoats put them to the sword. Every one of them and without mercy.

Grant felt the bile rise in his throat. He wanted to charge to the rescue, to use his broadsword to slash and kill the soldiers, but there were more than a dozen of them. He had learned a great deal about fighting in the past six months as he followed Charles Stuart into England and back again and he knew that to show himself now would be a futile gesture, he would be just one more body left to rot in the glen. One more victim of the Duke of Cumberland's retribution. Keeping low, he turned and began to make his way back through the gorse and into the darkness. Better to live and fight another day.

Maddie opened her eyes and stared at the faded hangings around her bed. This was not the lodgings in Inverness that had been her home for the past twelve months, but that was not what caused her to feel uneasy. It was the unusual silence and stillness within the room.

She pushed back the hangings and saw immediately that the truckle bed in the corner was empty. Slipping out of her own bed, she went over to it. The rumpled sheets were cold, suggesting that Edie, her maid, had left it some time ago. A quick glance showed her that the cloth bag Edie used for her possessions had gone, too. It was inevitable really. They were but three miles from Edie's home and she should not be surprised that her maid had left and gone back to her family.

Maddie dressed quickly and went downstairs, where she soon confirmed that the maid was not in the building. And she had taken the pony.

'I remember her saying yester evening that she had family in this area,' said the landlady, serving Maddie with her breakfast. 'Perhaps she has gone a-visiting.'

'Perhaps.'

It was unlikely, since the maid had left no word, but Madeleine wanted to believe it. She remained at the inn for as long as she dared, but at last she knew she must move on. The landlady looked concerned when Maddie asked to have her pony saddled.

'You'll never be riding off alone, mistress,' she exclaimed, shocked. 'It isn't safe for ye, what with the redcoats everywhere.'

'I have no choice,' replied Madeleine. 'I cannot go back to Inverness. Since the battle, the area has been crawling with redcoats. But neither can I stay here.'

'No, that is true enough.' The landlady sighed and gave her a pitying look. 'Ye must move on, but it would be dangerous to use the road, for you are sure to meet soldiers if you do. There is an old track not half a mile from here that will take you across the hills to the next change house at Kildrummy. Young Robbie, the groom, will set you on your way.'

Two hours later Maddie bade farewell to the groom, tossed him a coin and turned her horse on to the barely discernible track. She was well aware that soldiers of Charles Stuart's army who had escaped the carnage of Culloden might well be hiding in the hills, but she was sure they posed less of a threat than the marauding government troops who were terrorising the country.

It was growing dark by the time Grant arrived at the change house. A couple were standing outside and they watched his approach with anxious eyes. Not unexpected, he thought, in these troubled times. Any stranger was a threat, even one dressed as a gentleman—albeit a ragged one—in top boots, breeches and a riding jacket.

When they would have turned away, he hailed them cheerfully.

'Good day to you! Would you be the landlord, sir?'

'Aye.'

It was a cautious reply, but Grant was not deterred.

'I wonder if I might get a little food here.' He gave a shrug and a wry smile. 'I would willingly work for my supper. I can clean out the stables, cut you some peat, or chop logs for your fire.'

'I—'

The man's response was cut short by raised voices from inside the inn and the sound of smashing crockery. Grant's brows rose.

'That will be the soldiers.' The landlord looked nervous. 'Three of them.'

'Ah. Then perhaps I should wait.' He had barely finished speaking when a woman screamed.

Without hesitating, Grant dragged out his sword. He pushed past the landlord and strode into the inn. A redcoat was in the narrow passageway, leaning against a closed door and drinking from a wine bottle. Grant quickly lowered his sword arm so the weapon was concealed by the skirts of his coat. The soldier spotted Grant and pushed himself upright, swaying slightly.

'Try the taproom at the back of the house,' he said, his words slurring together. 'The parlour's occupied. My friends are taking their pleasure.' Another cry rang out and he bared his teeth in a lecherous grin, his hand going to his crotch. 'I'll be getting my turn next.'

Grant came closer, smiling. 'Lucky fellow.'

The man never noticed the swinging sword hilt until it caught him squarely on the jaw. He reeled away, already unconscious, and Grant neatly caught the bottle as it fell from his hand. Pausing only to remove the fellow's sword and drop it and the bottle out of sight behind a wooden bench, he stepped over the inert body and went into the parlour.

He took in the scene in one glance: discarded red coats, swords and belts thrown over a chair, muskets resting against the wall by the door. One man slumped in a corner, a bloody handkerchief pressed to his head. A second soldier struggling with a woman, forcing her back over a table.

Grant fell upon the attacker, dragging him off the woman and giving him a blow that sent him crashing to the floor, where he joined the plates and tankards already scattered there. The other soldier struggled to his feet, but Grant was standing, sword in hand, between him and the weapons.

'You are wise to hesitate, I'd like nothing more than to run you through. You are a disgrace to your uniform. Damme, sir, if I was your commanding officer I would have you flogged!'

Grant's clipped English speech and natural authority had its effect—the man glared at him, sullen but wary. The other soldier was stirring and Grant nodded towards him.

'Help your friend to his feet.' He picked up the coats and tossed them across. 'Here. You will find your guard in the passage, senseless with drink. Leave this place and take him with you.'

'But we cannot leave without our arms,' protested one.

'You can take the muskets, nothing more.'

The men looked at him, aghast.

'No cartridges? We will be virtually unarmed!'

'Aye, so you'd best rejoin your regiment with all speed,' Grant replied coldly. 'If you make it back alive, you may refer your commander to me, I am Colonel Rathmore of the Fourteenth. Now get out before I change my mind and kill you anyway.'

Such was his assurance the men did not question him. They shambled out of the room and closed the door behind them. Grant listened to the sounds from the passage, then moved to the window, watching until he saw the men riding away. Only then did he turn his attention to the woman.

She was still leaning against the table, but she had straightened her disordered gown and was currently engaged in retying the ribbon around her dusky curls. All the time she was watching him, her eyes wary. Deep blue eyes, he noted, like the colour of Loch Ardvarrick on a summer's day.

'Madam, are you hurt?'

'I am not,' she told him brusquely. She added, as an afterthought, 'I am obliged to you.'

'Pray think nothing of it,' he said politely.

'But it was three against one.'

'Two,' he corrected her, smiling a little. 'You had already dealt with one rogue, had you not?'

'I broke a water pitcher over his head.'

'Good for you.' He righted an upturned chair and set it before her. 'You are very pale. Understandably so, in the circumstances. Will you not sit down and I will fetch you a glass of wine?'

'I do not think—'

'You need not be fearing they will return for a while,' he interrupted her. 'It will take them some time to reach their quarters and even more to discover I duped them.'

His voice had slipped back into a softer, Highland lilt and she frowned at him.

'You are not Colonel Rathmore?'

'I am not even an Englishman.' Grant shrugged. 'Well, my grandmother was English, but I hold no affinity with that country. I was not sure they would believe me, but they are young and inexperienced.'

'They were also vilely drunk!'

'Yes, which made it easier to overpower them.' He said again, 'Will you not sit down, madam?'

Madeleine hesitated. The terror was fading and this man, rough as he looked, spoke gently. His face was covered with thick, dark stubble, suggesting it had not seen a razor for some time, but that was not unusual. Mayhap he was an honest traveller, although in her experience, there were precious few of those around.

At that moment he intercepted her appraising look and smiled. For the first time she noticed the golden flecks in his deep brown eyes and she could see only kindness and concern in his face. Madeleine wanted to trust him and decided to do so, at least, for the moment. She perched herself on the edge of the chair.

'Now,' he said, 'I will find our host and tell him to bring in some wine.'

When he had left the room she felt a slight resurgence of fear and crossed her arms tightly, willing herself not to tremble. Her gown was not torn, but she could still feel the soldiers' hands scrabbling at her bodice and dragging up her skirts. She felt dirty, unclean, but the thought of bathing was inconceivable. She had no maid, no one to guard her door. She was very much alone.

Her thoughts went back to her rescuer. He had seen off her attackers, but to what purpose? It was a month since the government troops had routed the Jacobite army and the land was crawling with soldiers, both hunters and the hunted. The victorious army was scouring the land, pursuing their enemy with a ferocity that left everyone in fear of their lives. No one was safe, as she had discovered.

She flinched as the door opened.

'I beg your pardon—did I startle you?' The man came in carrying a bottle and two glasses. 'I thought it would be quicker to bring these myself. The landlord has set the tap boy and stable hands to keep watch, just in case our friends should return.'

'Are you sure he is not in league with them?' she replied, unable to keep the bitterness from her voice. 'He did nothing to help me.'

'The poor man was terrified. He was afraid for his wife and children, too.' He filled the glasses and handed one to her. 'They are trying to make up for it now and are busy in the kitchens, organising dinner for you.'

'For me?' She watched him over the rim of her glass. 'And what of you, sir, do you not eat?'

'Later, perhaps.' She did not miss his slight hesitation, the way his hand flattened against his coat pocket. Could it be he had no money?

'You might dine in here,' she suggested.

He shook his head. 'This is a private parlour and you have hired it.'

'That is so, but after the service you have rendered me, the least I can do is to buy you dinner.' When he hesitated, she added, 'I should be grateful, too. I would rather not eat alone tonight.'

'Very well, I shall accept your offer and thank you for it, ma'am.' He glanced around, his mouth twisting. 'The landlord has promised to send the maid in before too long. She will clear up the room and prepare the table.'

'Good. We may tell her then to set another place for you. In the meantime, perhaps you, too, will take a chair.' She waved him to a seat. 'I should like to know to whom I am indebted?'

'I am Grant Rathmore, ma'am, of Ardvarrick, but there is no debt.'

'You are very kind, Mr Rathmore.'

'I am also curious,' he said bluntly. '*I* should like to know what you are doing here, alone and unaccompanied.'

Madeleine inclined her head, thinking quickly. She decided the truth would serve her best, although she would tell him as little as possible.

'My name is Madeleine d'Evremont.'

'The landlord tells me you are travelling alone, Mistress d'Evremont. Is that wise?'

She bridled at that. 'Of course it is not wise! My maid was with me when I left Inverness, but when we reached Balvenie, she slipped away. Her family live nearby and I suspect she has returned to them.'

'Forgive me, madam, but a lady, even one accompanied by her maid, should not be travelling without an escort.'

'I can take care of myself!' Recalling what had just occurred, how he had rescued her, she realised that sounded very foolish. 'In *general* I am very capable of looking after myself,' she amended. 'However, I have no choice but to continue my journey.'

'And where is your destination?'

That was not something she wished to share with a stranger.

'I am going south,' she said vaguely. 'To stay with friends.'

He was leaning back on his chair, his long legs stretched before him and his booted ankles crossed as he regarded her with a touch of scorn in his deep brown eyes.

'And what kind of friends is it that lets a young lady travel without an escort?'

Maddie hesitated, then admitted, 'They do not know I am coming—'

She broke off as the door opened and a young serving girl entered. Her companion looked up.

'Ah, here is the maid come to tidy the room and we shall be very much in the way here. Shall we go over there and sit by the fire?'

Madeleine's brows lifted. 'But there is no fire.'

'It has been prepared, so I can soon light it and then we will be out of the girl's way.'

They moved their chairs nearer to the hearth and made innocuous conversation while the maid bustled about, clearing up the broken dishes on the floor and setting the table. When she had finished the girl bobbed a curtsy and would have left, but Grant Rathmore stopped her. He glanced at Madeleine.

'Perhaps, ma'am, you would like to go to your room to wash your hands before we dine? The maid might go with you, if you would rather not be alone.'

She was touched and not a little surprised by his consideration. He was clearly not such a vagabond as his untidy appearance suggested.

She rose. 'Yes, thank you, Mr Rathmore. I shall not be too long.'

He rose, too, and bowed. 'Take all the time you need, Miss d'Evremont.'

* * *

Alone in the room, Grant walked over to the window. Outside, the shadows were lengthening in the yard and, although there was some time yet until sunset, Grant decided he would fasten the shutters. The landlord had assured him he would keep his men on watch throughout the night, but one could not be too careful. He would keep his sword with him, too, in case of attack, although he hoped he might at least enjoy his meal in comfort and peace, for once. Truth be told, he was looking forward to dining with the lady.

Miss Madeleine d'Evremont. The name suggested she might be French and he thought he had detected the slightest accent in her speech. She had left Inverness with her maid, but no escort. Did that mean she was a fugitive, like himself? Grant shrugged away the question. The answer was no concern of his. He had no time to worry over a stranger.

Yet she was a pretty little thing. She spoke well, too, in a pleasingly musical voice. An educated lady, he thought, and she could not be without funds, if she could afford to bespeak this parlour. The devil of it was, with her dainty figure and heart-shaped face she would always be at risk from men, especially soldiers whose blood was up.

Having satisfied himself that the shutters were secure, Grant turned away from the window and his thoughts returned to the lady. She would attract trouble like a magnet! He had enough problems of his own and was not in a position to shoulder those of anyone else. He would enjoy dinner, thank Miss Madeleine d'Evremont for her hospitality and be on his way.

* * *

When Maddie returned to the parlour the candles were burning and casting a soft, golden glow over the room. A branched candlestick stood on the table, throwing extra light on the two places set. Her fellow diner was putting more logs on the fire, but at her entrance he rose and dusted his hands.

'In good time, Miss d'Evremont, our host is about to bring in the dishes. A ragout of some sort, I believe, but perhaps we should not enquire too closely.'

He held her chair for her and poured them each a glass of wine before sitting down and engaging her in conversation. His polite manner soon put Maddie at her ease, which she suspected was his intention. He must know as well as she how improper it was for a lady to be dining alone with a man she barely knew. Just because he had saved her from the redcoats did not mean his intentions were any more honourable.

'You are frowning, madam, is aught amiss?'

'Only that I know so little about you, Mr Rathmore.'

'In these troubled times, perhaps that is for the best.'

'Perhaps, but that does nothing to quench my curiosity.'

She gave him an encouraging smile and in response his eyes gleamed, but he shook his head.

'Nay, madam, let it suffice that I am a traveller, making my way to the east coast. I am no one of note. Hardly worthy of your attention. I suggest we talk of more interesting matters.' He reached for the bottle and refilled their glasses. 'For instance, your English is excellent, but it is not your native language, I think?'

She raised her brows a little. 'You tell me nothing of yourself, but expect me to divulge my history?'

'That would be far more interesting to me.'

She laughed at that and blushed a little. 'Very well, sir, since *I* have nothing to hide! You are correct, I am French by birth, but France is no longer my home. I have been travelling through Europe for the past four years.'

'With your parents?'

She took a sip of wine while she considered how best to answer him.

'With my father. My mother died when I was a child and when I reached seventeen Papa deemed me old enough to come with him on his travels. They have been extensive, Dresden, Vienna, Rome. Even London, for one brief period. For the past year we have been in Inverness.'

'He is an ambassador, perhaps?'

The thought made her want to laugh. It was quickly stifled, but she saw his look of surprise.

'Now, what have I said?' he demanded.

'My father has many traits that would be useful for such a post, but, alas, no.' She took another sip of wine. 'He lives by his wits. His income is, to say the least, erratic.'

'A gambler, then.'

She heard the minatory note in his voice and said, with a little touch of hauteur, 'Nothing sordid, I assure you. Papa is connected to some of the major aristocratic families in France.'

She had no idea if it was true. Papa had told her it was so, but he was always embroidering the stories of his past. However, for some reason it was important that this man did not think her low-born.

'And what brought you and your father to the Highlands?'

'Papa has friends here. He never explained it fully.'

That at least was the truth. Maddie knew it would be better if she stopped there. It was safer if she said no more, but for some inexplicable reason she felt she needed to speak, to tell someone.

'Papa left Inverness two weeks before the battle and I have not seen him since.'

'He was caught up at Culloden? My condolences—'

'No, no, you misunderstand. He is not dead. He sent me a note, when it was clear the Jacobite army had been routed, explaining that he could not return and instructing me to make my way to…to a house where I might be safe.'

'You told me earlier you were going to stay with friends.'

'Alas, I am not acquainted with these people.'

'But they are friends of your father?'

'I believe so…it is possible that Papa will be waiting for me there.'

'But even on that point you cannot be sure!' Grant gave an exasperated hiss. 'What was your father about, to leave you alone, with the country in such turmoil, and then to send you to a place you do not know, to people whom you cannot trust to help you—it is unforgivable!'

She fluttered one hand. 'It is not the first time Papa has had to disappear. Or that I have had to rely upon the goodwill of his…contacts. I am grown used to fending for myself, although I confess, this time, it was a blow to lose my maid.'

'Was your father involved in the recent uprising?'

She was growing accustomed to his blunt manner. What surprised Madeleine was that she felt comfortable enough to confide in him.

'Possibly, although he did not tell me the nature of his involvement.' She sighed. 'I cannot deny Papa likes living by his wits. He positively enjoys the thrill of high-risk ventures, although the rewards never turn out to be as great as he believes they will be at the outset.'

'He has no right to drag you into his schemes.'

She smiled at that. 'What else was he to do with me? We have no close family who would take me in— besides, I have been mistress of my father's household for years now. I should not take kindly to being under another woman's thumb.'

Grant could well believe it. There was a self-sufficiency to Mistress d'Evremont that intrigued him. From what she had told him she could not be more than two-and-twenty, but she had the assurance of someone much older—witness how easily she now turned the conversation towards less personal matters.

He followed obligingly. They talked of food, of wine and the weather, neither of them mentioning the recent Jacobite defeat or the current apprehension that gripped the land as government soldiers roamed at will, striking terror into the local inhabitants with their violence and lawlessness. However, he guessed it was still in the lady's mind, as it was in his. A constant, menacing presence, hanging around and over them like an ugly cloud.

At last the meal was done and Grant reluctantly acknowledged that he could delay no longer. He wiped his mouth with the napkin and put it down on the table.

'I am done. My grateful thanks for your hospitality, Miss d'Evremont, but alas, I cannot stay. The moon, such as it is, will be rising now and I must be on my way.'

'You are going?' She looked and sounded surprised.

He shrugged. 'I have a long journey and I am travelling on foot. Besides, in these lawless times it is safer to travel at night. And if you will take my advice, you will not delay in setting off tomorrow.' He pushed back his chair and stood up. 'You should ask our host to let one of his men go with you, or two if he can spare them. It is not safe for a woman to be travelling alone.'

The easy mood had gone and she regarded him solemnly, acknowledging the danger they had tried so hard to ignore for the past few hours.

'You are quite right, I need an escort.' She raised her eyes to his. 'Would *you* come with me?'

Chapter Two

Madeleine could not read the look in Grant Rathmore's dark eyes and his untidy beard concealed any clue to his expression. She thought he was going to refuse and she hurried on.

'It is not so very far out of your way and I can pay you. I will cover all your expenses for the journey and give you another ten guineas when we reach our destination.'

'Which is?'

'A house in Glen Muick. I understand it is only some twenty miles south of here.'

'Twenty miles of rough track,' he told her. 'And if that were not bad enough, the route will be swarming with redcoats. Glen Muick is south of the River Dee. Any crossing is sure to be heavily guarded.'

'Are you suggesting this to make me increase the payment?'

'Not at all. I do not want your money.'

So, he would not come with her. Maddie's disappointment was surprisingly strong but she thrust it aside. She would not show him any weakness.

'I have told you, I am quite capable of looking after myself. I shall avoid the soldiers and find an unguarded place to cross the river. I beg your pardon, Mr Rathmore. I should not have asked it of you.'

Grant watched her as she rose and she came around the table towards him, holding out one dainty hand. He took the proffered fingers and gazed at the lady. She was very calm, there was no hint of anything but polite indifference in her face as she dismissed him.

'I will bid you *adieu*, Mr Rathmore, and wish you a safe journey.'

When she tried to pull her hand away, he tightened his grip.

'No, wait. I will escort you to Loch Muick.'

She inclined her head and thanked him politely. He caught the faintest flicker of relief in her eyes, then it was gone.

'You will need a mount, of course.'

'I am sure our host can find me something. A garron would be best—a Highland pony. They can carry a man for many miles and over the roughest ground.'

She nodded. 'I bought two when we left Inverness. Unfortunately, Edie, my maid, has taken one of them.'

'If you have the means, then we can buy another. And talking of means, I will need a room for the night.'

'Very well. I will go and see our landlord now.'

As she opened the door, he stopped her.

'Perhaps you would ask him to supply me with a razor.' He grinned and rubbed a hand over his beard. 'If you are paying my shot here I can at least make myself presentable for you.'

Madeleine inclined her head, but she did not smile.

'I will instruct our host that he is to supply you with everything you need.'

When she had gone out, Grant poured himself another glass of wine and sat down again, wondering just what he had done.

Grant Rathmore was already in the private parlour, breaking his fast by candlelight, when Madeleine came in the next morning. For a moment she did not recognise him. Gone was the dark growth of beard, exposing the smooth lines of a lean, handsome face. His auburn hair was brushed until it shone and neatly confined by a ribbon at the back of his neck.

He looked up as she entered and, when he smiled, Maddie was shaken by the jolt of attraction that shot through her.

'Good morning, ma'am, I trust you slept well?'

He jumped up and pulled out a chair for her. Madeleine was glad to sit down, she was still reeling from the effect of his smile. It made her feel as if her bones were melting. She hid her confusion behind a scowl.

'I did, until I was so rudely awakened!' Heavens, even common civility was beyond her! 'I assume it was on your instruction that I was obliged to get up at this ungodly hour?'

'It was.' He resumed his seat, seemingly unperturbed by her irritable manner. 'I told you last night we must make an early start. Now, what will you take for breakfast? There are eggs and bread, of course, but I am afraid there is no ham. The landlord tells me he was obliged to give that up to the soldiers who came by here last week. However, the salmon is freshly caught and quite delicious. You should try it.'

She allowed him to put a little fish on her plate and Grant went back to his own meal, hoping her bad mood would pass once she had eaten something.

'How soon must we leave?' she asked him later, when he refilled their coffee cups.

'As soon as you have finished your meal,' he told her. 'The landlord is saddling the ponies as we speak.' He glanced up. 'I understand you have no lady's saddle.'

'No. It is more practical to ride *en cavalier*.'

'Is that not a little…revealing?'

'Not at all,' she replied coldly. 'I wear silk breeches beneath these skirts.'

Grant's lips twitched and a teasing riposte came into his head, but the steely look in the lady's eye prevented him from saying anything more. She would not appreciate being teased and, curbing his smile, he merely nodded and stirred his coffee.

'Good idea. The tracks are very rough here.' But his particular demon of mischief was hell-bent upon provoking her and he added, 'Even for a man.'

He heard her sudden intake of breath, the cold, haughty note in her voice as she responded.

'I have ridden with my father through the Alps, Mr Rathmore. I can assure you I managed the mountain passes very well.'

'I am sure you did, but I doubt you were being pursued by murderous redcoats at the time!'

He braced himself for another sharp retort. To his surprise, she laughed.

'No, although Papa and I were chased by brigands upon several occasions and once by wild animals!' She pushed away her empty plate. 'My father also disliked

females who kept him waiting, so off you go and prepare yourself for the journey, Mr Rathmore, I shall be
with you in a trice.'

Heavy clouds obscured the rising sun and it was in
a grey twilight that they set off from the change house
some half an hour later. Maddie was glad of her thick
cloak to ward off the morning chill. It would also protect her from the rain she felt sure would fall before too
long. Their ponies were sturdy creatures, well suited
to the rugged terrain, and she was quite comfortable in
the saddle, but she wondered how her companion was
faring. Grant Rathmore was taller than average and
she guessed he was more accustomed to riding a much
larger horse. She glanced across, taking in the straight
back, the proud way he held his head. His speech and
manner suggested he was an educated man of good
family—if his dress was a little shabby, that was to be
expected of someone travelling on foot. He had told her
he was from Ardvarrick, wherever that may be, but he
had said it with confidence. Was he a landowner, then,
or a landowner's son? She found herself wondering if
he was married. He was certainly attractive enough to
steal any woman's heart.

As if aware of her scrutiny he looked around at that
moment and Maddie quickly averted her gaze, but not
before she had seen the gleam in his eyes.

This will not do, she scolded herself. *This is no time
for dalliance with a handsome stranger!*

Yet she could not stop the heat suffusing her cheeks
and was mortified that he should see her blush.

*Whatever he might once have been, now he is noth-
ing more than a hired servant.*

That was a much better thought. She was accustomed to dealing with servants.

'Will you tell me now just exactly where we are going?' he asked her.

'I am paying you to take me to Glen Muick, Mr Rathmore. What more do you need to know?'

'It would be helpful to know the name of the house and the family you are to meet there. I did not press you for the information before, I quite understand that you would not want to say too much at the inn, but now we are alone I think you should tell me.'

Damn him, he sounded so reasonable.

'My father has instructed me to go to the Lochalls in Glen Muick.'

'Jacobites?'

She bit her lip. 'He does not say as much, but it may well be so.'

'You still have his letter?'

'No. He instructed me to burn it once I had read the contents.'

'Which suggests it might incriminate you if you are stopped by government soldiers. Hell and damnation, what was the man thinking of, sending you such a way?'

'That is not your concern,' she retorted.

'It very much is my concern if I am to keep you safe! Well, there is no help for it now. We must press on.'

Maddie glared at him, wanting very much to tell him to go to the devil, but the truth was she needed his help, so she kicked her little pony into a trot and went on ahead in what she hoped was a dignified silence.

They had not gone far when Grant caught up with her.

'If you have finished sulking, we need to cross the river here, where it is shallow.'

She thought it best to ignore the first part of his speech.

She slowed her pony. 'The road is on this side of the water, Mr Rathmore, and it is the route we will take. I am assured that by going this way, we can reach the crossing at Dinnet by nightfall.'

'The landlord told me of a lesser-known trail. It is a little longer, but it will be safer.'

'But it is not the route that I was advised to take.'

'And I am telling you 'tis the one you should use if you want to avoid trouble.'

She put up her chin. 'Then why did the landlord not tell me of it yesterday, when I told him where I was going?'

'He directed you to the next change house at Dinnet, I suppose? Yes, of course. He could scarcely do anything else for a lady travelling with only her maid for escort. But, trust me, we will be much safer if we head east rather than take the route he described to you.'

She said stubbornly, 'Then why did he not say as much to me? I am perfectly capable of following directions.'

He gave her a look that showed plainly he doubted it and her temper rose.

'This is also the route my friends in Inverness described to me and I believe we should follow it. I am informed that it avoids those roads most used by the military.'

'In normal times, perhaps, but since the last battle, government troops are everywhere and especially the glens to the west of here. The area will be crawling with soldiers.' He gave a sigh of exasperation. 'By heaven, madam, did your encounter yesterday not teach you anything?'

'Yes!' she retorted. 'It taught me not to trust anyone!' His mouth tightened and she was suddenly stricken with guilt. She hurried on. 'I beg your pardon. You came to my aid yesterday when you did not need to do so and I am truly grateful for that.'

'You have a strange way of showing it, madam!'

Maddie pressed her lips together. He was angry, she could understand that, but trusted friends had advised her to take this route. For all his chivalrous actions towards her yesterday and his handsome good looks, Grant Rathmore was a stranger. She narrowed her eyes to regard him. It was a look guaranteed to quell upstart servants and she was taken aback when he laughed suddenly.

'You would very much like to tell me to go to the devil, would you not? I confess I would like to do the same to you! I do not know when I have ever met such a stubborn lass or one so determined to have her own way. But you hired me to escort you and I cannot, will not, allow you to ride into danger.'

Still she hesitated and after a moment he exhaled, looking up at the sky before turning to address her again.

'You are not in Inverness now, Miss d'Evremont. You are a stranger to this country, but I am a Highlander. I understand this land and its people. I know how best to keep you safe. Trust me in this.'

Could she trust him? Madeleine looked into his eyes. Instinct said she could do so, but the events of the past few days had unsettled her and her head urged caution. True, he had saved her honour, perhaps even her life, but she knew nothing of him. Yet what choice did she have, other than to turn him off and proceed alone?

'Very well, sir. We will try your way.'

She would go with him, but she would be on her guard and take note of the route, that she might turn back if necessary.

They set off again, crossing the burn to follow a faint track that took them up and through the hills. They passed an abandoned village, the houses burned-out shells and the fields scorched and blackened. Madeleine drew rein and stopped.

'*Mon Dieu*, what has happened here?'

'British soldiers. They are supposedly looking for rebels, but they slaughter the men indiscriminately, throw the women and children out of their homes, torch the houses and burn the crops.'

She looked about her in horror. 'I cannot believe they can be so...so merciless.'

'No? I have seen it. I have seen how they take pleasure in their vicious deeds. The army is laying waste to my homeland and the British government condones it.'

He was looking at her, his eyes blazing with such cold fury that she recoiled and looked away.

'It is barbaric,' she muttered. 'I had no idea.'

'It is war, *mademoiselle*. Cumberland wishes to be rid of the rebellious Highlanders once and for all.'

He sighed and she felt the tension around them lessen, but his anger and pain were almost tangible. She was emboldened to reach out to him.

'I am so very sorry.'

The words were woefully inadequate. She watched

him as he stared at her hand resting on his sleeve, wishing there was more she could do, more she could say to comfort him. At last he raised his head and his face was shuttered, blank. He would not accept her sympathy.

'We should get on,' he said. 'We have a long journey ahead of us.'

They set off again, moving higher into the hills and as the land became more barren Madeleine gazed around her with growing anxiety. Apart from the occasional bird of prey wheeling high overhead she saw no signs of life. Below them were empty valleys while bare, craggy mountains towered above. At last she was moved to speak.

'Are you sure you know where you are going, Mr Rathmore?'

'If you mean have I travelled this way before, ma'am, then, no, but we are heading in a southerly direction, which is what is required.'

'But it could take us miles out of our way!'

'The army will be patrolling the main routes, the drovers' trails, so we are safer keeping to the mountains.' He threw her a glance. 'Your experience of Alpine bandits may prove useful.'

'Pray do not tease me.'

'I am not teasing. Many poor souls fleeing from that last bloody battle dared not return to their homes and they have taken to living in the hills. However, they should not trouble us.'

'Because you are one of them,' she guessed shrewdly. 'Are you, too, fleeing from Culloden?'

'Aye, madam, I am.'

She waited, hoping he would say more, but when

he did not, she found her curiosity was too strong to remain silent.

'But you are not dressed as a soldier, or even a Highlander. You wear clothes more fitting for a clerk, or a gentleman's gentleman.'

'I came upon an inn shortly after the redcoats had called.' His mouth twisted. 'No one was alive there. These clothes were in one of the guest rooms.'

She gave a little gasp and he turned his head to look at her.

'I did not remove them from a corpse, if that is your worry! Let us just say their owner had no more use for them.' Maddie felt a little sick and she put a hand to her mouth. He said, roughly, 'Would you rather I had not told you? I might have lied and said I bought them.'

'No, thank you, I prefer the truth. I had heard tales, rumours, of the army's brutality, but I assumed it was a few rogue troops. Even after my own experience I did not quite believe it.'

'Then believe it now. The Scots are to be made to suffer the consequences of defying the government and, from what I have witnessed, vengeance is not confined to Jacobite supporters. The people have moved from their homes to hide out in the hills and moors. The soldiers are more wary of following them there for fear of attack.'

'But it can be bitter here, even at this time of the year.' Maddie shivered and pulled her cloak more tightly around her. 'It is summer now, but how will they survive in winter?'

'Many will perish, but they will take their chances with the weather rather than the soldiers.'

As if to prove his point, they soon found themselves

enveloped in cloud. Maddie strained her eyes as she looked around, expecting at any moment to see the blur of redcoats appear through the mist. Even when they had crossed the hills and moved down to the tree-covered slopes there was no relief.

The dank weather dragged on her spirits and the path seemed never ending. Madeleine felt exhaustion creeping through her body as she followed Grant Rathmore through woodland where the lichen on the trees seemed to glow greeny-grey in the half-light. She was hungry and her aching bones screamed for rest. When he eventually came to a stand, she brought her pony alongside his.

'The day must be very far advanced now, Mr Rathmore. We should—'

'Hush!'

His urgent hiss silenced her. He was tense, alert and she felt the hairs rising on the back of her neck. She nudged her pony even closer, straining eyes and ears for the slightest sound.

Then she saw them. Shadows emerging and turning into solid shapes. Burly Highlanders, each one bristling with murderous-looking weapons.

Grant heard his companion's sharp intake of breath as the figures emerged out of the mist.

'What's your business here?' One of the men stepped forward, his hand resting on the hilt of his broadsword. He was a large fellow and looked older than the rest, possibly the leader, Grant decided.

'Peace, my friend, we are merely travellers, trying to avoid the redcoats.' He took a chance and added, 'As are you, I suspect.'

'Who are ye and what d'ye want?' demanded the man again.

'I am called Grant Rathmore.'

'Rathmore, did ye say?' Another man stepped forward. 'There was a soldier o' that name at Fort Augustus, after the battle.'

'Aye, that was me.'

'Let's have a look at ye.'

Grant took off his hat and looked down as the fellow stepped closer to peer at him.

He said, 'I left, as you did, when the Prince told us it was every man for himself.'

The man looked him up and down. 'Ye look mighty different now.'

'Aye, well, I have been shifting for myself since I left there. I thought I'd be safer without the beard. And if I wasn't wearing the plaid.' Grant noted their attention had shifted to his companion and added, 'This lady is travelling under my protection.'

The older man's shaggy brows rose. 'Is she now?'

'Aye.' Grant looked the speaker in the eye and moved one hand to his own sword. 'She has had a taste of English manners. I assured her Highlanders do not behave like such savages.'

'Indeed, we do not.' The fellow spat on the floor before looking up again. 'So, what are your plans, where do ye stay tonight?'

'Under the stars, if we cannot find someone to give us shelter.'

'Ye'll no' find habitation before nightfall. You and the lass are welcome to eat with us at our shelter and to rest there the night.'

Grant glanced across at the lady. She looked calm enough, but her face was unreadable.

He nodded. 'Aye, we'll sup with you and gladly. Lead on, man!'

Chapter Three

Madeleine did not understand a word and she could only guess from their movements and the tone of the conversation that her escort had managed to allay their suspicions. The look he had given her was reassuring and when they set off again, she kept her pony alongside his so that she might speak to him.

'Well, Grant Rathmore, who are they, what is happening?'

For a moment he looked nonplussed, then he laughed.

'I beg your pardon; we were speaking the Gaelic and I had not realised!'

'I have noticed it with other Scots,' she said. 'They slip easily between languages.'

'Aye, I suppose we do. But to answer your questions, we have been invited to dine with them. As to who they are, my guess is they are fugitives, like myself.'

'Jacobite soldiers.'

He looked at her, his eyes narrowing. 'You would like to ask me if we will be safe with such outlaws, would you not? I hope we shall be.'

One of the Highlanders had dropped back and

now he turned and waited until the riders caught up with him.

'Ye've no need to be afeared of us, my lady,' he addressed Maddie in a heavy brogue. 'When Angus Gillies issues an invitation, we all abide by it.'

'Thank you.' She smiled at him. 'What is your name?'

He touched his cap. 'Dougal Hepburn, madam. Late of Colonel Anne's regiment. So ye see, we have great respect for the ladies.'

'Lady Anne Mackintosh,' explained Grant, seeing her bemused look. 'She raised a regiment for the Prince, despite her husband being a Government officer.'

The Highlander grinned. 'Aye, a fine grand lady she is, Lord bless her!'

He turned away, quickening his pace to catch up with his companions and leaving Grant and Maddie to follow on.

'Is your mind easier now?' he asked her, smiling.

'A little. Although I am not sure I shall ever be completely easy again.'

'War is a terrible business. My father knew it. He tried to discourage me, when word went out that the Prince was in Scotland and raising an army.'

She heard the sombre note in his voice. How old would he have been a year ago, when he marched off so eagerly to follow Charles Stuart, two- or three-and-twenty? He could not be many years her senior, but the lines around his eyes and mouth hinted at hardship and made him look older, as did the air of world-weariness that hung about him.

'But you would not heed his advice. I believe it is often so, with young men and their fathers.'

His mouth twisted. 'I was two-and-twenty. Not so young, just damned foolish.' He glanced up. 'It grows dark. I hope we shall reach our destination before too long.'

He had changed the subject and Maddie accepted it with an inward shrug. She had paid him to escort her to Glen Muick, nothing more. And she was not sure she wanted to know too much about this man.

They followed the Highlanders through a murky twilight and Madeleine had to concentrate to keep her pony from stumbling on the rough terrain as the track wound upwards along the side of a steep hill. She was about to ask how much further they must go when she noticed that the men at the front of the group had disappeared. A few yards more and she saw the dark, yawning mouth of a cave ahead. The leader, Angus Gillies, waited for them to come up to him.

'Ye are welcome to our abode, such as it is.' He spoke in English, his brogue thick but understandable to Madeleine. 'Come ye in. Dougal will look after your ponies. Dinnae worry, they'll be safe enough and ready for ye to be on your way in the morning.'

Madeleine was so tired even the sparse amenities of a bare cave were a welcome respite from riding. Her vision soon adjusted to the dark interior as she and Grant were escorted inside and they found themselves in a long, twisting tunnel. There was a faint smell of smoke and her eyes detected a glow ahead of them that had not been visible from the entrance.

A few more yards and they were in a large, cavernous space illuminated by rush lamps and the flames of a cheerful fire. Smoke curled around a large pot suspended on a trivet over the flames and moved on upwards until it disappeared into the darkness above. Two women were tending the fire and they looked up briefly as everyone came in.

Maddie could not understand what Angus Gilles said to the women, but it seemed to satisfy them, for they returned to their cooking and paid no more heed to the newcomers.

'All the comforts of home,' remarked Grant.

'Aye, well, we have no home but this, now,' retorted Angus.

The rest of the evening passed in a blur to Madeleine. A welcome meal of venison was served up by the women, who refused her offers to help them and waved her back to her seat on a rocky ledge beside Grant. She tried to listen to the conversation, but it was mostly in Gaelic and apart from the odd word she could not understand it. She grew sleepy and drifted off, waking up some time later to find her head resting on Grant's shoulder.

She sat up quickly. 'Oh, I beg your pardon.'

'No need.' He put his arm about her and pulled her close again. 'Rest now, while you can.'

She was too tired to argue and sank back against him, dozing until they were shown to a corner where there was a covering of bracken and heather on the floor. It was clear they were expected to share the makeshift bed, but before Madeleine could say anything Grant spoke.

'You can sleep here, *mademoiselle*. I have my cloak and shall manage very well in front of the fire.'

Maddie glanced around the cave, noting the dark passages, the distance from the cooking area where the fire was now just a dim glow. She shook her head.

'No. They clearly expect us to share this bed and, to be frank, I think I would like to know you are nearby.' She drew herself up and looked him in the eye. 'I hope you will not abuse my trust in you, Grant Rathmore.'

'You could be the handsomest lass in Scotland and ye'd be safe enough!'

She saw the gleam of his teeth in the dim light.

'What I mean is, you may sleep easy, madam. I am far too exhausted to have any designs upon your virtue tonight!'

They set off again at dawn after a slight confrontation when Maddie offered to pay for their night's shelter. At first Angus Gillies was inclined to take it as an affront to his hospitality, but Maddie insisted.

'Whisht now,' he said, looking at the coins she pressed into his hand, 'What am I supposed to do with these? They are no use to us here, in the mountains.'

'Not yet, perhaps, but you may use the money later, God willing.' She closed his fingers over the coins and held them, saying earnestly, 'It is not much, sir, and I do not wish to cause offence, but I would very much like you to take it.'

The brawny Highlander flushed slightly and raised her hand to plant a clumsy salute upon her fingers.

'Then I shall tak' it in the spirit in which it is given and I will thank ye, mistress, and wish you Godspeed on your journey.'

* * *

As they rode away from the cave, Grant laughed.

'I think you have gained an admirer in old Gillies, mistress. If I had offered him payment, he would have run me through.'

'They were so kind; I could not leave without showing my gratitude. I only hope they live long enough to spend it.' When he looked surprised, she met his eyes steadily. 'I am acutely aware of their predicament, sir, even though I am a stranger here and do not speak the Gaelic.'

She dropped back, indicating the conversation was at an end. Grant pondered her words and found himself wondering at the lady's self-possession. The assault by the redcoats was enough to shred any woman's nerves, but the very next morning she had set off into the unknown with a stranger and maintained her composure even when they had met the Highlanders and she had no idea of what was being said.

'You laughed out loud, Mr Rathmore.' She trotted up beside him. 'What is it that has amused you?'

'I was just thinking what an unusual female you are, Miss Madeleine d'Evremont.'

Her dark brows rose and he found himself being scrutinised by a pair of deep blue eyes. 'Now why should you say that?'

'You are travelling alone with a man you do not know, through a country turned upside down by war, and you show the most admirable sangfroid.'

'I cannot see that hysterics would do me any good at all in my present predicament.'

'True, it would make my escorting you damned difficult!'

That made her laugh this time. 'Indeed, it would. My father said very much the same before he agreed to let me accompany him. He needed a housekeeper, he said, not a watering pot.'

'Are you very close to your father?'

She wrinkled her nose. 'Not particularly—in fact, he can be the most infuriating man, but the alternative to remaining with him would have been going to live with my aunt, who is something of a recluse.'

'From what I know of you that would not have done at all!'

He was pleased when she responded to his grin with a wry smile.

'No, although I think sometimes Papa wished he *had* left me behind, especially when I disagreed with him.'

'Aye, arguments with a parent are the very devil,' he admitted, with feeling.

'Forgive me, but did you quarrel with yours? You said your father did not wish you to fight.'

'He did not.'

Grant closed his lips, but he could not close his mind to the regrets that had plagued him for months. His father had been right, the cause had been lost from the start and the retribution would be—was—bloody.

'So why did you fight for the Stuart Prince?'

Grant sighed. 'A friend was in a rage to go. I had no plans to join the army, but he kept on at me, day after day, persuading me it was my duty to join the cause and put a Stuart back on the throne. Eventually I gave in. I knew my parents would disagree so I gave them no opportunity to stop me. I slipped away.' His mouth twisted at the memory. 'Like a thief in the night. It is my biggest regret, that I did not take my leave of anyone and did not say a proper goodbye, because I can never go back.'

'Pray do not say that. I am sure, one day—'

'No.' Grant interrupted her. On this point he knew he was right. 'Ardvarrick and my family are lost to me now, even if I could be sure of their forgiveness. It is almost inevitable that everyone and everything I hold dear will be punished severely for my actions. One thing is certain: if I go back, the army will follow. The best thing I can do for Ardvarrick is to stay away. That is why I am making my way to the east coast, to secure a passage to France. I have friends there, contacts I made during a brief sojourn in Paris at the age of nineteen, when my father sent me away to broaden my education.'

'I am pleased you will know someone there,' she replied. 'And have you sent word of your intentions to your family? They will want to know you survived the battle.'

'No.'

Grant's jaw was so tight he could barely utter the word as he tried to suppress the guilt, the shame he felt. He often imagined his father's disappointment, his mother's heartbreak at the way he had left them, without a word. He had disobeyed his father and joined the Stuart Prince and even the initial euphoria of those early days, of capturing Edinburgh and the victory at Prestonpans, had never quite dispelled it.

He said now, 'There is little point in telling them anything, until I am safely abroad.'

Maddie recognised the finality in his voice and she said no more. She wanted to urge him to write to his parents, to let them know that at least he had survived

Culloden, but it was no business of hers. She did not know the man well, he would not appreciate her interference, but it cost her an effort to hold her tongue. She maintained her silence as the track took them high over barren hills where the wind blew without ceasing. Maddie was relieved when they dropped down again to take a path through the ancient woodland, even though they had to force their way between the trees in places.

After what seemed like hours, they stopped to rest the ponies and eat the oatcakes and sliver of cheese the Highlanders had given them from their meagre supplies. Neither mentioned their previous conversation and the mood between them was companionable as they sat together, sheltered from the wind by a large boulder projecting from the hillside.

'If I recall correctly what Angus said, we should soon reach Tarland,' Grant told her. 'After that it is but a few miles to the river.'

'Then when you are rested, we had best get on.' She began to pack away the remains of their food. 'All the cheese is gone, but we will save the rest of the oatcakes for later. After all, it is not certain we shall find lodgings tonight.'

It was another full hour of riding before they came to a wide valley. They stopped at the edge of the trees and Maddie could see in the distance a small settlement, smoke curling up from the houses.

'Is that Tarland at last?' she exclaimed. 'Thank heaven! It will be a relief to get back on to an open road again.'

She was about to move forward, but Grant put his hand on her reins.

'Wait.' He was staring towards the settlement. 'There is an unusual amount of activity down there.'

'Perhaps it is market day.'

Madeleine wanted to be sanguine, but she, too, began to feel the first stirrings of alarm as she saw the tiny figures bustling around below them.

'Wait here.'

Grant dismounted and moved cautiously towards the edge of the trees. Maddie paused only to secure the ponies before she joined him.

'I think I can make out splashes of red between the houses,' she murmured, straining her eyes in an effort to see better. She clutched his arm. 'Grant! There are soldiers. Hundreds of them.'

'Aye, and from here they will be patrolling the river for miles in both directions.' She heard him curse under his breath, then he took her hand and pulled her back into the shelter of the trees.

'What do we do?'

'The first thing is to get away from here,' he said grimly. 'Come. We will have to go back and skirt around them. If we keep within the trees, with luck they will not see us.'

They had reached the ponies before she realised he was still holding her hand. When she tried to pull away his grip tightened and he stood for a moment, looking down at her fingers.

'This setback will add considerably to our journey. I am very sorry about that, Madeleine.'

The use of her name and the humble note in Grant's voice twisted something inside her. It was as if an iron band was squeezing around her heart, which alarmed her. And she wanted to comfort him, which alarmed her even more.

'You could not have known.' Gently, she disengaged her hand. 'If we had followed the valley route, the way I wanted to go, we might well have ridden into them. That would have been a great deal worse.'

'Is that an admission that you were wrong, Miss d'Evremont?'

Her lips twitched, but she said with mock severity, 'It is, Mr Rathmore. Now let us mount up and be gone from here before I rescind it!'

They made their way back through the woods until Grant judged it safe enough to turn again.

'We will head east,' he decided. 'We can cross the river further downstream, possibly beyond Aboyne, and approach Glen Muick from the south side.'

She considered this, then nodded. 'How much longer will that take?'

'That depends upon where we can cross the river without being seen.'

'We might try to cross after dark.'

'That is a possibility, but I fear it will add an extra day to our journey, at least.'

'Oh, dear. This is taking more of your time than you had bargained for, Mr Rathmore.'

'Aye, but you have promised I shall be paid for my trouble. Besides...' he looked at her, a gleam of humour lurking in his deep brown eyes '... I cannot abandon a lady in need.'

Maddie looked away, feeling again the tightness

around her heart. If only he would not smile at her in that way! She drew in a long breath to steady herself.

'I have told you before, sir. I can take care of myself.'

'Yes, I remember you saying so, ma'am, more than once. Very well, let us get on!'

Grant's words and the laugh in his voice did much to dispel the unfamiliar feelings. In fact, she thought, with growing indignation, she had a strong inclination to box his ears for teasing her!

There was no more opportunity for idle banter. They kept to the wooded slopes, but it was necessary to stay alert for army patrols. Thankfully, the redcoats who were on the hills saw no need for caution and crashed their way through the trees, giving Grant and Maddie time to conceal themselves in the undergrowth.

It made for slow going and they were not even within sight of the river by nightfall.

'With this cloud cover it will soon be too dark to see,' remarked Grant. 'We must consider stopping soon. We should look out for a hut or barn to shelter for a few hours.'

'I think we would be safer here among the trees,' said Maddie. 'We have seen so many soldiers today that they are very likely to be making use of any building themselves.' She glanced about her and pointed to one side. 'There is a rocky overhang there, which will offer us a little protection from the weather and it is well screened by the surrounding woodland.'

Grant nodded. 'That will suit us very well.'

It did not take them long to see to the horses and make themselves comfortable against the rockface, wrapped in their cloaks. Maddie rummaged in her saddlebag and pulled out what was left of the oatcakes.

'They are a little broken, I'm afraid,' she said, unwrapping the muslin and offering the crumbly remains to Grant, 'but we shall not starve.'

'I am only sorry it is too dangerous to light a fire,' he remarked. 'However, I do have this to keep out the chill.' He pulled a small flask from his pocket and offered it to Madeleine, who eyed it suspiciously.

What is it?

'Uisge beatha,' he said. 'Whisky.'

She took the flask, raised it to her lips and took a sip. The fiery liquid burned her throat as she swallowed.

'Oh!' She drew a long breath, taking in the pungent aroma that lingered in her mouth. 'That is certainly warming.'

He laughed. 'Have you not had whisky before?'

'Never. I believe it needs to be drunk with some caution.'

'You are very right.'

She took another sip, this time rolling the liquid around her tongue. 'However, it is not unpleasant.'

She handed the flask back to him and saw the flash of white as he smiled.

'We will make a Highlander of ye yet, lassie.'

She munched on an oatcake, deciding it was safer to ignore his impertinence.

The darkness settled around them and soft sounds filled the night: the snuffle of the ponies tethered nearby, the occasional hoot of an owl and the rustle of small animals. The noises were reassuring and Madeleine felt quite comfortable sitting beside Grant, their shoulders almost touching.

'This place was a good choice, Miss d'Evremont,' he remarked, in a tone of approval. He offered her the flask again. 'I doubt we could have found a better spot.'

She took another sip of the fiery spirit. It was most assuredly warming.

'I am not totally without experience,' she told him. 'My father and I were obliged to sleep out of doors on more than one occasion.'

'Evading brigands?'

'Not always, sometimes my father was avoiding the law.'

'What a colourful existence you have had, ma'am.'

She shrugged. 'Papa always said he only did what was necessary to survive, although I might wish that our life had been a little more conventional.'

'I fear you would find *conventional* very dull.'

She laughed. 'Possibly.'

'Would you like another dram?'

'Thank you, no. I must not. I need to keep my wits about me.'

'I am not trying to make you intoxicated, Miss d'Evremont.'

'You would not be the first man to make the attempt,' she flashed back at him, embarrassed that he had guessed her thoughts.

Suddenly, the darkness and their isolation felt much more dangerous.

'I should inform you that Papa has an advantageous match planned for me,' she told him. 'A suitor from a minor branch of the Bourbon dynasty, so I am not minded to throw myself away on just any man.'

His response was little more than a grunt, which sounded almost derisive. How dare he! After a moment she continued.

'I must say, though, that some of my suitors have been *most* attractive.' She added with an air of superiority she knew would irk him, 'Very rich and exceedingly handsome.'

She smiled in the darkness when she heard his little growl of annoyance.

'Perhaps I should set your mind at rest,' he said. 'I find females with an independent, managing disposition most unattractive. They are not at all in my line. Especially foreign women with a dubious history.'

She winced, but could not really blame him for retaliating.

'I am glad to hear it,' she retorted. Then, deciding it would not be wise to pursue the argument, she said, 'Now, one of us will need to be awake at all times, so will you take the first watch or shall I?'

They agreed that Grant would sit up first. Madeleine wrapped herself in her cloak and settled down on the ground, using her saddlebags as a pillow.

'Independent, managing,' she said to herself as she tried to get comfortable. The words rankled and she wished now she had not teased him. Not even the knowledge that she was safe from his advances made her feel any better.

Grant huddled into his cloak and sat quietly, watching and listening for danger, while their conversation rattled about in his head. So, he was neither handsome nor rich enough for Miss Madeleine d'Evremont! Not that it mattered one jot to him. She was spoiled, hot-tempered and far too strong-willed for his tastes. The sooner he handed her over to her friends in Glen Muick, the better!

Chapter Four

'Madeleine. Come along, wake up now. We must be moving.'

There was a hand on her shoulder, gently shaking her. Madeleine sat up, rubbing her eyes and blinking in the grey light.

'It is almost dawn. I was supposed to take a watch, Grant. Why did you not wake me?'

'You were sleeping so peacefully I thought you would benefit from a longer rest.' He handed her the water flask. 'As soon as it was light enough, I walked on a little way to see if I could ascertain where we are. Good news, the river is much closer than we thought when we stopped last night. I think we might try to make a crossing now.'

'By all means.' She shook off her remaining sleepiness and scrambled to her feet.

'I have already saddled the garrons, so let us be gone with all speed.'

Maddie wanted to object to him doing so much while she slept, but instead she merely thanked him. He had used her name again this morning and she had used his. It felt natural, comfortable and she was reluctant to upset the new camaraderie.

Soon they were picking their way through the trees and down the hill to the water's edge. A pre-dawn half light covered the land, but it was possible to see the river gleaming silver-grey as it wound its way through the valley.

'The water is quite shallow here,' said Grant as they made their way to the bank. 'The bed is rocky, so we will have to take care, but the trees and the natural bends of the river will give us some cover. With luck no one will be watching at this time in the morning.' He paused and looked across at her. 'Are you ready?'

Madeleine swallowed nervously. If there were soldiers guarding this stretch of the river, then they would soon know of it.

She nodded. 'Lead on, sir.'

'Good. Follow close behind me, now.'

Once they had slithered down the bank into the water, the sure-footed ponies made easy work of the river, although for Madeleine the crossing seemed to go on for ever. She was aware of the birdsong in the trees, the noisy gurgle of the water as it splashed and danced around the rocks on the riverbed, but she was tense, her spine stiff as she anticipated any moment hearing a shout or a shot.

The ponies picked their way over the loose scree on the far side of the river and scrambled up the bank. Soon they were once more hidden among the trees. Only then did Maddie realise she had been holding her breath. She closed her eyes and clung to the saddle, head bowed.

'Madeleine? Are you ill?'

Grant came up beside her and caught her arm. She put her free hand over his and gripped it, drawing comfort from his very real and solid strength.

'No, only relieved that we are once more under cover. I fear I would not make a very good soldier.'

'You have shown great courage.'

In one swift movement his fingers twisted beneath hers and he lifted her hand to his lips. The gesture was so unexpected that it startled Madeleine. She was more accustomed to Grant teasing her. Indeed, she would have preferred him to make a joking riposte. His quiet words made her heart soar, yet at the same time she wanted to cry, although she was at a loss to know why.

Grant cleared his throat and carefully released her hand. 'We had best be moving on.'

He led the way, weaving between the trees and bushes, Maddie following in his wake, unable to forget the way he had kissed her hand. She found herself reliving the moment, feeling again the delicious, aching lightness inside that made her want to hug herself. She looked at the man riding ahead of her. She was paying him handsomely for his escort, but she did not think that was the reason for his kind words. She did not believe he would speak anything but the truth, so did he really approve of her? She squirrelled the idea away, afraid to put too much store by it, but hoping it was true.

They pressed on through the morning and into the afternoon. Grant spoke to the tenants of a small farm and purchased fresh bannocks and cheese, which they stopped to eat about a mile further on.

'From what the farmer told me, I think we are little more than ten miles from Loch Muick,' said Grant.

'Do they know that is our destination?'

'No, but even if they did I doubt they would betray us. They made it clear they have no love for the army.' He added, to reassure her, 'A few more hours will see you safe.'

Maddie merely nodded and continued to nibble at a piece of cheese. They had found a grassy bank, sheltered from the wind and overlooking the River Muick, to sit and eat. It was strangely peaceful and she was moved to remark upon it.

'The sun has rarely put in an appearance on this journey. In fact, until now the skies have been mostly leaden ever since I left Inverness. I have never known a country so cold and wet.'

'Ah, but there is nowhere better than the Highlands when the sun shines,' murmured Grant, lying back with his hands behind his head.

'It is the rarity that makes it so prized,' she declared. 'And the biting winds seem to blow all year round.'

She waited, expecting him to defend his homeland, but when she turned to look at him she saw that he was fast asleep. A wave of tenderness washed over her. He had stayed awake all night, keeping vigil. He must be quite exhausted.

Gently, she removed the uneaten bread from his fingers and rewrapped it.

'Sleep now,' she murmured, reaching out to smooth a stray lock of auburn hair from his brow. 'It is my turn to keep watch over you.'

* * *

They reached their destination as the sun was heading towards the western mountains. Lochall House was a substantial property on the edge of a wide glen that looked like a haven of green tranquillity. The house itself was built in the old style, a rectangular block with two square towers set diagonally on the corners, but lime harling and the addition of an extra wing had softened the old lines.

'That is a welcome sight,' remarked Maddie, drawing rein to look out over the prospect before they descended to the valley.

Grant stopped beside her, his keen gaze taking in the tended fields and smoke rising from the bothies in the small settlement at the edge of the loch. It appeared as yet untouched by the troubles.

'Looks can be deceptive,' he warned her. 'We will approach with caution.'

Thankfully his fears were unfounded. Upon arrival they were shown into the drawing room, where their hosts were waiting for them.

'Mistress d'Evremont! I am delighted to see you have arrived safely.' Lady Lochall hurried towards Madeleine, a smile on her kindly features and her hands held out in welcome.

'Thank you, ma'am.' Maddie looked about her, an anxious note in her voice. 'I had hoped to find my father here… '

'Alas, no, my dear child. All we have is his letter, telling us to expect you. It appears he was obliged to return to France upon a delicate family matter.'

'It is a pity he could not have let his daughter know of it sooner,' remarked Grant.

Lord Lochall looked at him, his brows raised in enquiry, and Maddie hurried to make an introduction.

'May I present Mr Grant Rathmore, my lord? He kindly agreed to escort me here from Kildrummy.'

'Any relation to Logan Rathmore, of Ardvarrick?' asked Lord Lochall.

Grant bowed. 'His son, my lord.'

His Lordship's manner softened a little more. He appeared reassured by Grant's answer and Maddie wondered if her escort was not such a lowly traveller as he had made out.

'But are you not on your way home, sir?' Lord Lochall asked him. 'Miss d'Evremont said you had come from Kildrummy. This is a mighty long way in the wrong direction.'

'I am not going to Ardvarrick. I am heading for the east coast and France.'

'Well now,' exclaimed Lady Lochall, 'What a blessing it would have been if only Yves d'Evremont had known of that, Mr Rathmore—'

'My dear, you are too precipitate,' cut in Lord Lochall, frowning at her. 'I am sure we do not need to bore our guest with these tedious matters.'

'No, no, of course not, how silly of me!' Lady Lochall laughed and fluttered about them, shepherding them further into the room, encouraging them to take a seat.

'But you said you have heard from Papa, my lord,' said Madeleine, remaining on her feet beside Grant. 'Odd that he could not find the time to write to *me*.'

'Perhaps he considered the situation in Inverness to

be too volatile to risk a letter,' suggested Lord Lochall peaceably. 'And from his missive, I believe his return to France was a matter of some urgency.'

'It is always the same with Yves,' declared Lady Lochall, laughing gently. 'He is forever telling us that he is engaged upon some delicate matter, or something of vital importance to France, and it is always of the utmost secrecy!'

'You would appear to know my father rather well, ma'am,' Maddie remarked.

'Yes, indeed, we knew Yves d'Evremont even before he married your dear mama. We have kept in touch with him ever since, although we have not met for some time.' Lady Lochall gave an airy wave of one hand. 'We attended their wedding, in Dijon. Do you remember, my lord? A long time ago now and, alas, we have seen little of Yves since then. Those were such *good* days... But enough of that! Your dear papa gave us no idea of when to expect you, which is why you find us in such disarray and rooms not prepared. Yves wrote that you would be travelling with your maid.'

'She was reluctant to come.' Maddie gestured towards her companion. 'Which is why I was glad to enlist Mr Rathmore as an escort.'

He caught her hand and carried it to his lips. 'And it has been an honour to be of service to you, Miss d'Evremont!'

She saw the wickedly teasing gleam in his eye, but it was the kiss on her fingers that made her snatch her hand away. She could still feel it, tiny darts of fire piercing her skin and travelling up her arm. The sensation was disconcerting. It made the breath catch in her throat and threw her off balance.

A servant had come in with refreshments and while Lord and Lady Lochall were distracted Maddie took the opportunity to glare at Grant.

'I am not paying you to flirt with me, sir!' she hissed.

She turned away, but not before she saw a shadow of surprise cross his face. Immediately she was contrite. What was wrong with her, that she must rip up at him over such a trifle? It was most uncivil of her to remind him that he was little more than her servant. Really, she was becoming quite a harridan.

Lady Lochall came bustling up.

'Come, come now, I pray you will both sit down with us and take a glass of wine while bedchambers are prepared for you!' She carried Madeleine off to a sofa and sat down beside her. 'My dear, what a time you have had of it, being alone in Inverness with the battle virtually on your doorstep! Thank heaven you reached us safely. Let me look at you, for I have not seen you since you were in your cradle! Yes, you have your dear mama's colouring, such a shame she died so young, for I am sure she would not have allowed Yves to bring you to Scotland at such a time! But enough of that. You are here safe and that is all that matters. Now, I am sure you would like to try one of these little cakes, nothing too much, of course, or they will spoil your appetite.'

Lady Lochall rattled on and Madeleine responded when necessary, aware that their host was engaging Grant in conversation on similarly innocuous subjects. It was clear that nothing more was to be explained about the arrangements for her flight to France, for a while at least.

* * *

Grant responded mechanically to his host's attempts to converse, his true thoughts concealed beneath a look of polite interest. His spurt of anger against Madeleine d'Evremont had quickly faded into rueful acceptance. Having delivered her safely to Lochall House, he had allowed himself to relax his guard and it had been in a playful mood that he had kissed her hand. He had known almost immediately he had made a mistake, for there had been such a jolt of attraction as his lips touched her skin. He had known a sudden desire to pull her close and capture her mouth with his own. Her swift rebuke had been a brutal reminder of what she thought of him. Theirs was a business arrangement. He had been at fault and would take care not to put himself in that position again.

At last a footman came in to announce that rooms were ready and they all rose. Lady Lochall waved towards the servant.

'Samuel will escort you to your room, Mr Rathmore, where I trust you will find everything you need. If we have forgotten anything, pray do not hesitate to ask. I shall tell Cook to set back dinner and we shall meet here again in, say, two hours. Will that suit you, sir?'

Grant bowed. 'You are all kindness, ma'am.'

He followed the servant out of the room, aware of his relief that the Lochalls were treating him as a gentleman. And why should they not? After all, he was still Grant Rathmore, heir of Ardvarrick, whatever Mademoiselle Madeleine d'Evremont thought of him.

When Grant had gone, Madeleine felt bereft, desolated that she had not been able to apologise to him, but she hid it beneath a smile when Lady Lochall took her arm.

'I shall escort you upstairs to your room myself, Miss d'Evremont. You will feel so much more comfortable when you have had a little time to refresh yourself.'

Chattering, her hostess swept her out of the room and up a wide staircase. Maddie glanced up, hoping to see Grant ahead of her, but he had already disappeared and she tried to concentrate upon what her hostess was saying.

'I had Tomson, my abigail, look out some clothes for you. They belonged to my daughter, before she was married, and you are not so very different in size, although she was a little taller, I think. Tomson is an excellent seamstress and will add a little tuck here and there to make them fit you.'

'But I could not possibly impose in this way, my lady!'

'My dear Madeleine—I may call you that, may I not?—it is no trouble at all, I assure you. Your father hinted that you would be travelling light and I feel sure you would like to change out of your riding clothes, if for no other reason than to prettify yourself for Mr Rathmore.'

At this Madeleine stopped. She felt a slight embarrassment that her hostess had seen Grant kiss her hand, but that was nothing to her mortification at the cruel way she had rebuffed him.

'Lady Lochall, please believe that I have no interest at all in Mr Rathmore, nor he in me. I *paid* him to escort me here.' She managed to laugh. 'Goodness, it has come to a pretty pass when one cannot hire an escort without tongues wagging.'

Lady Lochall looked as if she would say more, but something in Madeleine's manner prevented her. She merely sighed and shook her head, and they continued up the stairs.

It was a full two hours before Madeleine was ready to make her way back to the drawing room. Her hostess had been a little optimistic in comparing Madeleine's petite figure with that of her daughter and it took the long-suffering maid a great deal of expertise and ingenuity to adjust a green satin robe to fit. She was just putting the finishing touches to Maddie's hair when Lady Lochall knocked on the door.

'May I come in? I have come to fetch Miss d'Evremont down for dinner, Tomson, if you have finished.'

'I have now, my lady,' replied the maid, stepping back and critically surveying her handiwork. 'I think she'll do now.'

Maddie rose from the dressing stool, laughing and blushing at the same time as Lady Lochall clapped her hands and exclaimed that she had never seen the closed gown look better.

'Tomson, you are a miracle!'

'She is indeed, ma'am,' agreed Madeleine, 'and I am most grateful to you for allowing her to dress me, although I did not mean to keep her here for so long. After all she is your maid.'

'Do not fret, my dear, the second housemaid helped me dress, which was all that was required today, and I am delighted with what Tomson has achieved for you. I shall have her look out more gowns tomorrow. And

I will not be gainsaid, Madeleine, because they are doing no good shut away in a trunk so you had best make use of them.'

Maddie's stuttered thanks were cut short as the abigail grimly reminded Her Ladyship of the time.

'Oh, heavens, yes, thank you, Tomson. Come along, my dear, the gentlemen will be waiting for us!'

Grant had been shown into a small but well-appointed guest room. He shrugged off his coat and gave it to the servant to take away and clean it up as best he could, then he made use of the ewer of hot water to wash off the dirt of travel before stretching himself out on the bed. He was asleep almost immediately, only to be woken some time later by a soft scratching at the door.

As he sat up, a small man in a black suit entered.

'I beg your pardon for disturbing you, sir, I am Bailey, His Lordship's valet. He asked me to bring your change of clothes.'

'My what?'

The valet ignored the question and reverently laid the garments over a chair.

'I took the liberty of looking these out for you, sir, and I trust they will fit you. I judged your size from your existing coat.'

'Mighty good of you,' muttered Grant. The way the fellow said the last words suggested he did not approve of the shabby frock coat with a musket ball hole in the skirts.

Bailey gently laid a pair of tartan stockings on top of the pile, then turned to Grant.

'Will that will be all, sir?'

'Aye,' growled Grant, swinging his legs off the bed. 'Thank you, but I don't need you to help me dress.' The man bowed solemnly and as he moved towards the door, Grant called after him. 'Pray thank His Lordship for his kind consideration.'

At the appointed time he presented himself in the drawing room, where he found Lord Lochall waiting for him. He bowed slightly and waved a hand towards his attire.

'I am indebted to you, my lord, for supplying me with fresh clothing.'

'It is nothing.' The ghost of a smile appeared on His Lordship's thin face as he handed over a glass of wine.

'I take it you had exchanged your Highland dress for those rags you arrived in.'

'It was…expedient.'

'You were at Culloden?' The blunt question surprised Grant, but he answered calmly.

'Aye. A foot soldier.'

'An officer, surely.'

Grant shook his head. 'I left Ardvarrick with hardly a penny to my name and joined up. I'd not use my father's money for a cause he did not support.'

'And that is why you are not going home.'

Grant hesitated. 'I have a fancy to see something of the world first.'

He was not sure his host believed him, but he could not bring himself to admit that he felt too guilty to return. He had taken no Ardvarrick men with him, but Jamie Cowie had been accompanied by twenty or more from neighbouring Contullach and less than a handful had escaped with their lives. How could he go back, when others, young men he had known all his life, could not?

He thrust the thought aside and tried to concentrate upon his host, who was reminiscing about his own Grand Tour. Grant encouraged this theme, interjecting the occasional question or remark and the subject lasted them until the ladies came in.

Grant was relieved to be nothing but a spectator for the first few minutes of their arrival. Madeleine had changed her shabby riding gown for a robe of pale green satin, closed at the front by yellow bows and with a muslin fichu draped about her shoulders. Her wild curls had been tamed and confined by a green ribbon. There was a delicate flush to her cheeks when Lord Lochall complimented her upon her appearance, but Grant noticed a slight air of distraction, as if she had something on her mind, and no sooner had Lady Lochall claimed her husband's attention than Madeleine came over to him.

'I am very sorry for the way I spoke to you earlier,' she murmured, eyes downcast.

'Think nothing of it, madam.'

'I was impolite. I beg your pardon.'

He put up his brows and said lightly, 'Can one be ill mannered to a lowly hired hand?'

Her eyes flew to his face and he cursed himself for allowing his hurt to show.

'You know I do not think of you like that,' she murmured.

'And now it is my turn to beg your pardon.' He resisted the temptation to reach for her hand and contented himself with a smile. 'Cry *pax* with me, then, lady, and we will forget this matter.'

'Yes.'

As if by magic her face cleared and it felt to Grant as if the sun had come out from behind a cloud.

'Yes. Thank you.'

Lady Lochall called her name and Madeleine moved away. Grant watched her, glad to see her sunny spirits restored. Her blue eyes sparkled with merriment as she laughed at something her hostess was saying and she presented a very pleasant picture, one Grant would have been happy to study in silence for some time. However, good manners dictated that he should join in the conversation and he did his best. Fortunately it was not long before they went into the dining room, but if he thought he might be spared the distraction of Madeleine's animated countenance he was disappointed, for they were seated opposite one another.

The dinner was a good one. They had not eaten so well since leaving the Highlanders' cave and he had to concentrate to prevent himself bolting his food down greedily. A glance across the table told him Madeleine was coping much better. She looked quite at home, picking daintily at her food while keeping up a conversation with her hostess.

She looked quite at ease in her borrowed finery, conversing as if she had not a care in the world. She really was an exceptional woman, he thought. And quite pretty, he decided, in an unconventional sort of way. Not his sort, of course. He did not favour small, dark-haired women with decided views and sharp tongues.

'And you, Mr Rathmore—' Lady Lochall's voice cut

into his thoughts and brought him back to the present '—perhaps you will tell us how you come to be escorting our young friend?'

Across the table, Madeleine sent him a warning glance which he acknowledged with a smile before responding to his hostess.

'We met at Kildrummy, ma'am. Miss d'Evremont's maid had left and there was no one at the change house who could escort her, so I offered to undertake the task.'

Maddie breathed out, relieved he had not given too much away about their first encounter. She did not wish to be reminded of the way the soldiers had attacked her, or her own folly in putting herself into such a vulnerable position.

'I am very grateful to him for delivering me here safely,' she said now. 'The journey was not without its difficulties. Mr Rathmore must be happy to be relieved of the burden.'

'You could never be a burden to me, madam.'

She felt a sudden breathlessness. He spoke lightly, as if the words were mere politeness, but the message in his eyes was very different. She had seen such a glow before in a gentleman's eyes when he was attracted to a woman. He did not look as if he was teasing her, but surely he could not be serious! She felt a tiny frisson of excitement.

When Maddie had entered the drawing room she had thought how well Grant looked in the tartan short-coat and coloured breeches. He had brought no clothes with him so she could only surmise that Lord Lochall had looked them out. They were a fraction on the small side, she had noted, for the coat was strained across

Grant's broad shoulders and she remembered how she had been obliged to avert her eyes from the tight breeches, which left little to the imagination.

The thought of those muscled thighs now brought the heat rising through Maddie, setting her body on fire. This would not do at all! She must keep the conversation light-hearted or she would be lost.

She managed a little laugh. 'You flatter me, Mr Rathmore. You know I did not take kindly to your advice, when you insisted we avoid the main tracks.'

'But you were very wise to do so, Miss d'Evremont,' put in Lord Lochall. 'I have heard the redcoats can be a little...unruly.'

'I believe they can be,' returned Maddie, keeping her eyes lowered.

'We have been very fortunate here,' Lady Lochall informed them. 'Ormskirk, the Captain of Dragoons, is a very civil young man and keeps his men under very strict discipline.'

'That is not to say he poses no threat,' said her husband, his eyes flickering towards the servants standing by the door. 'We must all be cautious. Miss d'Evremont, may I help you to a little more of the ragout? You appeared to enjoy it.'

The conversation shifted to food, but when the gentlemen returned to the drawing room later that evening Maddie took the earliest opportunity of speaking to Grant.

The servants had withdrawn and their hosts were engaged in discussing the merits of serving claret— His Lordship's preference, and smuggled into the country—against the Rhenish, which was my lady's choice of wine.

Maddie walked across to Grant, who was studying one of the portraits on the wall, and said a quiet thank-you.

He turned to her. 'For what?'

'For not disclosing what happened at Kildrummy. I am ashamed that I allowed myself to fall into such danger.'

'I do not think you could have prevented it.'

'I might have done so. I was too complacent, you see. If I had dined in my room, rather than insisting that I have a private parlour, I might well have avoided their attention.'

'I doubt it. Those men were drunk and intent upon mischief. I am only glad I was there to step in.'

'So, too, am I.'

She smiled and briefly placed her hand on his arm before turning away and going back towards the fire, where she sat down beside Lady Lochall.

The touch was fleeting but, combined with her smile, the effect had been powerful. His heart was still racing and he was only too aware of the little arrows of fire that her fingers had sent through his sleeve and into his arm. They were even now coursing through his body, playing havoc with his peace of mind.

Grant exhaled slowly. Inconvenient, to say the least. The lady had made it clear she would not welcome his attentions, so it would be madness to read too much into that little exchange. Despite her apology before dinner, he knew she thought of him as little more than a servant.

'Rathmore, what are you doing there in the shadows, sir? Pray come and sit down with us and allow me to refill your glass.'

His host's call roused Grant. He summoned a smile as he crossed the room towards them.

'You were looking at the portrait of my husband, were you not?' Lady Lochall asked him. 'It was done several years ago. There is a much finer one in the morning room, by Ramsay of Edinburgh. It was painted a couple of years ago. But perhaps you did not see it, it is over the door.'

'Aye, but I did, ma'am. I also noted its partner, the portrait of yourself on the opposite wall. Both excellent likenesses.'

Grant did not add that Ramsay had also painted his portrait. His father had most likely removed it to the attics now. Putting the picture of his disgraced heir out of sight. Putting him out of their life. He had lost not only Ardvarrick, but his family, too. Regret sliced into him like a dirk as he thought of it.

Lady Lochall was asking Madeleine if she had ever had her likeness painted.

'Yes, in Rome, but I have no idea where the painting is now. Possibly at the house of my aunt, in Dijon. My father arranged for it to be shipped there, but I have not been back to France since.'

Lady Lochall gave a sigh and caught her hands. 'Ah, poor child, to wander Europe like a nomad!'

Madeleine looked a little uncomfortable at this show of sympathy.

'Think of it another way, my lady,' Grant said, 'such a nomadic life means that Miss d'Evremont has not been *bored*.'

As he had hoped, Madeleine laughed.

'No, indeed, I should hate that above all things!'

There was gratitude in the look she threw him and he sat back in his chair, sipping his wine, wondering if anyone could be bored in her company.

Chapter Five

The next morning Maddie awoke to find another gown laid out for her. The young maid who came in with her morning chocolate explained.

'Mrs Tomson worked on it during the night, ma'am, and Her Ladyship sent it up with her compliments, only you was sound asleep then and she had said I wasn't to wake you.'

'Pray thank Lady Lochall and Tomson for me.'

Maddie took the cup of hot chocolate with a murmur of thanks, but the maid did not move away from the bed. Instead she dipped a little curtsy.

'I am to wait upon you, if you please, so shall I fetch up the hot water now?'

When Madeleine was at last washed and dressed she made her way downstairs, where she found Grant and the Lochalls in the sunny morning room and she was swift to thank her hosts for their kindness.

'To be offered an excellent breakfast in the privacy of my room and to have a maid, and fresh gowns, makes me feel thoroughly spoiled. It is especially welcome after the travails of the past few weeks,' she told them.

'I am glad—I should not wish any daughter of mine to find herself in your predicament. To be without the protection of a parent in such times as these must be very worrying.'

'I confess I was a little anxious, with the battle so close to Inverness and not to have any further word from Papa. I can only thank Mr Rathmore for giving me his escort to get here.' She bent a swift smile in his direction. 'I fear I have seriously delayed your own journey, sir. No doubt you will be relieved to be on your way again today. I am grateful that you waited, that I may take my leave of you.'

Lady Lochall spoke up. 'As to that, we have persuaded Mr Rathmore to remain with us until tomorrow, to rest himself properly.'

'I am very glad to hear it,' exclaimed Madeleine, genuinely pleased at the thought. 'That is, if it does not upset your plans?'

'Not at all,' Grant replied. 'Another day here or there will make no difference to me.'

'And you young people will be company for one another this evening,' declared Lady Lochall, beaming at them.

Madeleine blushed and then hated herself for showing such weakness. She moved off to sit down upon a chair, where she busied herself arranging her skirts.

'Talking of journeys, how soon do you expect to hear from Papa, my lord?' She noted Lord Lochall's hesitation and added, 'I do not believe we have anything to fear if we speak frankly before Mr Rathmore.'

His Lordship acknowledged this with a nod. He said

heavily, 'Your father's note said it would take time to put his plans in place, Miss d'Evremont. He insists he will arrange everything, but we have yet to learn the details. Once we do, we can make arrangements for you to travel onwards.'

Lady Lochall beamed even more. 'In the meantime, my dear Madeleine, we are delighted to have you here with us, is that not so, Lochall?'

'Of course. I—'

He broke off as the doors flew open and a bluff, good-humoured voice declared, 'So you are at home, my lord. I thought I should find you here!'

His back to the door, Lord Lochall muttered in exasperation and threw a look of apology mixed with warning towards his guests. Maddie watched as a large, fashionably dressed man entered the room and stopped just inside the door, a look of almost comical consternation on his round features.

'By heaven, Your Ladyship, I beg your pardon! I did not know you had visitors. Why did that fool butler of yours not tell me?' He gave a loud, rumbling laugh. 'But then, I did not give the poor fellow time to catch his breath! I thought it would be safe to find you and Lochall alone at this time in the morning and said there was no need to announce me.'

The speech was delivered without pause as the man came across the room to kiss my lady's hand, talking all the while. Lady Lochall recovered from her surprise and responded with a smile.

'Why, Mr Sumington, it is quite delightful to see you here, indeed it is.'

'Ah, you are all kindness, my lady.' The newcomer beamed at her a moment longer before straightening and directing his enquiring gaze towards Maddie. 'Now, won't you make me known to your young friends?'

Lord Lochall obliged with introductions, alluding to Madeleine as a young protégée of his lady and vaguely describing Grant as the son of an old friend. Then, in turn, he explained that Mr William Sumington was his neighbour.

'Neighbour and *friend*, Lochall. Why, blow me, man, we have known each other these past forty years, ain't we? And that is why I am here. I don't stand on ceremony with such an old acquaintance.'

'No, indeed not.' Lady Lochall smiled and encouraged him to go on.

'Well, 'tis like this, ma'am, Mrs Sumington is craving a ball. Now 'tis no good my telling the wee wifey that this isn't the time for such merriment, she thinks a little dancing is just what the young ones need—I have two sons and two daughters, you see, Miss d'Evremont, and they are desperate to stand up with partners other than their siblings, so we fixed on Thursday to invite a few close friends and neighbours.'

Lord Lochall put up one hand. 'Do you mean tomorrow, sir?'

'Aye, my lord, that is correct. Which is why I am riding about the countryside today, to give the invitation to our neighbours. Short notice, I know, and whether anyone will care to join us for an impromptu gathering is another matter, but I am hopeful some will come. At least enough to make up a second set. And I see now it was Providence that brought me here today,' he concluded, beaming at Madeleine and Grant, 'because some new young blood is just what is required!'

Maddie felt quite battered by Mr Sumington's cheerfulness, but when Lord Lochall glanced at her, one brow raised in enquiry, she gave the tiniest nod.

'My lady and I will be delighted to come over, sir, and to bring Miss d'Evremont with us. However, Mr Rathmore will be resuming his journey in the morning.'

'Alas, that is true,' replied Grant, 'Else I would have been only too happy to join you.'

'Ah, that is a pity, but I quite understand,' declared Mr Sumington. 'However, if you change your mind then you will be very welcome, young man. Very welcome. Now, I will not impose any longer upon you and your guests. I shall report back. No, no, I shall not stay for refreshments, my lady, I have more calls to make yet! We can converse more tomorrow, what?'

And with that Mr Sumington bowed low and swept out again, leaving a marked silence behind him.

'Well,' declared Lady Lochall, throwing herself back into her chair and plying her fan vigorously. 'I vow that man goes beyond what is pleasing, walking in here as bold as brass! What was Roberts about, to let him come in like that? I suppose he had gone to some other part of the house and left it to one of the under-footmen to answer the door. I shall have words with him!'

'I believe Sumington is sound enough,' replied her husband. He turned towards Grant, 'Although I should have preferred him not to know of your presence here. He is bound to carry the news back to Sumington Lodge and I don't doubt one of the family will mention it at the ball.'

'Not quite a ball, my lord,' Grant corrected him with a smile. 'Your neighbour distinctly told us it would be nothing but an impromptu gathering.'

'But word spreads far and wide from these affairs,' replied Lady Lochall, uncharacteristically serious. 'It was my plan to keep Miss d'Evremont here quietly and pass her off as the daughter of an old friend. Oh, my dear, what a pity I did not think to tell Mr Sumington that you were in mourning. We could have invented some relative for the purpose.'

Despite her anxiety, Maddie laughed at the lady's speech.

'What is done is done, ma'am,' she replied. 'I must make the best of it.'

'You are quite right, Miss d'Evremont,' agreed Lord Lochall. 'Now, if you will excuse me, there are letters I must write. It is a fine day and my stables are at your disposal, Mr Rathmore, if you would like to ride?'

'Thank you, sir, but after all the riding we have done these past days I would appreciate a day *out* of the saddle.'

'Then might I recommend a walk in the gardens. They have recently been remodelled to my own design.'

'Perhaps Miss d'Evremont would like to join you,' put in Lady Lochall. 'The new paths are very well drained now and even though we had heavy rain in the night, it will be quite safe to walk upon them. And there is a delightful little wilderness that you might enjoy.'

Madeleine hesitated, but when Grant added his voice to the invitation she accepted and ran upstairs to fetch a shawl.

Outside, the air was fresh, but a bright sun shone down and, where there were high hedges to provide shelter, it was pleasantly warm.

Grant was very conscious of the young lady on his arm, but he reminded himself that they must soon part and he must not allow himself to enjoy her company too much. Not that he would be tempted to delay his departure. The longer he remained in Scotland the greater the danger.

'What do you make of our hosts?' Madeleine asked, interrupting his thoughts as they strolled along. 'Do you think I can trust them?'

He hesitated. 'I believe so. They are old friends of your father, and he has consigned you to their care.'

'My father is not always the best judge of character,' she told him. 'I noted the white rose and the thistle on the wineglasses at dinner last night. I know that can be a sign of Jacobite supporters, but His Lordship has been very circumspect in his conversation.'

'My presence might account for his reticence. It is also likely he prefers that the servants remain ignorant of any plans, as much for their own sake as his.'

'There is that,' she admitted. She gave a sigh and turned her face up to the sun. 'What a relief it is to be out of doors and able to speak freely.'

'You trust *me*, then?' he asked, pleased with the idea.

Her face softened into a smile. 'How could I not, after your service to me? Which reminds me.' She stopped and pulled a small red leather purse from her pocket and held it out.

'What is that?' He made no move to take it.

'The ten guineas I owe you. I promised to pay it once we reached here.'

'I had forgotten all about it,' he confessed.

She pushed the purse against his chest. 'Take it, Grant. It was honestly earned.'

But it did not sit well with him, taking money from a woman.

'It is not necessary; I have sufficient to get me to the coast.' It was a lie and Madeleine's look told him she knew it.

'I want you to take it. We agreed the sum.'

Grant noted the stubborn set to her dainty chin, but still he shook his head.

'I do not want it.'

'You have a long journey ahead; you will need it.'

'I shall manage,' he said impatiently. 'Put your money away, Madeleine.'

She drew herself up, her eyes flashing. 'I will be in no man's debt!'

With that she pushed the purse into the pocket of his jacket and stalked off.

For a stunned moment he watched her walk away, the skirts of her gown catching the light with every sway of her hips.

'Madeleine, wait!' Grant muttered a curse and ran to catch up with her. 'Of all the hot-at-hand females… *Stop*, damn you!' He caught her arm, his free hand diving into his pocket to retrieve the purse and thrusting it back at her. 'I have said I do not want this and I will not take it! I have friends near Aberdeen who will help me, *if* I need funds. You, on the other hand, may need every last groat to pay for your safe passage to your father. Now for heaven's sake stop being so foolish and put your money *away*!'

Her eyes positively blazed with fury and he braced himself for a tirade, but to his astonishment she remained silent. The fire in her eyes was doused by gleaming tears and his own anger died as quickly as it had come.

'Oh, Madeleine!' He cupped her face and gently wiped his thumbs across her cheeks. 'I beg your pardon. I would not for the world make you weep.'

'I am not w-weeping,' she retorted, pulling away from him and dashing her lacy handkerchief across her eyes. 'I detest such weakness!'

That made him smile.

'I am sure you do,' he murmured.

She was looking about her with the air of a hunted animal and he said gently, 'If we go back to the house with you showing such signs of distress it will very likely cause comment. I suggest we continue our walk.'

She did not resist when he pulled her hand on to his arm and they set off again, this time away from the house, taking a path that ran between beds of spring flowers encased in low box hedges.

'I should beg *your* pardon,' she said, after a few moments. 'I should not have ripped up at you. My father has always deplored my fiery nature, he says it comes from my mother.'

'My hot temper is inherited from *my* mother,' he told her. 'She is a true redhead.'

Maddie gave a watery chuckle. 'It would seem we are destined to fight, then.'

'Could we not declare a truce? After all, I am leaving in the morning.'

'Then I think we might. We should be able to remain polite to one another for the rest of the day.'

A half-hour wandering through the gardens saw harmony restored, so much so that all thoughts of returning to the house were forgotten. They walked every one of the many paths and even then Grant was reluctant to turn back towards the house.

'Lady Lochall mentioned a wilderness,' he said. 'If you are not too tired, we might take a look at it.'

'I should like that,' she replied. 'Although why one would want to create a wilderness inside the grounds when there is already so much *outside* is beyond my comprehension!'

When Maddie finally went to her room to change for dinner she was refreshed and happier than she had felt for weeks. She had enjoyed walking in the gardens with Grant, once they had resolved their differences. Neither of them mentioned their little contretemps and she resigned herself to the fact that he would not take payment for escorting her to Lochall House. She blamed it on his particularly strong sense of honour and, although she wondered if there was some way he would accept the money without wounding his pride, she did not want to risk the delicate friendship that was growing between them. She knew he was leaving in the morning, but it felt important to her that they did not part on bad terms.

Another altered gown was awaiting her, this time a cream satin, so exquisitely embroidered with colourful flowers and birds that it drew a little coo of pleasure from Maddie when she saw it. When the maid had helped her into the gown, she sat before the looking glass and decided she might be a little more frivolous with the arrangement of her hair this evening. Instead of brushing her dark curls into a tight knot at the back of her head, she coaxed one glossy black ringlet to drop to her shoulder.

'There,' she murmured, turning her head from side to side to study the effect. 'Will I do, do you think?'

The housemaid clapped her hands and gave an ecstatic sigh.

'Och, ma'am, ye look like a princess, as fair as can be!'

'Thank you!' Maddie rose and shook out her skirts. 'Let us see if Lord Lochall and Her Ladyship will agree with you!'

When she reached the hall there was a servant waiting to show her into the drawing room and she swept in, pausing for a moment when the door closed behind her, as if unsure of her welcome.

Grant, looking around at that moment, felt a little kick of pleasure. From her shiny coal-black curls to the slippers peeping out beneath her satin skirts, Madeleine appeared to glow in the summer sunshine that blazed in through the long windows. Her ivory shoulders rose from the corsage unadorned, but her flawless skin needed no enhancing, and his eyes followed their line to the slender column of her neck and onwards, up to her face.

She was not beautiful in the accepted use of the term, her mouth too wide, the little chin too determined, but there was a delicate flush on her cheeks and the high cheekbones and straight little nose commanded attention. Even her eyes were shining like sapphires.

Grant saw the admiration in Lord Lochall's face as he moved forward to greet her and was not surprised. She was very striking and would command attention in any society.

'My dear, your walk in the garden has done you a great deal of good.'

She laughed as she gave him her hand to kiss. 'Aided by finding another beautiful gown waiting for me, my lord. I cannot thank you and Lady Lochall enough for your hospitality.'

'Nonsense, my dear, it is the least we can do for you,' replied Lady Lochall, waving away her thanks. She glanced the clock. 'La, how the time has gone on! Shall we go in to dinner?'

It was the most enjoyable day Madeleine had yet spent since leaving Inverness. The good food and the kindly nature of her host and hostess put her at her ease, but it was the rapport with Grant Rathmore that made it so memorable. Perhaps it was knowing she would not see him again after tomorrow that made them so at ease.

Indeed, the conversation sparkled as they joked and laughed together like old friends. Afterwards she could never remember just what they had talked of, nothing of importance, she was sure, but the evening flew by. Lord and Lady Lochall were content to allow the young people to chatter away. It was not until they were all gathered together in the drawing room later that the conversation took another turn.

The gentlemen had just come in when a servant entered with a letter for Lord Lochall.

'A note, at this time of night?' remarked his lady.

Lord Lochall did not reply immediately, but something in his manner put Madeleine on her guard and she waited anxiously for him to speak.

'It is from Yves d'Evremont,' he said at last, looking at Madeleine. 'He sends instructions for your voyage to France.'

Watching her across the room, Grant found his mind racing with possibilities. There were plenty of small fishing villages along the coast where a rendezvous with a French ship might be arranged. He could go with her, see her safely aboard and perhaps even sail with her. He would like to see her out of danger and restored to her family.

'From Papa?' She was gazing eagerly at His Lordship, her hands clasped together. 'He has organised my passage to France?'

'He has, my dear.' Lord Lochall looked down at the paper he was holding. 'Naturally, he writes obscurely in case his letter should fall into the wrong hands, but it is very clear. The French are supporting the Young Chevalier and, despite the British Navy's best efforts, French privateers are getting through.'

Madeleine nodded. 'I have heard as much. When do I leave? Oh!' She laughed aloud and clasped her hands together. 'I beg your pardon, my lord, I must appear very ungrateful.'

'Not at all, my dear. I am sure you are most anxious to see your father. However, you must remain here for some days yet. There are arrangements I must make.'

'What arrangements?' she asked, puzzled.

'Travel in this part of Scotland is not easy at the best of times and at present one must be even more careful,' replied His Lordship. 'I must find you a guide and safe houses where you may stay.'

Grant stepped a little closer to Madeleine's chair. 'I will go with her. It is no more than fifty miles from here to the coast; with luck we can manage that in two days.'

'I regret it is not quite that simple,' replied His Lordship, adding drily, 'Yves d'Evremont's arrangements rarely are.'

Madeleine was shifting impatiently on her chair and Grant said quietly, 'I will withdraw, sir, if you would prefer to discuss this in private with Miss d'Evremont.'

'No, no, please stay.' She put out a hand to detain him. 'My lord, I have no secrets from Mr Rathmore. I believe we may trust him. And he will need to know everything, if he is to accompany me.'

'Ah, but there is the rub, my dear, I am not sure Mr Rathmore will be able to escort you. Your father's arrangements take you in the opposite direction. West, into Ross-shire. They are quite specific. There is a French ship sailing for Scotland with gold for the Prince's cause. Yves has secured you passage on it, but you must get yourself to the rendezvous for Midsummer's Eve. The Captain will be able to wait a few days for you, but it is not safe for him to tarry in those waters for too long.'

'Where am I to meet this ship?' asked Maddie.

Lord Lochall shook his head.

'Your father is too canny to put such detail into his

letter. He says you are to meet with his contact for your final directions at Kinloch, on the edge of Loch Òrail.'

'What!'

Grant could not help exclaiming when he heard the name. His Lordship was aware how familiar that place would be to him, but Madeleine, however, was looking at him, puzzled. He knew he must explain.

'I know Loch Òrail. It is but a day's journey from Ardvarrick.'

'Ah, I see.' Maddie nodded, her face grave. 'And you will not wish to travel so close to your home. I understand that.' She turned again to Lord Lochall. 'But why must *I* go so far? It must be all of a hundred miles from here.'

'More like one hundred and fifty,' Grant corrected her.

Madeleine had taken the letter from His Lordship and scanned it, but now she jumped to her feet.

'That is just like Papa,' she raged, waving the letter at no one in particular. 'He turns the simplest task into a mammoth undertaking!' She began to pace the room with quick, restless strides. 'I will not do it. A hundred and fifty miles—why, that is madness! I am convinced it would be better to go to the east coast and sail from there to France. There must be any number of vessels that could take me.'

'But the instructions are clear,' Lord Lochall insisted. 'Your father—'

'My father *abandoned* me!' Madeleine stopped her pacing and glared at him. 'He left me in Inverness, knowing a battle was imminent. He gave me no hint of what he was about. He did not even tell me he was returning to France! I knew nothing until I received his note, telling me to make my way here. And now he is saying I must retrace my steps, travel back to Inverness and beyond, risking my life in the hope that there will be a French ship waiting for me at some western port, if I should ever find it! I believe I shall have more success if I make my own arrangements.' She turned to Grant. 'You are bound for France; will you take me with you?'

She was looking at him, a small inferno of anger with her breast heaving and cheeks flushed. Grant knew getting himself out of Scotland would be dangerous enough, let alone taking a woman with him. Her father had contacts and must have paid well to arrange his daughter's passage whereas he, Grant, had only his wits to aid him.

Lady Lochall spoke up. 'I must say that appears to be the most logical solution.'

Her eyes, as well as Madeleine's, were on him now and he knew he was lost. He inclined his head.

'If you are determined to go your own way, then, yes, I will accompany you.'

'Very well.' She nodded. 'We will leave at dawn. I—'

'Oh, no, we will not!' he cut in quickly. 'If you want my escort, then we must plan this properly.'

'But you were planning to leave tomorrow, it can make little difference if I come with you.'

'I beg you will show a little sense, madam! It makes all the difference in the world. We must consult His Lordship; he will know the best way to go about it.'

Their eyes met and held. She was still tense with nervous energy, her eyes glittering dangerously. Grant knew the battle was as much with her own temper as anything he had said.

Lord Lochall cleared his throat. 'I cannot prevent you from going east, Miss d'Evremont, if you are set upon it, and I will give you every assistance. However, I believe Rathmore is right. You should delay your journey by another day at least.'

'I cannot see any reason for that.' She waved an impatient hand. 'I would prefer to be moving as soon as possible.'

'I am sure you would, but my neighbour Sumington was quite taken with you and, having agreed to go to the dance tomorrow, it would be remarked upon if you should disappear beforehand.'

Her anger was abating. The angry light had left her face and Grant could see that she was considering their host's words. When she looked towards him, her brows raised, he nodded.

'Lord Lochall is right, you should go. We can make an early start the following morning.'

Madeleine nodded. It was decided. The heated passion of the past half-hour had left her exhausted and she excused herself soon afterwards and retired to her room.

However, once she was alone, she was too restless to go to bed. She was ashamed of her angry outburst, her lack of restraint when she learned of the journey Papa had planned for her. Lord and Lady Lochall were old friends of her father, they must know he could be by turns fickle, contradictory and autocratic. She had read understanding in their eyes when she raged against Papa, but not in Grant's. All he knew was that she had a quick temper and she regretted very much that he had witnessed another example of it.

Later, lying in near darkness that passed for night at this time of year, even the warmed and comfortable bed she was in did not help her to sleep. She desperately wanted to apologise to Grant. To try to explain.

Chapter Six

An hour ticked by and, rather than growing sleepier, Madeleine became more restless. She heard the murmur of voices on the stairs, then firm footsteps passing her door. She knew it was Grant, on his way to his own bedchamber at the end of the corridor. She strained her ears, listening for the faint sounds of soft-footed servants, distant doors opening and closing. She waited until the house was silent, then she slipped out of bed, pulling on the silk wrap her hostess had provided. It was a little long and she was obliged to hold it up to avoid tripping as she quietly opened the door and moved silently along the corridor. At the last door she stopped and knocked softly, stepping back a pace as it opened. She breathed a sigh of relief when she knew it was the right one.

'Madeleine!' Grant was no more than a shadow against the dim light behind him, a tall figure in billowing shirt and tight breeches.

She said quickly, 'Good, you are not asleep yet.'

She stepped past him into the room.

'What madness is this?' Grant glanced along the

darkened corridor before quietly closing the door. 'You should not be here, if anyone sees you, your reputation will be in tatters.'

'I am aware of that, but I had to come, I needed to talk to you.'

'There is nothing that cannot wait until morning.'

'But there is!' She took a hasty turn about the room. 'I was angry earlier. I am so ashamed that I lost my temper with you. I wanted you to know that. And I wanted you to know *why* I was in such a rage.'

'Confound it, you have no need to explain anything.'

'But I *do*!'

Grant knew he should have sent her back to her room. He should still do that, but when he regarded the dainty creature standing before him, her thick dark tresses loose and cascading over her shoulders, hands clutched tightly together and her dark eyes fixed upon him so beseechingly, he could not bring himself to turn her away.

'Well, you are here now, so the damage may already be done. You had best sit down.' Grant waved her towards one of two chairs standing each side of the empty hearth and when he had shrugged himself into his coat he sat down opposite her. 'Now, tell me what is so urgent you have to steal into my room at this late hour?'

'It is barely midnight,' she retorted, showing her usual spirit.

'That does not alter the situation, Madeleine, and you know it.'

'You are right, but...' She twisted her hands together, then said in a rush, 'I cannot bear for you to think ill of me. At least, any more so than you do already.'

A reluctant smile tugged at his mouth. 'I do not think badly of you, Madeleine. You are a little impetuous, perhaps.'

'You think me obstinate and hot at hand,' she replied. 'And with good reason.'

She was troubled and he sensed she needed to talk.

'Very well.' He sat back in his chair. 'Tell me.'

The invitation did not appear to help her. She jumped up and began to pace the room. A single candle burned beside the bed and its flame threw her agitated shadow across the wall.

'Maddie, I understand your anxiety. It is natural that you should be concerned when you are about to undertake such a long and arduous journey and you were angry with your father for even suggesting it.'

'It is not that,' she waved a distracted hand towards him. 'I have made such journeys before. It is not the first time I have had to look out for myself. But this time——' Her pace slowed. 'My father is a dreamer, you see. He is constantly chasing some new idea, some plan that he believes will result in fortune, if not glory.' She added bitterly, 'His care of me has been haphazard, to say the least.'

'You said he was planning a great match for you. A prince of the blood, if I remember you correctly.'

She threw him a scornful glance. So, the minx had said it only to irritate him, as he suspected.

She said now, 'I am useful as a housekeeper and an occasional hostess, but I am aware that he sees me as little more than that.'

'Then why do you stay with him?'

'Where else should I go? The alternative is to return to my aunt at her dreary house in Dijon.' A sigh escaped her. 'I must confess that a little tedium would be welcome at the present moment. I am tired of the constant travel. Tired of always looking over my shoulder for strangers in the shadows. Papa swore to me that this visit to Scotland was purely for pleasure, to meet old friends. It was only when we reached Inverness that I began to suspect he was caught up in something more, possibly working with the French government against the British.'

'And hence supporting Charles Stuart?'

'Yes. Once we reached Inverness, Papa disappeared for days, weeks at a time. And there were callers late at night. I would hear the rumble of voices downstairs, long after I had retired.'

'Hardly social calls then,' Grant murmured. 'Was his disappearance a complete surprise?'

'Not exactly. After Inverness fell to the Prince's supporters in February, the nocturnal visits ceased but Papa continued to go away for a night, sometimes more. However, this last time I had no word for weeks and I began to wonder what had happened to him. Then, just when I was beginning to think something was seriously wrong, I received a message telling me I was to leave the town with all speed and make my way to Glen Muick.'

'And did he not say anything about himself, what he was doing, where he was?'

She had stopped by the bed, idly straightening one of the heavy curtains. 'It was written in haste. He said I was to come to Lochall House and wait. I thought he might join me here and we would travel to France together.'

'Instead he expects you to make a perilous journey alone.' He could not keep the condemnation from his voice.

'Yes.'

Her shoulders drooped and there was a wistfulness in that single word. She had lowered her guard and although she had her back to him, he glimpsed for an instant a vulnerable young woman behind the confident façade. He went over to her, putting his hands on her shoulders.

'But you are not alone now, Madeleine. I am with you.' He turned her towards him, putting his fingers under her chin and obliging her to look up. 'I will get you safely to France, never fear.'

She gazed at him, her eyes huge and luminous in the semi-darkness and in that long, silent moment, something changed. The room was suddenly still, expectant. And it was not only the air around them, he could feel it. Madeleine felt it, too, he knew it by the way her eyes widened. Her full lips parted in an unconscious invitation for him to kiss her. Invisible bonds were tightening around them, pulling them closer. She put her hands against his chest. It was a half-hearted attempt to hold him off.

She whispered, 'I should go.'

Neither of them moved. He could almost believe she wanted him to contradict her. An iron band was squeezing around his ribs, restricting his breath. Desire roared through him, he felt dizzy with it, unable to think properly. He was still gripping her shoulders and he could feel the bones beneath his hands. She felt delicate, fragile, and he knew he had to fight this, for both of them. It took every ounce of willpower to let her go, but somehow he managed it. He released her and stepped back, raking one hand through his hair.

'Yes, you *must* go. Dash it, Madeleine, what in God's name were you thinking of, to come here in the first place?'

He had not meant it to sound so harsh, but he was barely in control. She recoiled as if he had struck her. The hurt in her eyes flayed him and he had to turn away to stop himself reaching out to her again. He needed some defence and found it in anger. Damnation, did she not know how alluring she was, coming to his door with only that thin silk wrap for protection?

She whispered, 'I told you... I wanted to apologise—'

'By heaven, woman, do you think that is sufficient reason to behave so wantonly?'

It was his turn to stride about the room. Hot lust was raging through his body and he desperately needed to counter it.

'You are a damned fool, Madeleine. You are not a child; you know the dangers of throwing yourself at a man.'

'I d-did not throw myself at you! I came here as... as a friend.'

He laughed savagely and swung around.

'A friend!' She was standing close. Too damned close. 'Do you think a friend would do *this*?'

He dragged her to him, his mouth coming down on hers in a bruising kiss. He had meant only to punish her, but she did not recoil as he expected. It was he who broke off and pushed her away. He tried to steady his breathing while she stood looking up at him, her eyes wide. Slowly, she raised one hand and touched her mouth with her fingers, then, without a word, she fled.

For a long moment after she had gone Grant did not move. What in heaven's name had possessed him to kiss her? He was honest enough to know the answer to that. He had been wanting to do it for some time and had persuaded himself tonight that it was justified, that the experience would show her the danger and keep her safe in future. What a crass fool he was! She had come to him in friendship and by his outrageous actions he had destroyed all hope of her trusting him now.

Cursing softly, he punched his fist into his palm. He had also thought that one kiss would be enough to dispel his growing desire. That, too, was a mistake. He wanted her more than ever. The way he felt now, there was little chance that he would sleep tonight.

Back in her bedchamber, Maddie locked the door and stood with her back pressed against it, her heart pounding so much she could hardly breathe. No one had seen her precipitous flight along the shadowy corridor, there were no sounds of movement outside her room. She was safe.

Safe! The thick silence of the room mocked her. Quickly she scrambled into bed and curled herself into a tight ball. What had she done; how could she have behaved so recklessly? Entering a man's bedroom was a cardinal sin, she knew that. It was tantamount to inviting a man's advances. But she had not thought of that when she went to see Grant. She had been driven by the need for his forgiveness, frightened of losing his friendship. He had shown her in the most brutal way possible that she had already lost it. He had called her foolish, wanton, and how could she deny it? She had lost his good opinion.

Good heavens, had living with Papa not taught her anything? She had been his hostess long enough to see the contempt men had for women foolish enough to go beyond the bounds of propriety. Her father was a charming man and he had had any number of mistresses. He had never made any effort to hide the fact from her, nor had he concealed his disdain for those poor women when his interest waned, which it always did well before they had tired of him.

Madeleine had had her admirers, but she had never allowed them to go beyond a mild flirtation. No man had ever done more than press a chaste kiss upon her fingers. Until tonight. What shocked her most was not that Grant had kissed her, but the emotions he had aroused. True, she had been stunned by his sudden embrace, but she had been excited, too. Something inside had burst into life when their lips met. She had felt intoxicated, exhilarated. Rather than being outraged, she had wanted him to kiss her again. In fact, she had wanted him to sweep her up and tumble her on to the bed and do so much more!

With a groan she curled up even tighter as she relived those deliciously frightening sensations. For the first time she understood why her father's mistresses had followed him so relentlessly, begging for a little attention. Like moths around a flame, they could not help themselves. She had always pitied them.

Now, she pitied herself.

* * *

Madeleine awoke not much refreshed from her night's sleep and with a dull weight upon her spirits. She had made such a mull of things, not just with Grant, but her outburst in front of the Lochalls, too, showed a sad lack of good manners. What had happened to her these past few weeks, to turn her from a sensible, clear-headed woman into such a reckless, impetuous creature? She would very much like to hide in her room, but common sense told her that would not do. Everyone must be faced and the sooner she got it over with, the better.

She dressed with care and made her way downstairs, but when she reached the hall she came upon her hostess heading for the main door.

'Ah, good morning, Madeleine. You will find the gentlemen in the breakfast room. Do go on in, my dear.'

'Yes, thank you, but first will you allow me to offer you my apologies? I behaved very ill yesterday, ma'am, to you and Lord Lochall, when I learned of my father's plans for me. You have shown me nothing but kindness and I behaved like a fishwife.'

Lady Lochall patted her hands.

'Think nothing of it. To speak frankly, I was shocked at your papa's cavalier attitude and quite understand why you lost your temper, my dear. We have known Yves for many years and he has always been the most exasperating man. I am sorry to say that in the past we have been at pains to avoid becoming enmeshed in his schemes and stratagems, but we could not ignore it when he asked us to help his daughter. And you must not think we are regretting it. Not at all, I assure you.

You are very much like your dear mama, you know. God rest her soul.'

'Do you think so? I barely remember her, for I was very young when she died, but Papa always says I do not have her beauty.'

'She was a nonpareil, no one could compare,' Lady Lochall told her. 'But you are very like her and will never want for admirers, I am sure. And I do believe you have something of her wit and intelligence.'

'Do I?' Maddie blushed. 'Thank you, ma'am.'

My lady gave a sad little smile. 'We had hoped, when she married Yves, that it would tame him a little, but alas, he remained as restless as ever. Forgive me, my dear, I have always thought Yves d'Evremont a most charming man, but not, I fear, an ideal father, dragging you around Europe as he has done these past few years. And we heard he even purchased a gambling house and installed you as his hostess! Thank heaven *that* madness did not last long!'

Maddie could not disagree, but she tried her best to defend her father.

'Perhaps it has been an unusual life, ma'am, but I have enjoyed it, in the main.' She laughed. 'And I have learned a great deal. It is not every young lady who has been tutored in both Basset and Hazard.'

'Merciful heavens, never say so!' exclaimed Lady Lochall, shocked. 'I will not even allow Lanterloo to be played at my table! But never mind that, I must go. I am away to see the gardener. He wishes to know which flowering planters I want for the morning room. I should have done it yesterday only I was engaged with the housekeeper, inspecting the bedlinen. And when I get back I must see Cook to discuss the dinner menus.'

She gave a distracted little laugh. 'La, Madeleine, there are a hundred and one things to be done today!'

'Perhaps I might go to the hothouse for you, ma'am,' said Maddie, sensing an opportunity to put off the inevitable meeting with Grant. 'If you will trust me to choose the best blooms.'

'Oh, would you not mind? But what about your breakfast?'

'I think I should prefer a little fresh air this morning.'

'Oh, well. If you are sure.' Lady Lochall beamed. 'Bless you, my dear, I accept your offer. And you must take my shawl, too, it will save you running upstairs to fetch something.'

Her conscience eased by knowing she was helping her hostess, Maddie tripped out of the door and made her way through the flower gardens.

The meeting with the gardener took some time. When Madeleine showed an interest in his work, he was only too pleased to show her the various pots he had planted to provide a continuous supply of flowering plants for the house throughout the year. By the time she had selected the flowers for him to send up to the house, the morning was well advanced. Maddie recalled Lord Lochall had invited Grant to ride out with him and, coward that she was, she would be able to put off the inevitable meeting for a few more hours.

She strolled back through the gardens, glad of the solitude to collect her thoughts. She felt a little better, having made her apology to Lady Lochall, but she knew she would still have to say something to Grant. There was no longer any question of his escorting her to France, but she did not wish to part with him on bad terms, if it could be helped.

A movement ahead of her caused her to look up and with dismay she saw Grant striding towards her. There was no escape and after the merest break in her step she walked on, straining every nerve to appear calm.

'Miss d'Evremont.'

His greeting was formal, accompanied by a little nod, but as he was blocking her path she had no choice but to stop.

She said, 'I thought you had gone riding with Lord Lochall.'

'I had, but we returned early and now he wishes to discuss the arrangements for our journey to France.'

'*Our* journey? But I thought—'

'That is why I came to find you,' he interrupted her, his voice and countenance grave. 'I quite understand that you will not now wish me to accompany you.'

'I do not think it would be wise, sir, after what occurred last night,' she mumbled. Her cheeks on fire, she rushed on. 'I behaved outrageously!'

'I treated you abominably!'

They exclaimed together and both stopped in confusion.

'It was my doing,' she said quietly. 'I should never have come to your room.'

'And I should never have allowed you to enter. And I should certainly not have kissed you. I regret that, most bitterly.'

He is sorry he kissed you!

Maddie's head sank lower, her eyes fixed on the gravel path. There was a moment's silence, then he took a step closer and she found herself staring at the highly polished toes of his boots.

'Miss d'Evremont—Madeleine! If I swear to you that such a thing will not occur again, will you not change your mind and allow me to escort you?'

She hesitated. She did not relish explaining to Lord and Lady Lochall why the plans had changed so suddenly. And if Grant did not accompany her, she would need Lord Lochall to help her find another reliable escort.

Grant interrupted her thoughts, saying, 'Please, Madeleine, reconsider. We are both heading for France, it makes no sense to go off separately.'

A long and awkward silence ensued while Madeleine fought an internal battle. She knew the dangers now and Papa had always said knowing the problem was halfway to solving it.

'You are right,' she said at last. 'One must be practical about these things.'

He looked relieved. 'We should find a maid to go with you. Perhaps one of Lady Lochall's servants.'

'No, I would rather hire a local girl, once I am in France.'

'Then at least take one of the maids with you to the coast.'

'And have her travel back alone in these troubled times?' She shuddered, remembering her own encounter with the redcoats. 'It is too dangerous. No, if we go alone, we can travel faster. We both regret what occurred last night and that should be enough to ensure it does not happen again, should it not?'

She looked up, noting the faint crease in his brow and his unsmiling eyes as he made her a low bow.

'I give you my word upon it, madam.'

His words sent her spirits plummeting even lower. It was an easy promise for him to keep, because he had never wanted to kiss her in the first place.

Chapter Seven

The maid coaxed one glossy curl to fall upon Madeleine's bare shoulder and stepped back.

'There, mistress. I am done.'

Madeleine studied the result in her looking glass and felt a little kick of pleasure. Tomson had found another gown for her, a cornflower-blue satin trimmed with blond lace, and she rose, smoothing her hands over the skirts with satisfaction. It had only been a couple of weeks since she had left Inverness, but it seemed such a long time since she had worn anything so fine. She was almost glad now that they had delayed their departure until the morning.

Lady Lochall had given her a silk wrap to put over her gown and once she had thrown this around her shoulders she went downstairs. As she descended to the hall she glimpsed a figure in Highland dress standing in the shadows by the door.

Assuming it was Lord Lochall, she went up to him, saying cheerfully, 'Lady Lochall is not here yet, I see, which means I am not late— Oh! Gr—Mr Rathmore. I did not expect it to be you.'

'Evidently,' he replied. 'Lochall persuaded me to change my mind and accompany you. The idea of kicking my heels here alone this evening did not appeal.'

'I am glad of it.'

And she was. Maddie was genuinely pleased he was going with them, but even as she spoke he moved away from her, saying he must find the gloves Lord Lochall had looked out for him. She watched him stride away and felt her spirits dim a little. They had agreed the proprieties must be maintained and he was ensuring he was not alone with her. She sighed. So be it. She could expect nothing more.

Sumington Lodge was reached by a section of surprisingly good road that Lady Lochall explained was maintained by themselves and their neighbours for just such occasions as this. They were greeted cheerfully by their hosts, who swept Grant and Madeleine away for a round of introductions.

'The Sumingtons are good people and the guests friendly enough,' was Madeleine's verdict, when at last she and Grant could move away from everyone.

'And not at all inquisitive,' he replied. 'One could almost believe there had been no rising in the Highlands at all.'

'Would you rather they asked difficult questions?' she countered.

'Not at all. I understand everyone is here to enjoy themselves. No one wishes to spoil the evening with doubts and suspicions about their fellow guests.'

'About us, you mean.' She was serious for a moment. 'We are the only strangers here, even if we are under Lord Lochall's aegis.'

A warning glance put Maddie on her guard and she looked around to see Mr Sumington bearing down upon them, his eldest son and daughter following close behind.

'Well, well now, what is this? We cannot have you standing here when the dancing is about to begin! Here are Sukie and Douglas eager to partner you for the first reel.'

It was clear they would not be allowed to refuse, so Madeleine summoned up a smile and went off to do her duty.

For an hour Grant danced and smiled and said all that was proper, but all the time wishing he was anywhere other than in Sumington Lodge. His hosts had welcomed him cheerfully, brushing aside his apologies for turning up unannounced and declaring they were grateful for another guest to make up the numbers. Not that he was needed—the large room was quite full and he thought that Mr Sumington must be gratified by the response to his last-minute invitation.

He had allowed Lord Lochall to persuade him to come along with them, thinking it might help to ease the tension between himself and Madeleine, but when she had come down the stairs to join him in the hall, he had felt that familiar tug of attraction and had moved away before she could see it.

Now he was obliged to watch her laughing and smiling as she danced and he felt an irrational stab of jealousy that she was enjoying the company of other men when she was so ill at ease with *him*.

The music ended and he escorted his latest partner from the floor before wandering off to find the glass of wine he had left in one of the window embrasures. He should not have come. A good night's sleep would had been much more advantageous to him, for they had an early start in the morning. Lord Lochall had suggested they make for one particular small east coast fishing village, where he was sure they would find a vessel to take them across the German Sea. He would need all his wits about him for the journey through country that was known to be patrolled by British soldiers. And he would need to maintain his cool reserve towards Miss Madeleine d'Evremont. She must be given no cause to think he harboured any warm feelings for her at all.

Which he did not. Not in the slightest. Last night he had succumbed to the natural temptation any hot-blooded male would feel when a pretty woman comes to his bedroom in a state of undress. Although in general, wilful, spoiled, hot-at-hand brunettes were not to his taste at all.

If ever he was to take a wife—and heaven knew he was in no position to even think of that at the present time!—if ever he was to consider marriage, he would choose a quiet, biddable girl with whom he could settle down to a life of peace and harmony. A fair-haired beauty, like the English cousins he had met in London a few years ago. Or even a redhead like his mother. His bride would have to be a gentle, kindly soul, a good mother to their children and a capable housekeeper. A lady of whom his parents would approve.

He was so wrapped up in his thoughts that he did not notice Lady Lochall until she spoke his name. When he turned he saw that she had Madeleine with her, the two of them bright-eyed and rosy-cheeked from the dance.

'Good heavens, I had forgotten how much energy is

needed for a lively reel!' exclaimed my lady, collapsing on to the window seat and fanning herself vigorously. Grant immediately offered to fetch some refreshment, but she declined.

'Lochall is bringing us wine, I am sure he will be here directly. Madeleine, my dear, will you not sit down, are you not exhausted?'

Glancing at Madeleine, Grant thought he had rarely seen anyone looking less fatigued.

'Not in the least, ma'am,' she replied, a laugh in her voice. 'It is a long time since I enjoyed an evening such as this. I find it quite refreshing!'

He could not help but smile at her enthusiasm. She was clearly enjoying herself. Her countenance was positively radiant and her blue eyes had new brilliancy, their colour enhanced by the lustre of the jewels and her shimmering gown.

'The next is a strathspey,' said Lady Lochall, as the fiddlers prepared to strike up again. 'Have you been in the north long enough to learn the steps, Madeleine?'

'Indeed I have, ma'am.'

'Then you should tread a measure with Mr Rathmore.'

'With me?' he exclaimed, imagining Madeleine's dismay at such an idea. But far from being horrified, she was turning to him, a shy smile on her lips.

'Why, yes, sir, if you are willing.'

It was an olive branch and one he would accept gladly. He offered his arm and led her out to join the set. It was a slower, more stately dance than the previous reels and he had time to appreciate his partner. She was a graceful dancer, gliding and skipping across the floor with her dusky curls gleaming and the candlelight twinkling from the sapphires at her ears and throat.

He decided she would not have looked out of place in the finest ballroom in the land. Or even at Court. With such a partner it was easy for Grant to forget for a while the violent horrors of the past few months and the perilous journey ahead of them. His only regret was that the dance was over too soon. As the last bars faded, he bowed to Madeleine and led her from the floor, acutely aware of her dainty hand on his arm, the whisper of her silken skirts as they brushed his legs.

'I enjoyed that very much,' she told him. 'You dance well.'

'Thank you. I am much out of practice.' There had been little time for dancing in the past year.

'No one would know it.' She added, a note of teasing in her voice, 'You are very gentlemanly tonight.'

'In my borrowed finery.'

Maddie heard the bitter note in his voice and wished she could tell him how well he looked. She wanted to say that his lithe figure and air of assurance would mark him down as a gentleman even if he was dressed in rags. Instead she bit her lip. He would think she was flattering him, but it would be no more than the truth. In her opinion he was the most handsome man in the room. He wore no ornament and his auburn hair was held back in a simple ribbon, but, in the tartan jacket and small clothes that His Lordship's valet had cobbled together for him, Grant Rathmore would not have looked amiss in the finest ballroom.

'As am I wearing borrowed raiment,' she said instead. 'I am beholden to Lady Lochall for my costume.'

'Even the jewels?'

'No. Not the sapphires. They were a present from Papa for my coming of age, just over a year ago. It was one of the rare occasions when he was plump in the pocket and, so far, I have managed to get by without selling them.'

'I hope you never have to sell them,' he said. 'They suit you. They match your eyes.'

Madeleine did not know how to reply. The dance had restored some of the former easiness that they had shared, but she knew it must not go any further. It would not do to allow the attraction she felt for this man to show itself again.

Thankfully, they had reached the window embrasure where Lady Lochall was waiting for them and a response was no longer required. She dropped Grant's arm and stepped closer to my lady, who was full of compliments for their dancing. Maddie murmured her thanks, laughing away any suggestion that they made a splendid couple. She was about to change the subject when she realised Grant was gazing over her head across the crowded room.

'A damned Dragoon. That's torn it.'

His muttered words made her turn around and she saw their host approaching with a red-coated officer beside him. Fighting down her alarm, Maddie assumed a look of polite enquiry.

'Now here is Captain Ormskirk arrived, to add to our numbers!' declared Mr Sumington, in his genial manner.

Maddie studied the soldier while introductions were performed. He looked to be a serious young man, the lines about his eyes and a faint scar on his chin suggesting he was a seasoned officer, while a fresher cut on one cheek suggested he had been in action recently. She noted how his gaze sharpened when Grant was introduced.

'Rathmore, you say?'

Maddie held her breath.

'Aye, that's it,' declared Mr Sumington. 'Rathmore of Ardvarrick.'

Grant inclined his head, looking completely at his ease. 'You know my father, perhaps, the Laird?'

Laird! Maddie was obliged to hide her shock behind a bland smile. Was he bluffing? She thought not. Looking back, it all fitted—Lord Lochall's demeanour once he knew Grant's identity, his ease in polite company. Oh, good heavens! And she had treated him like a common servant!

Captain Ormskirk was staring at Grant, as if trying to recall some memory, and she held her breath, waiting for him to answer Grant's question.

'No,' he said at last. 'I have never heard of Ardvarrick.'

Their host laughed and continued to chatter.

'The good Captain's duties delayed him from being here sooner, but now he is arrived and ready to join in!' Mr Sumington turned to Madeleine. 'After watching your performance in the strathspey, Miss d'Evremont, he was eager to be presented to you.'

The Captain bowed to her. 'Indeed, ma'am, I am honoured to make your acquaintance.'

'You wish to dance perhaps, Captain?' suggested Lady Lochall.

Madeleine realised the lady was trying to divert the soldier's attention from Grant and she fixed what she hoped was an inviting smile upon her face.

The Captain bowed. 'Alas, ma'am, I have a leg wound that has not yet healed and cannot dance. However, perhaps Miss d'Evremont would care to take supper with me?'

'But you have only this minute arrived, sir!'

'Yes, but I was obliged to miss my dinner to come here tonight.' He held out his arm. 'Shall we? I caught a glimpse of the refreshments set out in the dining room.'

Madeleine knew she could not refuse. She accepted graciously and moved away on his arm, to all appearances delighted to be singled out by the Captain of Dragoons.

'You are related to the Lochalls, Miss d'Evremont?' he asked as they negotiated their way around the edge of the room.

'A friend of the family,' she told him, drawing on the explanation they had all agreed before setting off this evening.

'And do you make a long visit?'

'That depends,' she said cautiously. 'Until it is safe to travel.'

'Then you may be at Lochall House for some time, ma'am. With so many Jacobites on the run I would not advise anyone to venture far for the time being.'

He led her into the dining room which, with the majority of guests still dancing, was almost empty. They helped themselves from the dishes laid out on the sideboards and retired to a small table to sit down.

'And the gentleman in your party. Mr... Rathmore. What do you know of him?'

'Very little, I am afraid.' She adopted a dismissive tone, as if she had no interest in her fellow house guest. 'I believe his father and Lord Lochall are acquainted.'

She adroitly changed the subject and brought the conversation round to the Captain himself. By gentle questioning she kept him talking, discovering he was from Newcastle and the father of a young family. She was about to launch into more questions, confident that such a fruitful topic could keep them occupied for a long while, but the Captain forestalled her.

'I think you have heard enough about me, ma'am. I would like to know a little more about *you*, now. D'Evremont. That is a French name?'

'Yes. My father is French.'

'And he is not with you?'

'No.' She decided that the truth would serve her best. Or at least, as close to the truth as she dared admit. 'Papa is in France. I am on my way to join him.'

'I see. As I have already said, ma'am, these are dangerous times to be travelling.'

'They are dangerous times to be in Scotland, Captain.'

'True. And does Mr Rathmore accompany you?'

'Heavens, no!' She laughed and opened her eyes at him. 'Why on earth would you think that?'

'A young lady should not be travelling alone.'

'I have sufficient funds to hire an escort.'

'Perhaps you would allow me to arrange that for you.'

She said quickly, 'Thank you, but that will not be necessary.'

He sat back and looked at her.

'You appear…wary of me, Miss d'Evremont.'

'I will be frank with you, Captain. My last encounter with soldiers was not a pleasant experience.'

'Then I must show you that we can behave like gentlemen.' He raised his hand to a passing footman. 'More wine?'

By the time they rose from the supper table Madeleine was still smiling, but she felt exhausted at the verbal game of cat and mouse. Other guests wandered in and out again, but Captain Ormskirk showed no signs of wishing to leave. She lightly turned aside his questions, diverted him with amusing but carefully modified anecdotes of her travels in Europe. Captain Ormskirk listened, laughed and appeared charmed by her company, but at length he threw down his napkin and rose from the table.

'You are a most entertaining companion, Miss d'Evremont, but I think I have monopolised you long enough.'

She smiled up at him. 'We have been sitting here a great deal longer than we ought, Captain. I feel quite guilty that I have kept you all to myself for so long. Pray do not wait for me, but off you go and talk to the other guests, sir. There really is no need to escort me back to my party.'

'Oh, but there is,' he said, drawing her hand on to his arm. 'I cannot allow you to escape me quite so easily.'

The Captain spoke lightly, but Madeleine had the uneasy feeling that there was more to this than common politeness.

The fiddlers were playing a lively reel and Madeleine noticed that both Lord and Lady Lochall were on the dance floor. She pointed this out to the Captain and suggested she would wait there until the dance was concluded.

'Ah, but I see the fourth member of your party is standing alone on the far side of the room,' replied the Captain. 'It would be polite to join him, don't you agree?'

Across the room, Grant watched their approach and, as they drew near, he caught the warning glance Madeleine threw at him. It was unnecessary—he had been on his guard from the moment the Captain of Dragoons had appeared. Madeleine removed her hand from the Captain's arm and stepped into the empty window bay, as if in search of a cooler spot.

'I am glad to find you still here, sir.' Captain Ormskirk acknowledged Grant with a little nod.

'*Still* here?' Grant raised his brows. 'Where should I go without the rest of my party?'

'Where indeed, Mr Rathmore?' murmured the Captain. He took a few steps further into the square bay. 'I remember now where I have heard that name recently.'

Grant followed him. Not by the flicker of an eyelid did he show any concern. The Captain continued.

'Yes, there were reports of an incident recently, involving soldiers who were patrolling along the River Don. They talked of an officer calling himself Rathmore.'

Grant looked blank and shook his head. 'I am not aware I have any relation of that name in the military.'

'No, it is the strangest thing. No one I know has heard of a Colonel Rathmore.'

Grant laughed. 'But as you can see, Captain, I am not an army man.'

The Captain was regarding him steadily. 'The incident took place at the change house at Kildrummy.

I thought perhaps the tale had become muddled and it might be yourself, sir?'

'Kildrummy?' Grant shook his head. 'I did not come that way.' He laughed. 'I would not be surprised if it was some rascally fellow using my name. What is this…er… Colonel supposed to have done?'

He saw the Captain's eyes flick towards Madeleine, who was plying her fan and looking uninterested, even slightly bored.

'He assaulted three troopers and stole their weapons.'

'That is serious indeed,' said Grant. 'Do you know the reason behind the assault?'

The Captain ignored the question. He said, 'Patrols have since been increased in that area. I would not be surprised if we see more soldiers billeted here before too long.'

Captain Ormskirk walked to the window and stood looking out at the summer twilight, his hands clasped behind his back, and Grant exchanged a silent glance with Madeleine. All three of them were standing in the large, square bay window now, an almost tangible feeling of danger swirling around them. A few feet away, in the main room, the music and dancing continued, but it was as if that was another world. The Captain began to speak again.

'I believe the matter had something to do with a woman, although there is nothing of that in the official report.' He kept his gaze fixed on the window. 'It is difficult to discover the true facts, but from what I know of the men involved, and from what I have heard, the troopers were behaving disgracefully.'

'If that is the case,' said Grant, choosing his words

with care, 'one can hardly blame the man for coming to the aid of the lady.'

'True, such rogues deserve to be punished, Mr Rathmore. However, the law must be upheld.'

Madeleine sucked in an indignant breath and Grant shook his head at her, warning her to keep silent.

Captain Ormskirk continued. 'I have orders to report any strangers in the area. That was one of the reasons for coming here tonight. When I heard Sumington was holding a little party I thought it would be a good opportunity to make enquiries. It has been most…illuminating.'

Grant's hand moved instinctively to his side, but he was not wearing his sword. He and Madeleine maintained their silence and at last the Captain turned to face them. He stepped up and took Madeleine's hand in his own.

'It has been most enjoyable, too, but alas I must be going.' He bowed over her fingers. 'Thank you for your company, Miss d'Evremont. In other circumstances I should have been eager to further our acquaintance, but as it is…'

He let the words hang, but neither Grant nor Maddie broke the silence and after a moment he continued.

'I wish I could stay longer, but duty calls. However, I doubt I shall get around to sending off my report before tomorrow night.' He gave a little nod, half turned and stopped again. 'Oh, and I have heard they are stepping up patrols around Aberdeen and along the coast, too. I pity any poor devils who try to escape to France that way in the next few weeks.'

Another nod and he strode away.

'He knows.' Madeleine turned to Grant, trying to

keep her voice steady. 'I said nothing to give us away, I swear it. I thought, by keeping him by my side, I was protecting you. Us.'

'Perhaps you did. He has given us warning, has he not?' He broke off as Lord and Lady Lochall came up to join them.

'Captain Ormskirk has left,' said His Lordship, looking grim. 'I saw him here, talking with you both. That was most unfortunate. If I had known Sumington would invite the military, I should never have accepted.'

'As I understand it, he was *not* invited,' said Grant. 'He came here for information. But we cannot talk here—to see us huddled together might give rise to even more speculation. We should dance.'

Maddie shuddered. 'I am not sure my legs will support me!'

'Oh, I am sure they will. Come, let us show the world a brave face.'

Grant's smile was warm, comforting, and when she put her hand in his, she felt strength flowing through her. Head held high, she walked out with him to join the dancers.

Chapter Eight

It was not until they were travelling back to Lochall House that anything more was mentioned about their plans. Grant lost no time in explaining to Lord and Lady Lochall all the Captain had said to them.

'Oh, dear heaven, how unfortunate that he should attend tonight,' said Lady Lochall, gripping Madeleine's hand tightly. 'He may even now be on his way to Lochall House with a raiding party.'

Her husband shook his head. 'That is unlikely. Why would he be at such pains to warn them if that was the case?'

'I agree.' Grant nodded. 'His disapproval of the soldiers' behaviour was evident.'

'And he did seem very taken with Madeleine,' added Lady Lochall.

'Aye.' In the shadowy interior of the carriage, Grant's teeth gleamed in a sudden smile. 'She charmed him finely!'

Madeleine blushed and disclaimed. She was exhausted from an evening spent measuring every word, every response to avoid giving anything away. She said now, 'Can we trust him, do you think?'

She heard Grant huff out a sigh. 'We have no choice, but I believe so.'

'One thing is for sure,' said Lord Lochall. 'You must leave at first light.'

'But not together.' Madeleine was adamant about that. 'They will be looking for a man and a woman. And it is not safe to go to the east coast.'

The carriage had pulled up on the drive and Lord Lochall jumped out, turning back to hand down the ladies.

'We can do nothing more tonight and I think sleep would serve us all best now. We will all think more clearly after a few hours' rest.'

Madeleine agreed and went to her room.

Her nerves had been so on edge she'd thought it would be impossible to sleep, but it seemed that no sooner had she blown out her candle than the maid was gently rousing her. The little clock on the mantelshelf told her it was early but, as the memory of the previous evening returned, she lost all desire to close her eyes again and sat up to drink her hot chocolate.

The maid dipped a curtsy. 'His Lordship says to come down to the morning room as soon as you are dressed, ma'am.'

Her travelling dress, she decided. It was a little shabby now after the hard wear of the past few weeks, but it was the most practical of her gowns and heaven knew she would not be able to take more than could be packed into her saddlebags.

* * *

When Madeleine finally made her way to the breakfast room she found the others were already gathered around the table. Lord Lochall dismissed the servants and invited her to sit down.

'We dine in private this morning,' he told her as the door closed softly behind the footman. 'That way we can talk more freely and decide how best we may help you.'

'You have done more than enough already, my lord. I think the sooner I quit your house, the better it will be for you.'

'I do not think there is any immediate danger,' he responded. 'However, after what we learned last night, I believe it would be best to return to your father's original plan.'

'I think so, too. I hope you can provide me with a guide, sir, at least for the first part of the journey.'

'That will not be necessary,' said Grant. 'I know the way.'

'You?' Madeleine shook her head at him. 'No. Captain Ormskirk has made the connection between us. It would be far too dangerous to travel together.'

'I do not propose that we travel under our own names.'

'I doubt *that* will make much difference.' Her nerves were at full stretch and she found his smile infuriating. 'Grant Rathmore, I have told you, I do not *want* your escort!'

'But you *need* me, whether you like it or not.' He held her angry gaze for a moment longer, then said in a coaxing tone, 'Come, Maddie, listen to what I have to say before you fly up into the boughs. Finding a reliable guide to take you from here to the Western Highlands would be well-nigh impossible. I confess my knowledge of this area is limited, but once we cross the Ness you will be entering my world. I grew up there, I know most of the tracks and have more chance than anyone of getting you safely to Loch Òrail.'

'But you have said yourself you might be recognised if you go back.'

'That is a chance I will have to take.'

'No. It is still too dangerous. The soldiers will be on the alert.'

'But they will not be looking for two brothers, travelling together.' He smiled. 'You should not look so surprised. You have already said they will be looking for a man and woman. Therefore, we must do something different.'

Maddie's thoughts raced. It might work. She was already used to riding astride, like a man. And yet there were obstacles.

'I have no clothes...'

Lady Lochall leaned over and patted her hand.

'That is all settled, my dear. We keep a collection of servants' liveries and I had Tomson look out what we have in your size. She will have something ready for you when you go back to your room.'

Maddie sat back, considering what she should do. She did not want to accept their help, they had done so much for her already. She thought the best thing she could do for everyone was to slip away, and as quickly as possible, but when she looked at Grant it was clear he had read her mind.

He said, 'I am not leaving you to make that journey alone, Madeleine.'

'Rathmore is perfectly correct.' Lord Lochall dabbed at his lips with his napkin before continuing in his slow, precise way. 'It is imperative you have someone who knows the route and who better than a man who was born in that area?'

'It seems I have no option.'

'None,' Grant said to her. 'Now go and turn yourself into my little brother!'

Less than an hour later Madeleine returned to the morning room, transformed. An overlarge shirt was concealed beneath a plain linen cravat and a blue serge waistcoat, with a matching blue frock coat over all. She wore her silk breeches beneath the rough leather ones that had belonged to some long-gone stable boy and her black leather riding boots were considered masculine enough when worn with the pair of leather spatterdashes Tomson had looked out for her. The ensemble was completed by a cocked hat which she set upon her head at a jaunty angle, having brushed her hair back into a queue and secured it with a length of ribbon.

Not having a greatcoat in her size, Maddie had to make do with a cloak to protect her from the elements and she had wrapped it around herself when she left her bedchamber, lest her appearance give rise to comment among the servants. However, Lady Lochall had thought ahead and sent everyone out of the way and it was not until she entered the morning room that she had any reaction to her altered appearance.

Taking a deep breath, she put up her head and swaggered in, saying as she did so, 'Well, will I do?'

There was a moment's silence, then Grant slapped his thigh and gave a shout of laughter.

'Bless me, but you make a fine lad!'

A mischievous smile bubbled up. She swept off her hat and make him a low bow.

'Why, thank you, sir.'

'You need names,' declared Lady Lochall, entering into the spirit. 'Let me see, what shall it be: Douglas, Iain, Robert?'

'What about James?' suggested Maddie. 'That has a good ring to it.'

'No!' Grant's sharp rejection drew all eyes and he felt obliged to explain. 'I lost a friend of that name at Culloden.'

He still felt the guilt of it, having survived while so many of his comrades perished on Drumossie Moor.

'Oh. I beg your pardon.' Maddie was immediately contrite. 'What say you, then, what name would you suggest for me?'

He looked at her, considering the matter.

'Duncan,' he said at last. 'And I shall be Ross. Duncan and Ross... Malcolm. What think you?'

'I think it will do very well.'

'We are agreed, then. Now, we should be on our way.'

'You will need money,' said His Lordship. 'Allow me to fund you.'

Madeleine shook her head. 'Thank you, my lord, but that is unnecessary. I still have the funds I brought with me from Inverness. Sufficient for the both of us.' She sent a challenging look towards Grant. 'You will, of course, be reimbursed for escorting me.'

'Let us get to France first, then we will argue about payment.'

He turned away abruptly, not wishing her to see how

concerned he was about this journey. They had more than a hundred and fifty miles to cover just to reach the rendezvous. Their chances of making it safely to France were low.

Grant and Madeleine stepped out of Lochall House to find their Highland ponies ready and waiting for them on the drive. They took their leave of their hosts and scrambled into the saddles, stopping for a final wave when they reached the turn in the road. A steady drizzle had started to fall and Grant remarked that they should be thankful for it.

'The track will take us up into the low cloud, which will conceal us from prying eyes. His Lordship suggested we should head west before we cross the river, to avoid any extra patrols.'

'Very well.'

She sounded dispirited and he said in a rallying tone, 'What is this, Madeleine, you are not contradicting me. Are you quite well?'

She did not smile. 'I am afraid we have put Lord and Lady Lochall in great danger.'

'I agree. It is unfortunate, but there is no help for it. The best thing we can do for them now is to get as far away as possible and quickly. They will tell Captain Ormskirk, when he calls, that we have gone to Aberdeen and they know nothing more than that.' He reached across and clapped her on the shoulder. 'Chin up, young Duncan, we will win the day, never fear!'

The going was tough, constant rain turned the track to a muddy stream and the ponies slithered and stumbled their way up and down the hills. They sheltered at night in caves or under rocky ledges. The supplies Lady Lochall had given them lasted for the first two days. After that they were forced to seek out farms or inns where they might buy food.

It was a relief when the weather cleared and Madeleine's spirits lifted a little to see the battered castle walls of Inverness and the buildings huddled around it.

'Keep your hat low and your collar up,' Grant warned her. 'I do not want to risk your being recognised.'

'No one will expect to see me in this garb,' she told him. 'Also, most of our acquaintances left here in the weeks before the battle.'

'And no one offered to take you with them?'

'No. They were none of them particular friends. Papa never encouraged it. We never settled in one place for very long, you see.'

'I, on the other hand, lived at Ardvarrick for most of my life. Until I joined the army last year.'

'Did you lose many friends in the campaign?'

She saw the shadow cross his features. 'True friends? No, but that does not make it any easier to bear their loss. The thought that I am alive and they are not.'

He spoke bitterly and she could think of nothing to say to help him. The best she could think of was to change the subject.

'I shall be inordinately pleased if we can find a respectable inn for the night,' she remarked. 'I should so much like to wash and put on clean clothes. Perhaps even to take a bath! Now what in the world have I said to make you laugh?'

'You are my little brother,' said Grant, still laughing. 'Any bathing would have to be done in our shared room.'

Her eyes widened. 'Goodness, I had quite forgot that! Could we not bespeak separate rooms?'

'We are lowly travellers, not royalty!'

'Not *you*, perhaps,' she said in a teasing voice. 'Papa once claimed he is connected to some minor branch of the Bourbons.'

'That will not help us in our present situation,' he retorted. 'Such grandiose notions would rouse a great deal of speculation.'

'Yes, and I am afraid it is just another of his tales.' She sighed. 'Ah, well, if it must be a single room, then you will have to take yourself off for an hour.'

Inverness was very different from when Maddie had left it. The streets were overrun with soldiers and many buildings stood empty. They passed the house of Louis Haster, the elderly watchmaker she had visited when Papa had needed his pocket watch repaired. Then it had been as neat as wax and freshly painted. Today it was empty, windows smashed, door hanging off its hinges and she felt sick, imagining what might have happened to the kindly old man.

'At least the inns are still in business,' remarked Grant, looking around him. 'Let us see if we can find suitable lodgings for the night.'

They found two hostelries that looked in reasonable order and visited both for a tankard of ale, in order to decide which would be the most salubrious for their night's stop. They both agreed the one on Bridge Street was the best, the servants better dressed and the public rooms cleaner. An enquiry of the landlord produced the information that the inn was almost full, but by dint of a little charm and a few extra coins Grant was able to procure a private room for them, with the luxury of a peat fire burning in the hearth.

A bath, however, was not possible. The landlord could spare no more than two jugs of hot water and with this Maddie had to be satisfied.

She sent Grant away to the taproom while she stripped off her clothes and by the time he returned her shirt was hanging up to dry before the fire and she was wearing the fresh one from her saddlebag like a smock over her breeches.

She coloured when he came in, aware of her very informal attire, and rushed into speech.

'The boots has taken my coat off to be brushed and said he would do the same for yours, if you wish.'

'When we retire, perhaps, but for now we need to prepare for dinner. The landlord refused to have it brought to our room and I did not like to press the matter as that would only draw attention to us.'

Maddie looked about her.

'To be truthful, there would be no room here, would there? We should have to sit on the bed to eat.' That brought to her mind another delicate matter although she pretended such things were an everyday occurrence for her: 'And talking of beds, we should decide upon the sleeping arrangements.'

Grant waved a hand. 'That is all taken care of. I have asked them to bring in a truckle bed. I told the landlord you were a restless sleeper. Prone to kick.'

She smiled in response to the twinkle in his eyes. 'Quick thinking of you, sir.'

'On the other hand, the bed is quite large enough for both of us, if you would like to try it…?'

'I shall do perfectly well on the truckle,' she told him.

'Are you sure?'

The twinkle in his eyes had deepened. Maddie snapped off the smile and gave him a cool look instead.

'Perfectly,' she replied sweetly. 'Unless *you* would prefer to sleep in the stable?'

Grant opened his mouth to reply in kind, but he was silenced by a scratching at the door. Madeleine barked out a gruff and impatient 'Yes?' as she opened it.

The serving girl outside bobbed a nervous curtsy.

'Your coat, sir,' she muttered, handing over the garment before hurrying away.

Grant chuckled. 'Well, *Duncan*, I can see I shall have to teach you how to turn a maid up sweet if you are ever going to be a success with the ladies.'

She threw him a fulminating glance. 'I have no doubt you are an expert, *Ross*!'

'I am not sure about that, but I am happy to teach you what I know.'

He saw from the widening of her eyes and the sudden bloom of colour in her cheeks that the thought disturbed her. She was remembering that kiss, as he was, and it set alarm bells ringing.

Hell and damnation, if we do not take care, neither of us will sleep tonight!

He abandoned his teasing and turned away. 'Have you left me any clean water? Good. You had best make yourself presentable while I wash.'

Chapter Nine

They went downstairs to eat their dinner in the large public room. There was a constraint, but it was different from the tense awareness that had set them both on edge earlier. Grant had pulled the bed hangings together to provide a modest screen between them while he washed and Madeleine tucked in her shirt and finished dressing. However, when he had asked her if she was ready to leave the room her answer had been so timid, her look so conscious that he knew the disguise would not hold unless her spirits improved.

He gave a little tut of irritation.

'Hmm. I cannot possibly allow my little brother to go abroad looking like a ragamuffin.'

She took umbrage at that, as he knew she would.

'What is wrong with my appearance?'

'Your cravat is all wrong. Here, let me tie it for you.'

By the time he had rearranged its folds, muttering irritably all the time, the martial light was back in her eyes and she was glaring at him with ill-disguised indignation.

'There.' He stepped back, critically surveying her. 'That will have to do.'

'Do? We must look a hundred times more respectable than most of their customers!'

'And how else should a gentleman look? Appearances are everything, little Brother.' He opened the door and stood back for her to precede him. 'Come along, Duncan, jump to it!'

As he had hoped, her eyes flashed. She rose to the challenge, striding out of the room and descending the stairs with all the swagger and over-confidence expected of a young gentleman.

They found an empty table and were soon supplied with drinks and the food, when it came, was good.

'Not difficult to see the reason,' said Grant, when Maddie commented. 'Most of their customers are from the military. Officers with money to spend. Which is in our favour. They will not expect to find fugitives in their midst.'

'Fugitives!' She grimaced. 'Yes, I suppose that is what we are now.'

'I have been one since the army fled from Culloden.' He kept smiling, for the benefit of anyone looking their way. 'If we are caught, you would be condemned for merely being in my company.'

'Then we had best not be caught,' she replied, reaching for her tankard.

Any doubts Grant had that Maddie would be able to carry off the deception were soon put to rest. She took a chair opposite him and maintained her relaxed air, drinking confidently from the tankard in front of her and only the slight flicker of her lips disclosed she was not accustomed to supping ale. He had wondered if her hands were too dainty to bear scrutiny, but she had rubbed a little soot on the backs to disguise her smooth white skin. She had also applied the merest smudge to her chin and cheeks and, in the dim light, it gave a very convincing impression of the first emergence of an adolescent beard.

They enjoyed their meal uninterrupted and afterwards ordered coffee and more ale. They were both reluctant to return to their shared room, but thankfully, they had no trouble in finding topics of conversation. Around them the customers came and went, some to make their way home, others moving to the taproom once they had finished their meal until eventually only a few tables were still occupied. Two of these were in the far corners, where the men talked in low voices, but a third table was surrounded by a group of soldiers who had been drinking freely all evening and were now in boisterous mood. One, in an officer's uniform and with his wig askew, hailed the landlord and demanded more wine.

'We have the means,' he said, waving a fat purse in the air. 'We all took a share, didn't we, lads? After all, the poor fool won't be needing this now.'

'Or his timepieces, Major!' declared another, laughing and patting his pocket.

'Aye, they were a welcome bonus, eh, lads?'

Their host was approaching and the officer's companions tried to shush him, but he was in his cups and refused to be silenced.

'Why should I not say it? Damned traitor deserved to die!'

Another officer glanced up at the landlord and gave a nervous laugh.

'Old man who resisted arrest in Castle Street,' he explained. 'Tragic accident.'

Grant wondered if he should remove Maddie from their presence. She was sitting with her elbows on the table, hands around her tankard and a look of concentration on her face.

The innkeeper, stony-faced, placed three more wine bottles on the table and turned to leave. As he passed their table Madeleine put a hand out to stop him.

'Another flagon of ale here, landlord, if you please.'

Grant's brows shot up.

'Is that wise?' he asked her, keeping his voice low. 'It is time we retired.'

'Not yet.'

Her frowning glance flickered to the noisy group on the next table. Grant gave an inward shrug. The longer they remained below-stairs the less time they would have to spend alone in their room together. The less time for awkward moments.

The group beside them continued to drink, pushing their chairs back, untying stocks and loosening cravats as they sank lower in their chairs. It was clear to Grant that they were settling in for a night of drinking and he was about to suggest to Maddie that they should retire when something dropped to the floor. The soldier sitting nearest had drawn out a handkerchief to mop his face and the snuffbox caught up in its folds tumbled out.

Maddie swooped to pick it up.

She tapped the man's arm. 'You dropped this, Sergeant.'

'Why, thank 'ee, young sir. Much obliged.'

'Think nothing of it, sir. Always glad to be of assistance. 'Tis a fine piece.'

'Aye.' The Sergeant held the box up to the light. 'I won it from a young corporal back at Carlisle. At cards. Fair and square.'

'Cards, eh? My favourite pastime.'

Grant sat up, tense and alert. What the devil was she playing at?

Across the table the Major called out merrily.

'What is it, Sergeant? What is going on over there?'

'The young gentleman in the corner noticed I'd dropped my snuffbox, Major Albright,' replied the man, holding it up.

Maddie touched her hat. 'We were discussing cards, Major.'

'Cards, eh? Now there's an idea.' The officer cast a bleary eye about the table. 'Who is for a game?'

Most of the number laughed and shook their heads. A couple bade the company goodnight and left the table to stumble up to their rooms.

'There's still four of us. Wake up, Lieutenant.' Major Albright prodded his neighbour, who was head down on the table and snoring loudly, but got no response. 'Although only three of us are awake.'

'If we joined you, we might enjoy a game of Lanterloo,' offered Maddie.

'Loo?' The Major's brows shot up. 'Now what would a young fellow like you know of such things.'

She gave a modest shrug. 'Only the rudiments of the game, I admit, but I should like to play a hand.'

Grant began to feel some alarm. He said quickly, 'You must excuse my brother, Major, I fear his wits have gone a-begging. Come, Duncan, it is growing late and we should retire.'

'Nay, Brother, we have time for one game, surely?'

The look that accompanied this statement was so fierce that when the Major invited them to join him at the table Grant capitulated. He had no idea what Maddie was about, but he was intrigued. He was not overly worried; he judged they were not yet in so deep he could not extricate them.

'I think we have the opportunity here to win a little money,' Madeleine muttered as they rose from their seats. 'Suggest to them that we play five-card loo.'

Introductions were performed, the sleeping soldier was pushed to one side and Grant and Maddie took their seats around the table while Major Albright straightened his wig and sent one of his companions to find a pack of cards and counters.

After the cut Grant had the lowest card and dealt first, finally putting the remaining cards down and turning the top one for trump.

'Spades,' muttered the Major, studying his hand and shaking his head.

Grant won the first round when everyone passed, but in the next he failed to win a trick and was looed. As the game progressed the room became quieter, the players concentrating on their hands. Maddie, he noticed, was playing solidly, passing or exchanging her cards with considerable skill. She won several tricks, was looed once and did nothing to rouse suspicion in anyone but himself.

Since she still held the purse strings, he considered he was justified in being a trifle concerned. The light of battle was in her eyes and such a look of determined concentration on her face that he knew she was up to something. He just hoped it would fall short of ruining them.

He continued to play while keeping one eye on Maddie. More ale was called for, but he was relieved to see that she barely touched her tankard. Their companions, however, continued to drink steadily and, by the time the Major laid down his cards, face up, with a shout of triumph, he was the only player besides Maddie and Grant to be still awake and sitting upright at the table. Grant was not sure if it was by skill or good luck that they had managed to lose so little.

The Major nudged his companions to rouse them, but when he suggested another game they swore drunkenly and shambled off to their billet.

'You'll play again, Malcolm,' he declared, scraping together the cards.

'Three players is not enough.' Grant tried to keep the note of relief from his voice. 'I think it is time my little brother and I bade you goodnight, sir.'

'What? Nonsense!' Success had energised the Major and he was already calling for a fresh pack of cards. 'Another game. We will manage with three—'

'That would not be a fair contest,' Madeleine objected, her voice gruff.

'What shall it be then, Quadrille, if I can rouse my Sergeant?'

'Piquet,' Maddie suggested. 'Just the two of us. My brother would prefer to sit by the fire with his pipe, isn't that so, Ross?'

Major Albright laughed. 'Young Duncan is a spirited lad, Mr Malcolm, but you need to put him on a tighter rein. Keep him from trouble.'

'The boy is bent on his own destruction. He will not heed me.' There was more than a hint of truth in the words, Grant realised bitterly. 'But hark me now, Major. I will not be held responsible for any losses he may incur.'

He frowned at Maddie as he said it, but she responded with nothing more than an innocent look and a bland smile.

The officer looked disappointed. 'Would you not prefer to play in his stead, Malcolm?'

'Do you think I won't be a match for you, Major?' Maddie exclaimed, a laugh in her voice. 'I think I might surprise you.'

Grant shrugged. 'If the boy wants to lose his money to you, I'll not stop him. It will teach him a lesson.'

He drew a chair close to the sluggish fire and pulled out his pipe, then he stretched his legs before him and pretended to doze, but all the time he was watching, alert.

Madeleine, or Duncan as he should call her, had shrugged off her coat and was expertly dealing the cards. Despite this slight advantage, she lost the first *partie* of six hands. Grant groaned inwardly. It did not bode well. The next *partie* went better, with Maddie scoring a repique. The Major called for more wine, but Grant noticed that 'Duncan' was still drinking almost nothing.

His spirits rose when Duncan declared he held a *quatorze* of aces, only to be dashed again when a series of poor discards saw him lose the hand. The other tables emptied and the room was silent save for the players as they kept score. Grant's nerves were at full stretch. He wished he had insisted at the outset that Maddie let him take care of their funds, then he might have had some sway over her impetuous decision to play. Grant heard her declare a *tierce*, which the Major contested, cursing, and he noticed the pile of coins at her elbow begin to mount.

The landlord came in to replace guttering candles, but neither of the players paid him any heed. They were on the last hand of the final *partie* and there was little difference in their scores, although, having watched the game closely, Grant was confident Maddie would not lose. In fact, he thought her play had been near perfect and she might have doubled her winnings, had she wished to do so.

Where the devil had she learned to play like that?

The Major asked the same question as Duncan won the final trick. He swung around to glare at Grant. 'Were you helping him?'

'Not in the least. You will see that I deliberately set my chair so I could not read your hands. Neither could my brother see me without turning about.'

Grant kept his voice calm and unconcerned, but he was ready to act if necessary. If the mood turned ugly, this could all go very wrong.

The Major acknowledged his words with a grunt and turned back to the table. He scowled for a moment, then gave an uncertain laugh.

'I vow 'tis the first time I have been bested by such a youth! You must have had an exceptional teacher.'

'I have a good memory and I paid attention to mathematics at school,' said Maddie, gathering up the coins from the table and putting them in her purse. 'I am adept at calculating the odds, that is all.'

'Well, well, it has been an education to play with you, young sir, although my purse is a deal lighter for the experience!' Major Albright drained his wineglass and refilled it, clearly intending to finish the bottle before he retired.

Grant rose and put his hand on Maddie's shoulder. Time to get out of here.

'We will bid you a goodnight, then, Major.'

'Goodnight to you, Mr Malcolm. And I'd advise you to keep this young whelp under your eye. Such a gift for gambling could prove his undoing.'

'I am all too aware of that,' muttered Grant, only giving his young 'brother' time to put on his coat before ushering him out of the room.

He did not speak again until they had reached the seclusion of their bedchamber, where he locked the door before turning on Maddie.

'What the devil do you think you were playing at tonight?' he demanded in a furious whisper.

She had shrugged off her coat and waistcoat and was lighting the candles on the mantelshelf.

'I thought our purse could do with replenishing.'

'Damned foolishness! Idiocy! Not only did you draw attention to yourself, you risked what money we do have in a game of chance.'

'Oh, there was little chance involved. I could have taken every groat from Major Albright, but I thought it best to allow him to think he had come off lightly.' She tossed the purse over to Grant. 'Here, you keep this. I think we have sufficient now to get us comfortably to France.'

Her insouciance only enraged him further. He threw the purse aside and grabbed her by the shoulders.

'Can you not see how dangerous that was? What if they had realised you are not what you seem?'

'There was very little chance of that. My disguise—'

'Your disguise is no more than an illusion and a fragile one at that! In a smoky room with flickering candles it might fool soldiers in their cups, but what of the morrow, when they see you in daylight?' He dragged his fingers across her cheek, wiping away the soot. 'Do you think this feeble masquerade will save you then?'

'I will keep out of their way in the morning!' She tore herself out of his grasp. 'I had to do something, they were so loud and coarse, laughing about what they had done to a helpless old man.'

'What?'

She had lost him. He had not been attending to the soldiers' conversation, other than to know that it did not involve them.

Madeleine stormed over to the washbasin and began to wash the soot from her face and hands.

'The money they were spending so freely.' She threw the words at him over her shoulder. 'They said it came from an old watchmaker in Castle Street. Louis Haster. I knew him. I noticed his house as we rode in today, windows broken, door battered down. He was a gentle soul, harmless. And they k-killed him.' She picked up the towel and began to scrub her face. 'When I saw the brutes were using his money to pay for their revels tonight, I could not stand by and let it go unpunished.'

She buried her face in the towel, her shoulders

drooping, and Grant's anger drained away. He took a few steps towards her and stopped. Well out of arm's reach.

'I am sorry, Madeleine, I did not know.'

'How could you?' She took a moment to place the towel neatly back on its rail and said, gruffly, 'I am grateful to you for allowing me to play.'

'I could see you were determined.' He tried to lighten the mood by adding, 'You are so dashed wilful that, short of picking you up and carrying you away, I did not think I could have stopped you.'

'I doubt you could, without acting like a bullying older brother.'

She looked up, the candlelight playing over her face, showing him the wry smile curving her lips. If only she knew! The feelings she aroused in him were anything but brotherly. Even in a man's shirt and breeches she looked very feminine. Very desirable.

A series of thoughts chased through his mind, but he fixed on the safest one.

He said irritably, 'You still have dirt on your face.' He picked up the damp cloth from the washstand. 'Here, let me do it.'

Madeleine closed her eyes and stood patiently while he took her chin in his hand and rubbed at her cheek. She was exhausted by the run of emotions she had experienced that evening. Her nerves had been at full stretch as she had walked to the table where they were to eat, aware of the curious glances of their fellow diners. She had no illusions about the risks they were taking, she knew they should do nothing to draw unwanted attention, but the soldiers' callous talk, gloating over the fate of the kindly old watchmaker, had put her in a rage.

Ice-cold anger had carried her into the card game, but then she had had to school her mind to strict concentration while she played, judging the abilities of her opponents, winning by just enough to keep them interested, not enough to make them suspicious. There had been a certain satisfaction, even exhilaration, at proving she had not lost her skill, but now it was over and reaction was setting in. She could understand Grant's anger, but she felt too shaken, too drained, to fight it.

'There, that's better.' He turned her face this way and that, critically inspecting it before releasing her.

Maddie blinked her eyes open, ready to thank him, but the words would not come. Grant was gazing at her and she stood awkwardly, remembering the last time she had felt like this, as if a storm was about to burst over them. It had been the night Grant had kissed her and the fizzing, thrilling shock of his touch had run through her body.

And her body was now crying out for him to do it again. Her mouth was dry, her full breasts strained against the confines of the wrapping she had used to flatten them. She desperately wanted to step forward, to slip her arms about his neck and pull his head down until their lips met. She wanted to forget everything in another explosive kiss…

How long had she been standing here, staring at Grant? Could he read her thoughts, did he feel the same? Heart pounding, she watched his hand come up towards her cheek, then she saw his fingers close into a fist, slowly, as if he was exerting all his strength to pull it back down to his side.

As if released from a spell she took a hurried step back and at the same time Grant turned away from her.

'I beg your pardon!'

'It is very late!'

Their words collided with the violence of a thunderclap in the silence.

Grant cleared his throat. 'I will take the truckle bed.'

'We had agreed that I should sleep there.'

'That was before you treated those soldiers to a masterly display of skill that left them out of pocket!' He gestured towards the door. 'I will move the bed across the entrance, in case any of them try to sneak in and recover their money.'

His tone was sharp, indicative of irritation. Madeleine said quietly, 'Oh. Yes. Of course.'

'Besides, the bed hangings will give you some privacy.'

'Thank you.'

She climbed on the bed and pulled the curtains tight before changing into her nightshirt. She slipped between the sheets and listened to Grant moving about the room, heard the creak of wood and ropes as he finally lay down on the truckle bed. Then an awkward silence.

'Grant?' There was no reply, but she knew he could not be sleeping yet. 'I beg your pardon. Truly, I do not mean to make things so difficult for you.'

Grant listened to the words, uttered softly. He heard the note of regret in her voice. He was not sure if she was talking about playing cards or what had happened after, in this room, that flare of attraction that had caught him unawares. One moment he had been cleaning her face as if she was some tiresome and grubby brat, then his eyes had fixed upon her lips and all he could think of was kissing her. Desire had slammed through him, the violence of it rocking him off balance. Thank God they had both come to their senses! This attraction was beyond a mild flirtation now. It had become dangerously strong and he would have to be much more careful in future.

He said, 'Best get some sleep, we have an early start tomorrow. It is fortunate I paid our shot before we came upstairs. It means we can slip away early, before Major Albright and his cronies are awake.'

'Yes. Goodnight, Grant. And thank you.'

'For what?'

'For taking such good care of me.'

He responded with nothing more than a grunt and turned over in the hard, uneven bed. She had nothing to thank him for. The way the hot blood was coursing through his body, she was in as much danger here in this room with him as she had been playing at cards. At the thought of her, lying in that damned bed, almost close enough to touch, he almost groaned aloud with frustration. He turned over again, determined to put her out of his mind.

Confound it, the last thing he needed was to be distracted by a woman, especially one so rash, so impetuous as Madeleine d'Evremont. He encouraged the thought and tried to whip himself into a rage over her ability to upset his plans, but gradually he was forced to acknowledge a grudging admiration for the cool way she had dealt with the soldiers. She might well have learned the rudiments of piquet and loo at school, but where had she honed her skills to such a level? By heaven, there was even more to this woman than he had considered.

Grant turned over, thumping his pillow to make it more comfortable. He needed to rest, not to be thinking about the woman sleeping a few feet away. He tried to relax and lie still, but by the unnatural silence of the room he guessed that neither of them would rest well that night.

At last Grant drifted off, but his sleep was disturbed by dreams, all the very worst scenes that he had tried to forget but were seared into his memory. The violence and confusion of battle, charging headlong towards a wall of red coats, knowing comrades were falling, seeing Jamie cut down and expecting any moment to receive a mortal blow himself. Then he was alone in the dark, watching the destruction of a village, helpless to intervene and forced to listen to the screams and cries, his nostrils filled with the reek of smoke from burning buildings. He was in hell and there was no escape.

Somewhere beyond the carnage, Madeleine was calling to him. She needed him and he must help her, but he was powerless, he could not move. He tried to call, but his voice would not work, he could not reach her—

'Grant, Grant, stop. Wake up!'

He was thrashing around in his bed, tangled in sheets, but Maddie's voice was still there, closer now. The fog of sleep lifted. He felt the lumpy mattress of the truckle bed beneath him and opened his eyes to find a pale, wraithlike figure bending over him, gripping his shoulders.

'Madeleine.' He sat up and reached for her.

'You were dreaming,' she said, taking his hands. 'A nightmare.'

She did not resist when he pulled her into his arms. Still he could not quite believe she was safe.

'I beg your pardon,' he muttered. 'I have disturbed you.'

'No, no, I was not sleeping very well myself.' She held him, long enough for Grant to know she was real and for his terror to fade, then she gently pushed herself away. 'It is nearly dawn, and I was thinking it would be better if we were on our way before the others stir.'

'A good idea.' When she tried to rise, he held on to her hands. 'I will look after you and get you safely to your ship, Madeleine, you have my word on it. I will keep you safe or perish in the trying.'

He could not read her face, he could not be sure that she believed him.

'Thank you,' she said at last. 'And if at all possible, I would prefer it if you did not die, Grant Rathmore. You are far more useful to me alive.'

With her words the final shreds of his nightmare vanished. Nor was there any constraint in her tone. He let out his breath in a sigh of relief. They were friends again.

Chapter Ten

Grant was relieved to get away from the inn without mishap. With her hat low and a muffler around her chin, Madeleine attracted no second looks from the boots or the sleepy stable hand who witnessed their departure. They took the bridge across the River Ness and followed the road westwards. It was a blustery day, with fitful showers and occasional bursts of sunshine and they passed only a few travellers on the well-worn track, mostly farmers carrying their goods to the market.

They had just passed the ruins of the old abbey at Beauly when the low rumbling thunder of hooves alerted Grant to riders behind them on the road. His companion heard it, too, and looked back.

'Soldiers,' she said urgently. 'Three of them and moving fast… Grant! I think they are the ones from the inn last night!'

'There is no way our garrons can outrun their horses.' He looked about him and nodded towards the trees. 'Let us go that way, towards the river bank.'

Grant turned his pony and led the way off the track and down through a thin belt of trees to the water's edge.

'Perhaps they did not see us,' said Maddie as they dismounted.

'They saw us all right and they will follow.' He took the reins from her hand. 'Go and hide yourself over there. Far enough away that you can run, if you have to.'

'I'll not leave you—'

'Do as I say!' he ordered. 'I stand more chance of success if I am not worrying about you.'

She looked as if she wanted to argue, then with a nod she turned and disappeared into the undergrowth.

Not a moment too soon. At that instant the riders appeared, winding their way through the trees towards them. Grant recognised Major Albright with a lieutenant and the Sergeant close behind. His cronies from the night before.

'So, we meet again, Mr Malcolm.'

'Major Albright.' Grant finished securing the ponies to a branch as he weighed up the odds. Three against one and each of them armed with sword and pistol while he had only the dirk tucked away in his sleeve and his sword. They all looked heavy-eyed, though, which might give him a slight advantage.

'Where's your brother?'

Grant jerked his head in the direction of the river. 'He's gone to…er…relieve himself.'

The three soldiers dismounted and Major Albright ordered the Sergeant to stay with the horses.

'To what do we owe the pleasure, Major?' Grant enquired politely. 'Are you come to see that we are safely on our way?'

'Something like that.'

'I am honoured that you would take the trouble to come after us and to discover our direction.'

The Major shrugged. 'It was easy enough. You were seen crossing the bridge. It was a simple matter to guess which way you were going and to pick up your trail.'

'I am gratified by your interest in us, Major, truly I am, but there really was no need—'

'Oh, but there was.' The officer's voice was silky. 'Your little brother took a great deal of money from me last night, Mr Malcolm. I want it back.'

Grant shrugged. 'It was won in fair play, you admitted that at the time.'

'Perhaps, but I am loath to part with my money that easily.'

'Ah, but was it yours to lose?'

The Major drew out his pistol. 'I would advise you to hand it over.'

'Alas, Duncan keeps his own purse.'

'Then we will wait for his return.'

'As you wish.' Grant continued to adjust the harness, keeping the ponies between him and the soldiers.

'Come over here where I can see you better.'

Grant hesitated, his hand lingering on one of the saddlebags. 'Thank you, but I am content here.'

'Well, I am not! Over here. Now.'

Grant hesitated, glancing back at the saddle and moving only a step or two away from the ponies.

'What is in that pack?' demanded the Major.

'What? Oh, nothing of value.'

'He's mighty reluctant to leave it,' muttered the Lieutenant.

'Go and see what is in there.' The Major waved his pistol at Grant. 'You, move away.'

Grant shrugged and took another step to the side. The Lieutenant came closer, pistol in hand. Outwardly relaxed, Grant waited until the man was passing, then he leapt, swinging the soldier around in front of him. At the same time he caught his opponent's weapon hand in a vicelike grip and twisted. The pistol fell to the ground, clattering against a stone and, in the same instant, the Major fired. Grant felt the Lieutenant twitch and scream as the bullet caught him in the leg.

One man down and one with an empty pistol. Much better odds.

From the corner of his eye Grant could see the Sergeant reaching for his pistol, but he did not pause. He was already charging at the Major and he closed with him, delivering a heavy blow to the chin which sent his head snapping back. Major Albright crashed to the ground, stunned.

Two down.

Grant turned to face the last man, expecting to find the Sergeant levelling a firearm at him. Instead he saw Maddie standing over the soldier's body, a stout piece of a branch in her hand. As he ran across to her she looked up, her face pale.

'Is he dead? I crept around behind him.'

'No, he breathes. Well done.' He turned to the horses, slapping them hard on the rump to send them careering away, then he reached out and caught her arm. 'Come along, let's get out of here.'

Maddie glanced again at the body at her feet before moving away. She was reassured by the slight rise and fall of his chest. They passed the Major, too, stretched out on the ground, his eyes closed. Only the Lieutenant was conscious, clutching at his thigh and gasping with pain.

Maddie took one look at the blood-soaked breeches and dug in her heels. 'We cannot leave him like that!'

At that moment the man's head fell to one side and he passed out. Grant bent over the officer and looked more closely at the injured leg.

'It is only a flesh wound. He will survive.'

He straightened and would have moved on, but Maddie was already tearing off her cravat.

'He is bleeding profusely.' She sank down beside the man. 'We must try to staunch the blood.'

Grant curbed his impatience as she quickly tied her neckcloth around the man's leg. As soon as she had finished, he pulled her to her feet.

'There,' he muttered, 'That will do until his companions come around. Now let us get out of here!'

Maddie allowed him to bundle her on to her garron and send her trotting off towards the track while he untied his own pony. She heard him cantering up behind her and they had just left the shelter of the trees when there was a shot.

Grant cursed and, turning back, she saw he was clutching at his arm, wine-coloured droplets oozing between his fingers. Behind him at the water's edge, she saw that the Major had crawled over to his wounded companion and picked up his pistol.

'I should have remembered to throw all their damned weapons into the river!' Grant fumed. He nodded at Maddie. 'Ride on! We need to get out of here with all speed.'

'But your arm!'

'We'll deal with that later. For now, just ride!'

They set the ponies cantering away as fast as they could go. Maddie knew that without their horses and one man wounded, it would be some time before the soldiers could follow, but that did nothing to stem the panic swelling inside. Her spine tingled with fear as they fled along the rocky track.

She had no idea how far they had travelled before Grant slowed the pace. They were close to a loch and he rode to the water's edge before coming to a halt. Maddie noted with alarm how pale he was. She threw herself off her pony and ran over, ready to support him as he almost toppled out of the saddle. She helped him to the ground and unbuttoned his jacket.

'I am sorry if this hurts you, but we must see how bad it is.'

She closed her ears to his muttered curses as she eased the coat from his shoulder. The left shirtsleeve was already blood-red. She drew a small silver dagger from her pocket and hacked off the sleeve.

Despite his obvious pain, Grant laughed. 'Do you always travel so well prepared?'

'Of course,' she told him, using the small amount of unbloodied linen to wipe around the wound. 'We are fortunate, the bullet has missed the bone and come out the other side of your arm. I will need your neck-cloth to bind it up.'

'Since we used yours to bandage the wounded soldier, I suppose I cannot complain.'

'It is all my fault,' she muttered, close to tears. 'If I had not stopped to tend him, we would have been safe.'

'Stop that foolishness, do you hear me?' he barked at her. 'What's done is done.'

He was breathing hard, his eyes closed, and she glanced with concern at his grey face.

'We must find a surgeon for you. Perhaps we should return to Beauly.'

'No. We go on. There is a house I know. About three miles from here. Take me there.'

Maddie did not argue. This was Grant's country. She trusted he knew what he was doing and could only hope the family would be in residence. She bandaged the wound tightly, then helped him put his good arm back into its sleeve and fastened the coat about him, holding the injured limb in place across his chest. She knew he must be in pain, but, apart from a sharp intake of breath as she helped him to mount up, he said nothing.

Their progress was necessarily slow, but Grant directed her to move off the main track and they struck out into a narrow glen where the hills rose steeply from either side of a small loch. She glanced behind occasionally, but there was no sign they were being followed.

The route was little more than a sheep track beside the water, but after a mile or so the landscape softened and at the end of the loch there were fertile plains and a pale, turreted house standing tall against a backdrop of thick woodland.

'Calder House,' Grant told her. 'Sir Edmund McBinnie lives there. He knows me well.'

His words faded as he collapsed over the pony's neck. With a cry Maddie dismounted and ran to his side. With some difficulty she managed to lead her own pony while supporting Grant in the saddle for the final few hundred yards to the house.

She had no energy to skirt around to the service buildings at the back and took the most direct route to the main entrance. As she approached, the solid double doors opened and two liveried servants ran out. She called out to them.

'Quickly, we have been attacked and need help.'

Grant was already sliding from the saddle and they ran forward to catch him.

'Is your master at home?' asked Maddie.

She was about to explain that Grant was known to the family when two ladies ran out of the house.

'Good heavens, Mama, it is Mr Rathmore!'

'Yes, yes, so it is.' The older lady, a grey-haired matron, summed up the situation in a glance and immediately took charge. 'Robbins, take Mr Rathmore to the blue room, if you will, and ask Hanson and Mrs Forbes to attend him.' She turned to Maddie and gave her a kindly smile. 'You must come in too, young sir. Anne, take these animals to the stables, if you please. And send someone to find your father. He went off to the home farm this morning.'

Maddie realised she was still clinging to the ponies' reins and it took no small effort to make her fingers loosen their grip. She then discovered it was even more of a struggle to speak, but she forced the words out.

'Do I have the honour of addressing Lady McBinnie?'

'I am she.' The matron took her arm. 'Now, no more talking until we have you both safely indoors.'

Grant was close to collapse and more servants appeared to help carry him up the stairs. Maddie followed with her hostess, but when they reached the half-landing, Lady McBinnie detained her. 'We can safely leave Mr Rathmore to the ministrations of my husband's valet and my housekeeper. I assure you, he could not be in better hands. But you and I must talk. Come along, my dear.'

Maddie watched Grant being carried away before her hostess's grip on her arm tightened and she was escorted to what was clearly a lady's boudoir. When Maddie hung back in the doorway, Lady McBinnie regarded her with a frank look.

'I was only for a moment deceived by your male apparel, madam. Come in.'

They entered the boudoir and Madeleine heard the door click shut behind them.

'Now,' said Lady McBinnie, waving her to a seat, 'you will explain to me, if you please, who you are and how you come to be here, dressed in that outlandish manner. Oh, I am not shocked,' she continued, when Maddie blushed. 'With so much upheaval in the country nothing surprises me these days, but I should like to know the truth, then I can decide how best to act.'

She sat down, an enquiring lift to her brows, and Maddie perched on the edge of a chair, twisting her hands together as she considered just how to begin.

'My name is Madeleine d'Evremont. I am trying to get to France, to join my father, and Mr Rathmore agreed to help me. He—we thought it would be safer if I travelled as a boy. We pretended to be brothers.'

'I see.'

'Grant—Mr Rathmore—has behaved with the utmost propriety,' she said quickly. 'He was only trying to protect me. In fact, that is how he came to be wounded. We were waylaid by soldiers soon after leaving Inverness. One of them sh-shot him in the arm.'

Her head dropped and she rubbed her fingers across her cheek to wipe away a rogue tear.

Lady McBinnie pursed her lips. 'I have known the family for years and what you tell me is no more than I would expect from young Grant Rathmore. He was always a generous boy. And most loyal to his friends. Did the soldiers believe you were a boy? You are certain they have no suspicion of your true sex?'

'I am sure of it, but they will be searching for us.'

'Then it is clear you must change your disguise and become a lady again. The first thing we must do is to find you more suitable clothing. Ah, Anne, just in time.'

The door had opened and the young lady Maddie had seen earlier came into the room. She was a little younger than Madeleine, very pretty with a dainty figure and an abundance of soft, curling light brown hair. When she spoke, her voice was as cheerful as her countenance.

'The ponies are stabled, Mama, and young Seb has ridden out to find Papa. How is Grant, have you sent for a surgeon?'

'I do not believe his injury is serious enough to endanger his life, but Hanson and Mrs Forbes are looking after him, they will decide if he needs more expert help. I had him taken to the old nursery wing.'

'Oh, good. He can be safely nursed there without anyone knowing he is even in the house!'

'Quite.' Lady McBinnie rose. 'Now, my dear, will you please take *Miss* d'Evremont to your room? I depend upon you to find something in your wardrobe that she might wear.'

The young lady turned to stare at Maddie, her grey eyes wide as saucers, but she recovered quickly.

'It would be my pleasure, Mama. If you will come with me, Miss d'Evremont, we are much of a size and I am sure I can find a suitable dress for you.' She smiled. 'If Papa is to be believed, I have more gowns than I can ever wear!'

She carried Maddie off, chattering merrily, and almost before they had reached the bedchamber they were on first-name terms and getting on famously.

Anne insisted upon hearing Maddie's story in its entirety.

'You need keep nothing back,' she said as she began pulling gowns from the linen press. 'If you are travelling with Grant Rathmore, then we already count you as a friend.'

'You know him well?'

'Oh, I have known him all my life,' Anne replied. 'Our families have been friends for ever, you see. In fact…' She trailed off, colouring a little, before repeating the request that her new friend should tell her everything.

When Madeleine demurred, Anne insisted, and she capitulated. In truth, it was a relief to be able to talk to someone about what had happened to her since she and her maid had ridden out of Inverness. Maddie thought it best to leave out some details, such as the names of those who had helped them. She also omitted any mention of sharing a room with Grant. And that kiss. In fact, she was at pains to emphasise that she was paying Grant to escort her to the coast.

Nevertheless, the story was long and involved. Anne listened, and asked any number of questions, but all the time she was looking out suitable clothes for Madeleine and helping her to dress, so that by the time the tale was told, Maddie was fully attired.

'But will the servants not think it odd that I have changed?' she asked, gazing at her reflection in the glass. 'Will they not gossip?'

'Oh, no, they have all been with us for years and their parents, too, in some cases,' Anne told her. 'They know the importance of discretion and can all be trusted to keep secrets. Heaven knows we all have them.'

Maddie did not miss the downward lilt of Anne's last word, the almost imperceptible sigh.

'Even you?' she asked gently. 'Forgive me, I do not mean to pry, but…do you have a fondness for Grant Rathmore?'

The sudden flush on her cheek and look of alarm in Anne's grey eyes told their own story.

'I beg your pardon,' said Maddie hastily. 'I should not have spoken; it is none of my business!'

'I did not realise it was so apparent,' muttered Anne, looking bereft. 'I am generally so careful.' She perched herself on the edge of the bed. 'I *do* like Grant, very much, but he has never shown the slightest interest in me. He has always treated me like a sister. And that is just as well, really, because Mama and Papa have said how relieved they are that there has never been the least hint of anything stronger between us. Not that they will not do all in their power to help Grant, of course, but they had heard he went off to join the rebels, which puts his family and everyone connected with him at risk. So you see, it has all worked out for the best, a connection between us would not do at all.'

'I am so very sorry,' murmured Madeleine.

'There is no need,' Anne told her, pinning on a brave smile that did not quite reach her eyes. 'I am quite resigned to the fact that my feelings will remain unrequited.' She said anxiously, 'You will not say anything to my parents, will you, or to Grant?'

'No,' Maddie assured her. 'I shall not say a word to anyone.'

'Thank you. It would only cause them to worry about me, you see, and there really is no need. Now…' she jumped off the bed '… I think I have some red ribbon somewhere, that will look very well with that cerise gown!'

Thus it was that when the two young ladies went downstairs shortly before the dinner hour Madeleine was most suitably gowned in a crimson robe with white lace trim and worn over snow-white linen. They entered the drawing room to find Lady McBinnie already there, together with a thin gentleman in Highland dress whom she presented to Maddie as her husband, Sir Edmund.

He took her hand and bowed over it.

'Miss d'Evremont, I do hope you will forgive me for not being here to welcome you today.'

His kindly manner was very reassuring and Madeleine replied with a smile.

'Since you could not have known we were coming I could hardly expect it of you, sir. I am only grateful that you and Lady McBinnie are able to take us in.' She turned to her hostess. 'I must ask you, ma'am, how is Mr Rathmore? When may I see him?'

It was Sir Edmund who answered her.

'I looked in on him before coming downstairs, Miss d'Evremont. His wound has been dressed and there is no sign of infection, but he is very weak.'

'And may I see him now?' she persisted.

'Alas, my dear, I think it best to wait a little. Mrs Forbes has given him a sleeping draught and he would not know you.'

A servant came in to announce dinner and Lady McBinnie rose.

'You shall see him before the night is out, you have my word, but for now come along to the dining room. It would be a pity for Cook's efforts to be ruined by delay.'

Maddie swallowed her disappointment. She did not wish to appear ungrateful and she was indeed feeling hungry, so she allowed herself to be escorted to the dining room where she ate well and drank sparingly. Her hosts said and did nothing to arouse any suspicion. They were kindly, generous people and she felt herself beginning to relax in their company, although she could never forget that Grant was somewhere in the house, his arm ripped open by a bullet, and all because of her.

Once the meal was over and they had all returned to the drawing room, she felt sufficiently at home to voice her concerns that her presence was putting the family in danger.

'My dear, there is danger in merely being alive in these dark times,' was Sir Edmund's blunt reply.

'But I am a Frenchwoman,' she said, trying to make him understand. 'Our countries are at war.'

'You have been travelling in disguise,' argued Lady McBinnie. 'We must hope no one will connect our female guest with any skirmishes that have occurred recently.'

'It is more concerning that young Rathmore fought with the rebels,' put in her husband. 'However, we will take the risk and gladly.'

'You see,' said Anne, smiling at Madeleine, 'I told you they will do all they can to help.'

'Indeed, we will!' Her mother gave a heartfelt sigh. 'I saw Grant's poor mama shortly after his departure last summer. She told me he had gone quite without warning.'

Sir Edmund looked very grave. 'I have never seen Ardvarrick so shocked. We know so many families who were destroyed by the Fifteen Uprising and Ardvarrick has always done his best to keep his people out of the way of such things. He had no notion his heir would run counter to his advice and fight with the Jacobites. They will be fortunate to escape retribution now.'

'His heir?' Madeleine repeated, her heart sinking.

'Their only child,' explained Lady McBinnie.

Maddie felt matters were becoming even worse. If Grant had not changed his plans to help her, he might have been in France by now. He would have been able to inform his parents that he was safe, at least.

'They must be sick with worry,' Lady McBinnie continued. 'I am sure they would dearly like to see Grant again, just to assure themselves that he is well.'

'We heard from some of our people who saw him on the road last year,' put in Anne, looking up. 'On his way to join the Prince at Glenfinnan. He was with Jamie Cowie. They told us there were plenty of men from Contullach in the party, but no one other than Grant from Ardvarrick.'

'He mentioned a friend called Jamie,' said Madeleine. 'I believe he fell at Culloden.'

'As did so many good men,' remarked Sir Edmund. 'But that won't be the end of it. The British will exact the severest penalties from the families of all those involved in the uprising and from anyone seen to be supporting them.'

'All the more reason then that we should not be here,' Maddie persisted.

Lady McBinnie reached over to pat her hand. 'Patience, my dear. You must stay here now until Grant Rathmore is fully recovered.'

'But the soldiers might come here, searching. Even if they do not know *me*, they will certainly be suspicious of Grant.'

'I am sure they might be, if they found him.'

'This is all my fault,' exclaimed Maddie, jumping up. 'He would be safe in France by now, if it was not for me. As it is, he is severely wounded and in even more danger. I will never forgive myself if anything happens to him!'

'Hush now, nothing is going to happen, to either of you,' replied Lady McBinnie in soothing accents. 'You are both perfectly safe here.'

'Forgive me, ma'am, but how can you say that? There are soldiers patrolling throughout the Highlands. They are savage, merciless!' She shivered. 'I beg your pardon, but it cannot be right to put you in such danger.'

Sir Edmund gently but firmly escorted her back to her chair.

'*Nothing* is going to happen to anyone, Miss d'Evremont. You could not be in a safer house.' He chuckled. 'Did my wife not tell you? We have two English officers billeted with us.'

Chapter Eleven

Madeleine stared at him.

'English officers, here?' She looked about her, as if expecting them to step out from the shadows.

'They are here as our guests,' explained Sir Edmund. 'But it was an invitation we could not avoid extending to them. Colonel Sowton and Major Rutter arrived here two weeks ago. The rank and file are billeted in the village about two miles yonder, but it is a poor place with few good dwellings, so I was obliged to offer them hospitality. They were also grateful when I said Hanson would attend them. He is a very superior gentleman's valet and that makes them feel they are enjoying a stay in the country with friends rather than on military manoeuvres.'

'We made it clear that we did not have room for any more of their people, of course,' added his lady. 'Thus, we have avoided having their servants wandering around the house, spying on us.'

Madeleine stared at her in horror. 'And you took us in, knowing the danger?'

'What would you have me do? There is not another

house for miles I would trust to look after you. If you had carried on to the village, you would have ridden straight into the soldiers. No, I had no choice and when I saw Grant Rathmore, a boy I have known all his life, it was all the more imperative to keep him safe.'

Anne spoke up. 'You really do not need to worry, Madeleine. As I have already told you, there is not a servant in this house who would betray any secrets. And by having the officers here, under our eye, Papa can ensure that others are safe, too.'

Madeleine looked at the smiling faces around her and thought of Grant above stairs. She could ride away from here now if she so wished, but Grant was too ill to move again, at least for a few days.

She said, 'You are playing a very dangerous game, Sir Edmund.'

'I am aware, but there is little choice. And we are fortunate that our...er...guests are gentlemen. At least as much as one can expect Government soldiers to be.'

Maddie thought back to Captain Ormskirk.

'There are a few good, honest men in the army, I suppose.'

'We look after them, feed them well and they repay us with good manners and a modicum of protection,' Sir Edmund went on. 'As luck would have it, they rode out this morning and are not expected back until the morning.'

That, at least, was good news.

'Then they do not know we are here. I might stay with Grant, in the sickroom—'

'Alas, that will not do. Your arrival did not go unnoticed by one of my neighbours. He was up on the hills and saw two riders coming here. He was too far away to see clearly, but thought it looked suspicious and, being a well-meaning fellow, he came over earlier to enquire if all was well. Pray do not fret, I managed to convince him that I had sent a servant to escort a young relative here and he has gone away quite happy. But you see, my dear, we now need you to play the part.'

Maddie was not much reassured. 'And the officers, what will you tell them?'

'The same,' replied Lady McBinnie. 'You are my niece Fiona, come to stay.'

'You appear to have thought of everything,' murmured Maddie, her brain reeling.

'We are obliged to do so, in these uncertain times,' replied Sir Edmund drily. 'I suggest you retire early tonight and we will make sure our guests are apprised of your arrival. You need not meet them until the morning and by then my lady will have been able to tutor you in your role.'

'And Gr—Mr Rathmore?'

'We will keep him hidden and nurse him until such time as he may safely make an appearance. Do not worry, my dear, it is not the first time we have harboured a fugitive in this house. He will be quite safe.' He smiled at her. 'Would you like to assure yourself of his well-being before you retire?'

'I should, very much. Perhaps Anne would like to show me the way?'

But although Miss McBinnie threw her a grateful look, she shook her head.

'It is late and I am very tired. Mama will take you. I will visit Grant when he is stronger and able to receive visitors.'

'Yes, he will not want too many people fussing

around him. We will bid you goodnight, then.' Lady McBinnie rose and beckoned to Maddie, 'Come along, my dear!'

The sickroom was situated beyond the disused nursery rooms, reached via labyrinthine passages and windowless chambers full of unused furniture and old trunks. Madeleine thought it would be strange if anyone should find their way along here without good reason.

'The house has been searched on numerous occasions and no one has yet located this room,' Lady McBinnie told her as they headed for what appeared to be a gabled wall with a stone chimney running up through the roof. My lady went ahead and pushed on one of the support timbers. A section of wall opened to reveal a comfortable attic room where Grant was sitting up in bed, pale but awake.

'You see,' she said, 'our patient is very much alive.'

Maddie could not prevent a sigh of relief and Grant smiled at her.

'I told you it was the merest scratch.'

'It is a little more than that, Master Grant!'

Maddie jumped at the sharp words. She had not noticed the iron-haired woman in a black gown who was standing at the far side of the bed.

'You must be Mrs Forbes,' Maddie said now, smiling. 'You have worked miracles here. Mr Rathmore looks so much better than when I last saw him.'

The housekeeper looked nonplussed by the praise and shifted uncomfortably.

'Aye, well, it isn't as if I don't have enough to do without nursing young gentlemen who get themselves into trouble!'

Grant laughed. 'Do not be fooled by that stern manner, Miss d'Evremont. Mrs Forbes may scold me soundly, but this is not the first time she has had to fix me up.'

'No, I have tended more than enough cuts and bruises for you in the past, Master Grant, and that's a fact.'

The exchange did much to allay Maddie's worries and her smile grew. Grant put out his hand and she took it between both her own, unable to speak for the tumult of emotion raging inside. She had not realised how worried she had been until this moment. How alone she had felt without him.

Behind her, Lady McBinnie gave a little cough and suggested Mrs Forbes should accompany her downstairs.

'I will return shortly to escort you to your bedchamber,' she told Maddie before following the housekeeper from the room.

'How diplomatic of our hostess to leave us alone,' remarked Grant.

Maddie saw the glint in his eye and blushed. She realised she was still clinging to his hand and would have released him, but his fingers closed even tighter.

'No, please, do not run away.'

'I have no intention of running away,' she replied with as much dignity as she could muster, considering her burning cheeks and how hard her heart was thumping.

'I am glad to hear it. Pray, sit on the bed and talk to me.'

But that Madeleine would not do.

'If you let me go, I will draw up a chair,' she said primly.

Grant was reluctant to release her hand. He wanted to keep her close, to assure himself that she was really here, safe beside him, but he could not tell her that. He watched her fetch a chair and set it down beside the bed, enjoying the sight of her dainty form, the way her skirts swung around her as she moved.

'I like your gown.'

'Thank you.' She sat down and smoothed one hand over the red satin. 'Miss McBinnie gave it to me. She could not have been kinder.'

'Is she not a splendid girl? I have known her all my life. She has always been like a sister to me.'

Madeleine was looking down at her hands, clasped lightly in her lap, and Grant took the opportunity to study her, noting the long dark lashes that fanned her cheeks, the generous mouth, solemn now, but he had seen it stretch into a smile that could light up a room. Just the thought of it lifted his spirits.

I could sit and watch her for hours.

She looked up at that moment and he quickly averted his gaze.

'Lady McBinnie says they can keep you safe here, Grant, but as soon as you are well you should leave. I am sure Sir Edmund will be able to find another guide for me.'

'No. I promised to escort you and I shall finish this.'

'You have done enough for me. I cannot, will not, ask more of you.'

'I will finish what I started. Once I am up and about—'

She interrupted him. 'It is not *safe* for you to get up. There are two English officers staying in this house!'

'The devil there are!'

He jerked upright and sucked in his breath as pain shot through his arm. Immediately Maddie was on her feet and gently pressing him back.

'You must keep still or the bleeding will start again.'

'Blood and thunder,' he muttered, his teeth clenched against the faintness brought on by the agonising pain. 'I am as weak as a cat.'

'That is to be expected. You need to rest now. Once you are well enough to travel, then you should go home.'

Grant was resting with his eyes closed, but at her words he gave a bitter laugh.

'Home! I have no home now.'

'You do. Ardvarrick.'

'No. My actions will bring nothing but trouble to them. I fought for the Stuart and I made no secret of it. The soldiers will be sure to come looking for me.'

'But your parents will want to know—'

'Leave it now, Maddie. Confound it, woman, must you always argue with me? Do not meddle in things you do not understand.'

He spoke sharply and he saw her pressing her lips together. She did not want to upset him, even though it went against the grain to keep quiet. Should he apologise? No. It was better if she was angry with him, if she thought him ill-mannered and boorish. With any luck it would dull the edge of the attraction that had been growing between them. His own desires he could control, but he did not wish Madeleine to become too attached to him. He was a fugitive with nothing to offer and would surely break her heart.

There were voices, outside the door. Lady McBinnie had returned and Grant guessed she was speaking loudly to give them time to compose themselves. As he heard the scrape of the opening door, he schooled his face into indifference. He did not doubt she suspected she had happened upon a romance and had deliberately given them time alone.

Like a pair of lovers, which they could never be.

Maddie did not tarry in the sickroom once Lady McBinnie had returned with the elderly serving maid who was to keep watch on the patient until morning. Maddie waited only to assure herself that Grant would be in safe hands through the dark reaches of the night, then she was content to let her hostess show her to her own bedchamber.

She was exhausted by the events of the day, but she was also dispirited by her conversation with Grant. Her own situation was serious, but once she was reunited with her father life would continue much as it had before. Grant's plight was far graver. He might escape to France with his life, but he must leave behind everything he held dear, his home, his family and his friends. Her heart bled for him.

When Madeleine came down to breakfast the following morning, the McBinnies were already at the table, accompanied by two military men, resplendent in their blue-and-red uniforms. The officers jumped up as she came in and Lady McBinnie presented her to them as her kinswoman, Miss Fiona Dewar from Perth.

Madeleine responded calmly to their greetings. Colonel Sowton was a large, rather portly man with an air of good-natured geniality, but his gaze was shrewd and she decided it would be foolish to write him off as a buffoon. Major Rutter was a little younger, a tall, lantern-faced man who lacked his superior's bonhomie, but he politely held her chair as she took her seat.

'These are dangerous times for a young lady to be travelling alone, Miss Dewar.'

'Indeed they are, Major, but there was an outbreak of smallpox in the area and my father thought it safer for me to come here than to remain in Perth,' she replied, faithfully repeating the story she and Sir Edmund had agreed upon last night.

'A wise precaution by your parent,' he replied.

'Your aunt told us as much last night, Miss Dewar,' remarked the Colonel. 'We must hope the outbreak is of short duration.'

'I pray it will be, Colonel.'

'But I understand that there is also sickness in this house,' said the Major.

'Yes, one of the maids has come down with a fever, but it occurred only a couple of days ago, long after my niece had set out on her journey here,' replied Lady McBinnie. 'It is an inconvenience to have a sick servant, but it is not a serious ailment, Major, I assure you. However, we are keeping her well away from the family, as a precaution.'

She neatly changed the subject and Maddie gave a tiny sigh of relief, but it did not last. She was aware that Major Rutter was studying her closely. At the next pause in the conversation, he spoke again.

'Forgive me, Miss Dewar, but I can see little similarity between you and your aunt. You are very dark, while Lady McBinnie is so fair. And your manner, too, your voice. There is something more…exotic about you. A French connection, perhaps?'

'Rutter, really!' The Colonel objected with a blustering laugh, but the Major waved a hand at him, all the time keeping his eyes fixed upon Madeleine.

'We have orders that we are to be vigilant, Colonel, at all times. Well, Miss Dewar?'

Madeleine refused to be intimidated. She had already been looking amused by his speech, but now she threw back her head and laughed.

'France is hardly exotic, Major! Scotland has very strong links with the French, as I am sure you know. Going back generations, so I should not be at all surprised if there is some French blood on my father's side.' She lifted her coffee cup and regarded him over the rim. 'Or, perhaps you suggest that my mother played her husband false.'

Maddie knew it was an outrageously improper remark, but it had the desired effect of ending the interrogation. The Major flushed and disclaimed, Anne stifled a giggle and Lady McBinnie gave a little cry of protest.

Sir Edmund frowned at her, 'That is quite enough of your levity, Fiona. These Lowland manners do not sit well with us here.'

The Colonel rushed gallantly to her defence.

'It is entirely Rutter's fault for goading the lady. Come, sirrah, apologise!'

'I will unreservedly beg the lady's pardon if she is affronted.'

Madeleine inclined her head. 'And I must beg my

aunt's pardon for allowing my flippancy to make me speak so shamefully of her sister.'

She flashed an apologetic glance at Lady McBinnie, who waved it aside.

'You have your lively wit from her, my dear, which makes you all the more precious to us.'

Her smile was warm and understanding, relieving Maddie's fears that she had caused offence. Major Rutter, however, persisted.

'You are fortunate that you have an aunt who can offer you such comfortable surroundings, Miss Dewar.'

'I am well aware of it, Major.'

'Many families have lost everything, supporting the Jacobite cause.'

'Not all Scots support Charles Stuart,' she retorted.

'No.' He sat back, his gaze flickering around the table. 'Many are content to wait to see which way the wind is blowing. Hedging their bets, as they say.'

'I think you misunderstand us, Major,' murmured Lady McBinnie. '*Most* Scots prefer to lead a quiet life.'

'Perhaps you are right, ma'am, but the uprising has shown that a great many have been prepared to rise up against their rightful King.'

'To their cost,' Madeleine interjected. 'The reprisals being meted out by His Majesty's army are harsh indeed.'

'But necessary, Miss Dewar,' put in the Colonel. 'This insurrection must be quashed. We cannot have the rule of law overturned.'

'Some would say there is no law here but that of the sword!'

Madeleine regretted the impetuous words even as she uttered them.

'Miss Dewar is a stranger to the Highlands,' put in Sir Edmund, by way of explanation. 'Life here is very different from what she has known in Perth.'

'No doubt,' retorted the Major. 'However, I can assure the lady that those who are loyal subjects of King George need have nothing to fear.'

'No, indeed, which includes the present company, I am sure.' The Colonel beamed at them and pushed his chair back. 'Come along, Rutter, duty calls us forth.'

'There is no hurry. I gave the men their orders last night.' The Major was looking at Madeleine, who tried hard to ignore him. 'It is such a fine morning I thought Miss Dewar might like to take the air with me.'

Lady McBinnie responded, saying smoothly, 'Ah, how kind of you to suggest it, Major, and at any other time I am sure she would be delighted to join you. However, I am afraid I have need of my daughter *and* my niece today to help me in the linen room. With one of my maids having taken to her bed and requiring attention, there is a great deal to do...'

She let the words hang and the Colonel was quick to respond.

'Quite so, my dear lady, you are very right to remind us. We are most appreciative of your kind hospitality and must take up no more of your time. Come, Major, let us be on our way. It is up to us to lead our men by example, what?'

The two officers took their leave and as the door closed behind them, Anne let out an exaggerated sigh of relief.

'Oh, my goodness, that was an anxious time! I thought poor Madeleine was going to faint off when Major Rutter suggested walking outside with him!'

'I am very grateful for your mother's quick thinking,' replied Maddie.

'But you must be on your guard, Madeleine,' said Sir Edmund heavily. 'The Major is suspicious of you.'

'Not suspicious,' opined his lady. 'I believe she has piqued his interest. He is very taken with her.'

Anne chuckled, earning her a frowning glance from her mother, while Maddie shuddered eloquently.

'Whichever it is, you may be sure I shall be careful to keep away from Major Rutter. And the Colonel, too.'

Madeleine went off with her hostess to the linen room, where she dutifully helped with the sorting of the bed sheets. The task kept her occupied until shortly after noon and, Lady McBinnie having no more chores for her, she hurried away to the sickroom.

She found Grant looking much better. He was sitting up in bed, enjoying a plate of ham while a serving maid bustled about the room, clearing up after the night's vigil. He greeted her cheerfully.

'Have you come to keep me company? You are in good time, madam, for now Eilidh can attend to her work instead of dancing attendance upon me.'

He pushed the tray away and the maid came to take it, giggling and blushing as he smiled and thanked her.

Maddie made herself comfortable on the chair beside the bed and waited until they were alone before giving voice to her thoughts.

'I am quite dismayed by how much work our being in the house is making for Lady McBinnie's staff. After all, they also have the Major and Colonel to wait upon.'

'It is not all bad, you know. Eilidh confided to me that she hopes to be able to retire soon, with all the extra money she is earning from the officers. They are happy to pay for any information about the family and their guests.'

'Oh, no!'

He grinned. 'It seems the servants come up with quite ingenious ploys to induce the Colonel to grease their palms, but once the money has changed hands the reason for their suspicions proves to be nothing but rats gnawing in the stables, or an errant boot boy creeping about the house at night. They all think it a very good game to dupe the English officers.'

'I wish they would not,' she said seriously. 'Think what might happen if they are found out, or if they inadvertently divulge something important.'

'They know what they are about and are all very loyal to the family. But you are not enjoying the jest, Maddie. What is it—has anything happened?

She hesitated, not sure if she should worry him.

'The Major was very curious about me at breakfast this morning.'

'Perfectly natural, since you appeared out of nowhere.'

'Of course, but when we were talking, I am afraid I allowed my temper to run away. My answers to Major Rutter were a little…sharp.'

'You spoke your mind without thinking.' He smiled. 'I know you too well now to be surprised at that! Suspicious of you, is he?'

'Worse. I think he has taken a fancy to me.'

'What?'

'It is no funning matter,' she retorted, when Grant threw back his head and laughed.

Her anger died away and she sighed, putting one hand to touch the fichu around her shoulders.

'I was so careful to dress modestly this morning. And I thought I was safe enough, for I am not fair and pretty, like Anne.'

Grant was about to disagree, but he bit his tongue to stop himself. That gown would attract any man's notice, and when her temper was roused, her deep blue eyes sparkling and a delicate flush on her cheeks, she had something more than mere prettiness. However, the idea that the English officer had seen that fire in Maddie disturbed him and he shifted restlessly in the bed. Madeleine observed it and was quick to reassure him.

'There is no danger, none at all. The McBinnies have taken me under their wing and I do not believe the officers will wish to offend them, so you must not think I am concerned for my safety.'

'No, I know you can take care of yourself very well, as you have shown me on more than one occasion.' His lips twitched. 'Including our first meeting, when I came in to find you had smashed a jug over your attacker and broken his head.'

For once she did not smile. 'I hope I shall not be obliged to apply such drastic measures to Major Rutter. I fear he would make everyone in the house suffer for it. A better solution would be for me to keep out of the way when they are in the house.'

'That is simple, then. You can spend your days here, with me.'

'Here, alone with you? No, no, I could not. It would not be proper.'

'It is a *sickroom*, Madeleine. I need nursing.'

There was no mistaking the decided glint in his eye.

'You need nothing of the sort,' she said crossly. 'Lady McBinnie told me your arm is healing well and you will soon be able to leave your bed.'

'Ah, but not quite yet.'

'Very well, I will come back here this evening. When the officers have returned.'

'And not before?' He gave an exaggerated sigh. 'It is devilish dull here if I am alone all afternoon, Maddie. Do say you will stay. If you do not, then Lady McBinnie will insist that poor Eilidh or one of the other servants must be here to watch over me.'

'Perhaps Anne might do it,' she ventured.

She watched closely for his reaction, but he merely pulled a face.

'I think Anne finds it tedious to be with me. She came in earlier, to see how I go on, and we found little to say to one another apart from the mundane.'

'I expect she is shy.'

'Shy!' Grant laughed. 'And why should that be, when we have known one another for years? No, Anne is the most delightful girl and she is far too polite to say so, but she would prefer to be anywhere rather than sitting here entertaining *me*!'

Madeleine thought otherwise, but she could not say so, having given her word to Anne.

'Please say you will stay, Maddie.'

She wavered. Her head told her she should not be alone with him. He was too charming and his smile had a most disturbing effect upon her, bringing forth all sorts of wicked thoughts that had no place in the mind of a well-bred lady. However, she had to acknowledge that he still had dark shadows beneath his eyes and his arm might well be paining him.

'Very well,' she said at last. 'If it will allow the servants to go about their work, I will go now and ask Lady McBinnie if she has any objection to my sitting with you.'

When she had gone, Grant leaned back against the pillows. He would be very happy to have Madeleine's company. Happier than he dare say, knowing that she was as nervous as a bird around him, but he could not rest when she was out of his sight. He might not be in a position to protect her, but if she was here with him, if he could see her, at least he would know she was safe.

Chapter Twelve

'I can do this. I will *not* lose my head over this man.'

Madeleine repeated the words over and over as she went in search of her hostess. Grant Rathmore was in her thoughts far more than he should have been and she knew she must fight it. At first she had imbued him with heroic qualities after he had rescued her from her attackers at Kildrummy. Now he evoked her sympathy because he was wounded. Added to his undoubted good looks and his charm, it made for a dangerous combination.

She had seen women fall in love with her father because of his attractive manners or his apparent power and affluence, but once he appealed to their compassion they became slavishly besotted. She had seen through it, knowing the sad eyes, the apparent fortitude while suffering, was nothing but a ruse. Once his interest had waned, or their usefulness was at an end, Papa would cast off his devoted lover without a second thought. She had seen it often and often, and vowed long ago that she would not become one of those women.

* * *

Madeleine returned to the sickroom a short time later armed with an assortment of items that made the patient raise his eyebrows in surprise.

'There is mending to be done, torn flounces, ripped sheets and so on,' she told him. 'It will give me something to do while I am sitting with you and the light is good. It will not prevent my conversing, should you wish to talk. And I have cards, too, when you feel a little better.'

'Thank you.'

'But I could not bring you any books,' she went on. 'They are locked away and Sir Edmund is gone out. Anne said she would ask him to look out something for you, when he returns.'

'I hope he still has a copy of *Robinson Crusoe*. Anne and I read it together, when we were children.'

Maddie said nothing, busying herself with placing her sewing on a small table that she carried across to set beside her chair. Despite her assertion that she would not succumb to the attractions of this man, she could not ignore the stab of jealousy when he mentioned Anne.

'Do you know the book?' Grant asked her. 'I should like you to read it to me, an you would.'

The stab of jealousy melted into a little burst of pleasure.

'I have not read it and should very much like to do so. I will make enquiries as soon as Sir Edmund returns.'

The day passed quickly. Maddie had expected to feel shy in Grant's company, but although there was a little constraint at first, it soon disappeared. She experienced one difficult moment when Mrs Forbes asked for her help to change his nightshirt and rebandage his arm. She found her eyes drawn to his naked body, taking in the strong muscled shoulders, his broad chest shadowed with dark hair and the flat plane of his stomach disappearing beneath the sheet that covered his lower body. There were scars of old wounds, too, some not yet fully healed, reminding her that he was a Jacobite soldier. That his life was in danger.

Her hands trembled a little when the housekeeper asked her to bathe his injured arm, but she squared her shoulders and set to work. Grant was silent, his eyes closed, but a quick glance at his face showed her he was very pale and tense, his jaw clenched against the pain and that, as much as the ugly wounds, made her realise he was still a long way from well.

Mrs Forbes applied honey to his injuries and wrapped a clean bandage around his arm.

'There. Now we will pop him into a clean nightshirt and that will be that.'

'Must we disturb him again?' asked Maddie, glancing at Grant's white face.

'Lord love you, mistress, if we don't he will very likely catch a chill. This room gets very cold in the evenings.'

'Best do as Mrs Forbes tells you,' he murmured, giving the lie to her suspicion that he had fainted. 'I must wear a nightshirt to spare your maiden blushes, Maddie.'

The housekeeper tutted.

'Whisht, now, stop teasing the lass, Master Grant.

She is a very sensible young lady and I'm glad to have her here to keep an eye on ye.'

'So am I,' he replied. 'Truly.'

He opened his eyes and smiled at Maddie, all bland innocence, but she was not deceived. She glowered at him before fixing her mind solely upon helping him into his nightshirt. When it was done and Mrs Forbes went off, carrying away the bowl and all the dirty linen, Madeleine went around the bed, straightening the covers while Grant lay back against his freshly plumped bank of pillows.

'If that hurt you it is no more than you deserve,' she told him in severe tones. 'I am breaking every rule of propriety being here. It is no laughing matter.'

'This, from the woman who fleeced an army officer of his ill-gotten gains. While dressed as a man, too.'

'That was different.'

'Ah, yes. Of course it was.'

By this time she knew him well enough to hear the tired note beneath the mockery. Immediately her mood softened. He was reaching awkwardly for the water glass beside the bed and she hastened to hand it to him, slipping an arm about his shoulders to support him as he drank. She acted instinctively and it was only when she was holding him that she realised how intimate it was. With only the thin linen nightshirt over his skin she could feel the knotted strength of him, the hard muscles of his shoulders beneath her hand. Their heads were close together, too. Another inch and her face would be resting against his, or she might even turn and gently kiss his cheek...

The thought sent the blood rushing up through her, heating her skin, and she realised with shocking clarity that what she felt was pure lust. Her breasts and thighs positively *ached* with it. The idea frightened her so much that it was all she could do not to jump away from Grant. Only by a supreme effort of will did she manage to hold him until he had taken a few sips of water and she could ease him back on to the pillows. She hoped he would not see how her hand was shaking as she took the glass from him and set it down.

'You should rest now.'

He sighed. 'Aye. I am tired as a dog.'

He sank into sleep, his body relaxing, and she carefully pulled the covers up over his chest. The raging desire had died to a simmer, but now it was replaced with an overwhelming urge to protect and cherish this man. Tenderly she reached out and placed a light kiss on his cheek.

'Then sleep now. My Highland soldier.'

The days fell into a pattern. Madeleine broke her fast with the family and, if the officers were present, Lady McBinnie would discuss all that needed to be done that day. Rising from the breakfast table, Madeleine would follow her ladyship and Anne to the kitchens or the linen room, from where she could slip away to the sickroom.

At first, Grant slept a great deal and she spent most of the time at her mending, but soon he began to recover and required entertaining during his wakeful hours. Maddie read to him or they talked. He made no attempt to flirt with her and she relaxed in his company, happy to tell him more about her life in France, being schooled by a governess while living with Tante

Élisabeth in dull respectability, until Papa decided she was old enough to be useful to him.

'Useful?' Grant pounced on the word.

'Oh, there is no doubt he would have left me in Dijon if he had not needed a hostess. He had been dangling after a recently widowed *comtesse*, but it all came to nought so he decided to take me with him. You see, he needed someone to keep house for him and provide him with an air of propriety.

'Do I seem disrespectful? I know my father very well. He has had a string of mistresses, but he trusted none of them to run his household. He liked to keep them at a distance, so that he might cast them off more easily when he grew bored. You look censorious, but you need not be, Papa was always very generous. He never turned any one of them off without a sou.'

'That is very good of him.'

He sounded severe and she raised her brows at him. 'Did your papa never have a mistress?'

'Not to my knowledge. He and my mother have always been devoted to one another. They have never been apart for more than a few days.'

'Tiens!'

He grinned. 'Now I have surprised you! I thought it was quite normal, when I was growing up, but the more I have seen of the world the more I know that such happy, comfortable marriages are very rare. I have made up my mind that I shall not take a wife until I can find a woman who inspires just such devotion in me.'

Comfortable! Maddie bent her head over her darning. Yes, he would want a sweet, conformable wife. Not a hot-tempered, flighty piece who was constantly at odds with him. Someone gentle, well-mannered and cheerful. Like Anne McBinnie.

For a moment Maddie thought the loud sigh she heard was her own, but it was Grant and he followed it with a bitter laugh.

'Not that I am in any position to consider such a thing. And now I doubt I ever will be.'

Maddie snipped off her thread and carefully returned the needle to the workbag.

'It is illness that has dragged down your spirits,' she told him, keeping her voice steady, prosaic. 'You will come about again, Grant Rathmore.'

'Do you really think so?'

'I do.' She forced herself to meet his eyes and give him a reassuring smile before she said brightly, 'Now, I must go and change for dinner.'

After promising to look in again later, Madeleine went away and Grant settled down to wait for Mrs Forbes to bring in his own meal. He was glad Maddie was coming back and not only because he worried about her being in company with English officers. He could not deny that her conversation raised his spirits. Her life was so different from his own. She had been mistress of her father's household, attending glittering balls, mixing with exalted personages. She was very much a society lady, while he was scarcely a gentleman in her eyes. His Grand Tour had consisted of a mere three months visiting France and Italy and although he had spent two Seasons in London with his Hampshire relatives, he had not enjoyed it and it was with relief that he had returned to the Highlands and thrown himself into learning everything necessary to run Ardvarrick, when the time came.

Only now, Ardvarrick was lost to him. He could never return.

Madeleine slipped quietly along the corridors to the sickroom the following morning to find that Grant had left his bed and was sitting in a chair. She frowned at his pallor.

'Whatever are you doing?' she exclaimed. 'Are you sure it is wise to be out of bed so soon?'

'I am very sure! I cannot lie abed for ever. Hanson helped me, after he had shaved me and tied back my hair. I feel so damned helpless.'

'You are making good progress, but it is not yet a week since we arrived here.'

'But you cannot remain at this house much longer. I must get you to the meeting place.'

'You must not fret over that,' she told him. 'There is plenty of time yet.'

'Not for such a long journey. As I recall, your father's letter to Lord Lochall said the French ship will be at the rendezvous around midsummer.'

'Yes. More than two weeks away. And the ship will wait a few days for me,' she reminded him. Her brow creased. 'Midsummer's Day, that will add considerably to the risk, will it not? There will be no darkness to cover the ship's movements.'

'True, but I know that coast,' said Grant. 'It has the advantage of islands and inlets where a vessel may evade prying eyes. But that is by the by. I want you to promise me you will do nothing until I am well enough to escort you.'

'We will talk of that when you are better.'

He frowned at her. 'Do not try to fob me off, Madeleine! I want your word you will not set off from this house without me.' One look at her face told him that was exactly what she was planning and he added a warning. 'If you persuade Sir Edmund to provide a guide and leave here out of some misguided desire to protect me, be assured, madam, I shall come after you.'

The stormy look died from her eyes. She would stay, at least for the present. He felt himself relaxing, although he worked hard not to show it.

'We will discuss it when you are better,' she repeated stubbornly. 'Now, shall I read to you?'

That night Grant lay awake beneath the covers. Despite his being out of bed for the first time, he felt too anxious to sleep. He feared that Major Rutter was still showing an interest in Madeleine. Not from anything she said, but from her reticence. She appeared cheerful enough, but she was unusually restrained in her conversation.

A few more days and he should be able to leave off the sling. Then they must decide just what they would do to extricate Maddie from Calder House without rousing the suspicions of the officers. It would be difficult, all the more so because Madeleine was determined that he should not accompany her further. Well, he was equally determined that he would see her safe aboard the French ship. Whatever it cost him.

'Well, this is progress indeed!'

Maddie laughed as she watched Grant parade up and down the sickroom. It was a rare sunny day, but it was not safe for him to go outside, so she had opened the window to allow in the fresh air. The sounds wafted up to them from the courtyard below: laughter from the stable hands, the occasional bark of a dog. Grant was dressed in his own breeches and top boots, but his shirt and coat were beyond repair and although the voluminous cut of Sir Edmund's shirt presented no problem, his frock coats were all too tight for Grant to slip on without causing him pain, so he strode back and forth in his silk waistcoat, the shirt sleeves billowing out and concealing the fact that his arm was heavily bandaged.

Maddie watched him, thinking how much he had improved in the past few days. The gaunt, drawn look had gone from his face and he was moving again with the lithe agility of a cat. Only the slight stiffness with which he held his left arm gave any indication that he was injured.

'I am feeling much better,' he told her. 'We can now plan how we are going to get you away from here.'

She shook her head. 'No. We have already agreed we should part now.'

'We have agreed nothing of the sort! Quite the opposite, in fact. I am going to escort you.'

'We said we would discuss that when you were well enough,' she corrected him. 'And in the meantime, I have made my own decision. Sir Edmund will find me a guide. You must look to yourself and your family. You have said that you will not return to Ardvarrick—'

'I cannot return. For my parents to harbour a fugitive would be a disaster for everyone at Ardvarrick, if indeed it has not already occurred. I dare not take the risk of returning to them. However,' he went on, before she had a chance to speak again, 'I am the best person to take you west. I know the land and the best routes around it. More importantly I know the people.'

'But I have decided to decline your services.'

'The devil you have!'

Her chin went up. 'I shall pay you for your trouble so far—'

'Do not be such a damned fool, Madeleine. You know I am not doing this for the money.'

'I certainly did not ask you to do it for any other reason!'

That gave him pause. They were glaring at one another, but although he kept his eyes locked on hers, he was aware of the high colour in her cheeks, the way her breast was heaving beneath the modest muslin fichu she had draped across her shoulders. He clenched his hands at his sides lest he be tempted to reach out and shake her.

Or to drag her close and kiss her senseless!

'Very well,' he ground out. 'Let us not spend our time arguing. We will discuss the matter with Sir Edmund and let him decide.'

'Very well.'

He could see from her pursed lips that she was not wholly convinced, but he made no further attempt to persuade her. Instead he asked her to read to him for a while and later challenged her to a game of piquet, Grant's left arm being sufficiently healed to allow him to hold his cards, even if the shuffling and dealing were proving difficult.

They said nothing more about leaving Calder House, but Grant could not be easy. In his opinion, Maddie was looking prettier every day and he was concerned that the more the English Major saw of her, the more likely it was that he would try to seduce her. Or worse. The army's behaviour in Scotland had been less than exemplary, as he and Maddie had both witnessed. No, he must get her away and soon.

Madeleine continued to play the docile guest in the McBinnies' household, but she was growing increasingly restless. It would take several days, if not longer, to reach the French ship and she could not afford to miss the rendezvous. She approached Sir Edmund and asked him if he could find her a guide, but his answer was cautious.

'I could, of course, but I thought it was agreed Grant Rathmore will escort you. We expect him to be well enough for the journey very soon.'

'But you know how dangerous it would be for him to venture into an area where he might be recognised.'

'There is that,' replied Sir Edmund in his careful way. 'Although it might be worth the risk in order to see his parents one last time before going off to France.'

'Alas, that is one thing he swears he will not do. Which is why I would rather he did not put himself in such danger solely for my sake.'

She waited as her host digested her words, then he nodded.

'We must decide upon a reason for your departure. It will not do for you to slip away without notice.'

'Of course not. The officers would be obliged to raise the alarm and you and Lady McBinnie would immediately come under suspicion.' Maddie sighed. 'I can see this will not be easy, but I must go and soon.'

'I agree, but pray do not upset yourself. We will think of something.'

With that she had to be satisfied, but Lady McBinnie was growing anxious, too, as Maddie discovered when she helped that lady to collect flowers from the garden later the same day.

'I fear Major Rutter suspects something is afoot. He is perfectly civil, but he joked yesterday that the house must be in very fine order, for all the work you and Anne are doing.'

'Oh, dear. Do you think he suspects I am avoiding him?'

'I am sure of it,' replied Lady McBinnie. 'He said as much to me yesterday, but it is only natural that I should do my best to keep Anne and yourself out of harm's way. Och, if only they would move on! But, alas, I fear we have made them too comfortable. They consider themselves perfectly situated here.'

'It is very frustrating, especially when I need to organise my journey to the west.'

Lady McBinnie patted her hand and replied with a complacency that Maddie could not share.

'Well, we must see what transpires in the coming days. I am sure that between them, Sir Edmund and young Rathmore will come up with a plan. In the meantime, we must make the Major believe that you are truly very busy here. I shall take pains to tell him that you gathered all these blooms for the table. But what else can you do today? I have it! My tea service is in need of washing. If Major Rutter should ask me, I shall tell him that is what you and Anne are doing. If he has any pretensions at all to gentility, he will know Meissen porcelain is far too precious to leave such a task to the servants!'

* * *

'…repique and two *quatorzes*, plus a sequence of six and forty for capot… I win!' declared Madeleine, giving a little crow of delight. She glanced at her opponent as she gathered up the cards. 'Is your arm paining you, Grant? I do not usually best you quite so easily.'

'No, no, my arm is healing well now. But I beg your pardon, my mind was otherwhere.'

She looked up, enquiring, but he merely bade her deal again.

'Sir Edmund was telling me there are reports of a French frigate off the coast at Stonehaven,' she told him, keeping her voice casual. 'He says it is taking up Jacobites and he has contacts who could get you there. You could be safe in France in a sennight. You should go.'

'I will, an you will come with me.'

'My father has made other arrangements for me.'

'Which involve a perilous journey into the Western Highlands.'

'Sir Edmund will provide me with an escort.'

'No. I have promised I will take you.'

She thought of him injured, risking his life for her, and knew she could not bear it if he was to suffer more on her behalf.

She said firmly, 'And I have said I do not want you to do so. Pray you, Grant, do not argue further. My mind is made up. Now, shall we cut for the first deal?'

Grant shrugged and said no more, which was what Madeleine had asked of him, but somehow she felt no satisfaction in the victory. Knowing they would soon be going their separate ways did nothing to raise her mood, but she told herself it was for the best. She was enjoying his company far too much.

Madeleine lost the second game and they tied on a third, after which they agreed to stop. The next hour was spent in quiet companionship, Grant reading and Maddie with her head bent over her sewing. She looked up presently, and found Grant watching her. Under such scrutiny she felt the heat rising up through her body and attempted to conceal it with raised brows and a look of cold enquiry.

'I was thinking how unusual it is,' he told her. 'We have not said a cross word to one another all day.'

'Heavens, that will never do!'

'No, no, I am serious, Madeleine. I am enjoying it very much, just sitting here with you.'

His smile only heightened her confusion and she looked away.

'You would soon grow tired of this inaction,' she muttered, giving her attention to her mending.

'But at the end of a day spent out of doors, what could be better than to come in and sit like this? Quietly, with friends, and no need to put oneself out to make polite conversation. How comfortable that must be.'

Friends! Sudden tears threatened, but Madeleine blinked them away. Such contentment could not last. He would soon be calling her obstinate and quarrelsome again and wishing himself anywhere but in her company.

Which was good, she told herself, because she was the daughter of an adventurer, a man of precarious fortune who lived by his wits, while Grant Rathmore was the son of a laird. If he was ever to rebuild his life in

Scotland, he would need to ally himself to a woman of impeccable breeding and respectability. One with a good dowry, too. Someone like pretty Anne McBinnie, who had known him all his life and was so sweet natured that she never caused him to lose his temper. Anne would be the perfect match for him, if only he could see it.

The thought gave her no pleasure. In fact, it made her perfectly miserable, but she hid her feelings beneath a dismissive tone when she responded.

'Do you really think it would be an ideal life? I think it sounds decidedly...*provincial*.' She set the final stitches in her darning and snipped off the thread. 'There, another sheet mended. I shall go and add it to the pile in the linen room.'

'And then you will come back?'

'Not today. Mrs Forbes will be sending up your dinner soon and Sir Edmund said he would call in upon you this evening.' Grant was frowning, apparently deep in thought, and she gave in to the temptation to add, 'I suppose I *could* come back later and read a little more of *Robinson Crusoe*, if you wish. Grant, did you hear me?'

'Hmm? Oh, yes, that is kind of you, but perhaps you are right. Not tonight, Madeleine. By the time I have spoken to Sir Edmund it will be growing late.'

His smile was perfunctory, as if his thoughts were far away.

She was dismissed and it was hardly surprising, when she had been so dismissive of his company. *Provincial!* She had made it sound like an insult, which is what she had intended, even though she could think of nothing more delightful than to spend the rest of her days with Grant Rathmore. She should not feel guilty for planning to leave without him. He would be well rid of her.

The mood in the drawing room was definitely far more cheerful and relaxed when Maddie joined the family there before dinner. This was soon explained by the fact that Colonel Sowton and the Major were at the barracks and would not be returning until the morning.

'It will be so pleasant to take dinner *en famille*,' declared Lady McBinnie as they took their seats at the table.

Anne giggled. 'Mama! That is hardly complimentary to Madeleine.'

'Miss d'Evremont knows I meant no slight to her,' replied the lady, bending a warm smile upon Maddie. 'I consider her very much one of the family now.'

'Thank you, ma'am.'

'Perhaps Grant could come downstairs to join us later in the drawing room?' Anne suggested. 'What do you think, Papa?'

'I will ask him when I go upstairs,' replied her father in his solemn way.

'I believe it would do him good to see something other than those four walls,' Anne continued. 'We can alert the servants to keep watch, so that we are not taken unawares if the officers should return. It would be so pleasant to be able to sit together for an evening. What think you, Maddie?'

Quietly, with friends, and no need to put oneself out to make polite conversation.

Grant's words returned to haunt her. How could she have been so disparaging?

She said quietly, 'Yes, as long as there is no risk.'

Sir Edmund nodded. 'You are wise to be cautious, but I would vouch for all the servants within the house.'

However, when Sir Edmund came back from his visit to the sickroom he was alone.

'Rathmore thought it best to remain above stairs,' he told the assembled company.

'Perhaps the thought of the stairs was too much for him,' opined Anne, sighing.

'I shall ask Mrs Forbes to send up a cup of hot chocolate,' said Lady McBinnie.

She went to rise, but her husband waved her back to her chair.

'No need, my dear. Hanson is going up to help him into bed this evening. He will see to everything.'

Madeleine wondered if Grant really was too tired, or if he did not wish for her company. Perhaps that was the reason he had declined coming downstairs this evening. She was heartily ashamed of herself for such a lack of manners, but she could do nothing about it tonight and refused to make herself miserable over mere speculation.

Despite a dreamless sleep, Madeleine's first thought upon waking was that she needed to see Grant and as soon as possible. She must once again make her peace with him. She dressed quickly and went down to the morning room to collect a copy of the *Gentleman's Magazine* that she had seen there the previous evening. Sir Edmund had the periodical sent to him from London and she thought he would not mind if she took it upstairs to Grant. A peace offering. She hoped it might atone somewhat for her rudeness yesterday.

The route along the winding passages and through rooms full of trunks and abandoned furniture was very familiar to her now and she barely noticed them as she hurried to the sickroom. She reached the door and out of habit she stopped, looking about her and listening to make sure she had not been followed. Then she laughed at herself for being foolish. The officers were not even in the house, so there was no one to question her. Still smiling, she opened the door. Only to find that the room was empty.

Madeleine looked about her, feeling slightly sick. The bed had been stripped and all signs that anyone had recently occupied the room removed. It was as if Grant had never been there. She turned and rushed out. The maid was on her way up the stairs and Maddie stopped her.

'What has happened to Mr Rathmore, Eilidh, do you know?'

'Why, mistress, he's gone.'

'Gone!'

'Aye, ma'am. Late last night. The master said it would be safer for him to be going then, especially since the clouds were making it so dark.'

'Sir Edmund knows of this?'

'Aye, mistress, 'twas he who told me to clear the room first thing this morning.'

The girl smiled, bobbed a slight curtsy and moved on, leaving Madeleine to make her way down to the breakfast room.

* * *

Lady McBinnie was alone at the table, pouring herself a cup of coffee.

'Ah, good morning, Madeleine. Are you come to join me?'

'No, ma'am, I am looking for Sir Edmund.'

'Oh, dear, you have missed him. He has ridden out with his steward. I understand the recent rains have caused a deal of damage in the village. Is it important?'

'Grant has gone.' The look of surprise upon the lady's face told Maddie that Lady McBinnie knew nothing of it. 'Eilidh says he left last night and that Sir Edmund instructed her to clear the room this morning. I hoped he would explain to me what has happened.'

'Alas, he has said nothing to me, so I cannot help you. My dear, pray do not look so anxious. I am sure Sir Edmund would not have allowed Grant to leave if he had not thought it for the best. Will you not sit down and break your fast?'

But Madeleine could not share Lady McBinnie's complacency. Guilt had quite destroyed her appetite, Grant had left Calder House and she was very much afraid that she had driven him away.

Madeleine was surprised how much she missed Grant. She kept herself busy, helping Lady McBinnie, and, in the afternoon, working with Anne in the stillroom, but all the time she was thinking how much she would have preferred to be with Grant, reading to him, talking or even just sitting with him, watching him while he slept. She felt quite wretched, not knowing where he was, if he was well, if he was safe. Her misery was compounded because she had been unable to ask him not to think too badly of her.

She did not see Sir Edmund until she joined the family in the drawing room just before dinner and even then there was no opportunity to speak to him about Grant because Colonel Sowton and Major Rutter were present. She summoned up a cheerful smile with which to greet them.

'Have you been patrolling with your Dragoons, Colonel?'

'Ha-ha…no, mistress, I leave that to the Major, although he tells me it was dull work today. Ain't that so, Rutter?'

'It was an uneventful day, but tomorrow we will be patrolling north of here. There have been reports of Highlanders spotted in Glen Orrin.'

'Well, I hope for your sake this dashed rain has cleared by the morning,' replied the Colonel, glancing towards the windows. 'Why, 'tis as dark as winter outside now!'

Conversation moved on to the weather and Maddie was relieved there was no mention of the patrols having caught a wounded fugitive. However, her concern for Grant was not much allayed and she made an effort to converse with the officers in case she could glean even more information. In this she succeeded very well, but in trying to discover anything of interest, she knew she was treading a dangerous line. She did not wish Major Rutter to think she might encourage his advances and, after a few moments' tête-à-tête with him, she made an excuse to move away and join her hostess.

Just as she was approaching Lady McBinnie's chair

a servant opened the door and announced in a voice devoid of emotion, 'Mr John Lauder.'

Maddie's heart sank at the thought of meeting another stranger, someone else to fool with lies and false smiles. She turned towards the door, but the look of polite interest she had assumed froze on her face when Grant stepped into the room.

Her heart began to thud so hard she could not have spoken, even if she had wished to do so. In fact, it was as much as she could do not to collapse in a dead faint. She put a hand on the nearby mantelshelf to steady herself as she watched Grant sweep off his hat and bow low to Lady McBinnie, begging her pardon for arriving so late.

'Think nothing of it, sir.' Sir Edmund came forward before his stunned wife could frame a suitable reply. 'We are only glad that you are here safely and we can easily accommodate another guest at dinner.' He dismissed the footman with a nod and turned to Madeleine. 'Well, my dear, how happy you must be to see your betrothed.'

Chapter Thirteen

Betrothed? What madness was this now! Madeleine could feel the colour ebbing and flowing in her cheeks. Grant came up and reached for her hand, giving it a tiny squeeze as he lifted it to his lips. She must not betray him to the two officers, who were watching the little charade with great interest.

'I am, of course, delighted.' She strained her memory to recall how the servant had announced him. 'But, *John*, what are you doing here?'

'I have come to bring you word of your parents.' He smiled at her. 'The good news is they are both well and—no, before we go into that, I see Sir Edmund is waiting to present me to his guests.'

There was a roguish twinkle in his eyes and Maddie did not know whether to be relieved or irritated to see how at ease he was in this masquerade, how much he was enjoying himself. Just like Papa, she thought bitterly, as he turned away to make his bow to the two officers. So nonchalant, as if he had not a care in the world!

Grant looked every inch a gentleman of means in a

burgundy frock coat of fine wool decorated with gold embroidery and, apart from a trace of tightness in the sleeve, there was no sign of any injury. The coat and matching waistcoat threw into stark relief the snowy linen at his throat and the candlelight sparked red fire in his auburn hair, which was brushed back and tied with a black ribbon.

She listened intently as he answered the Major's questions. Papa had often been obliged to fabricate a history on the spur of the moment, becoming at various times such diverse characters as a rich landowner from Bergerac, a fashionable gentleman of Paris or even an inky-fingered scholar. Now she paid close attention to what Grant was saying. No, his journey here from Perth had been quite trouble free and, yes, he had been extremely fortunate not to meet with brigands or rebels wishing to relieve him of his purse, although he made it plain that it had cost him a pretty penny along the way.

While this conversation was going on Sir Edmund moved closer to Madeleine, keeping his back to the room and staring down into the fire as he murmured an apology.

'I beg your pardon, my dear. I had no opportunity to warn you of this. Rathmore and I agreed everything last evening.'

She gave the faintest of nods, her thoughts racing. Where had Grant spent the night, how had he obtained such fine clothes? Was his arm paining him? She must appear calm and at ease. She had been in similar situations before, with Papa, during their wanderings in Europe and she knew a cool head was essential. Although heaven knew where all this was going.

It was Major Rutter who asked the question she most wanted answered.

'And now you are here, Mr Lauder, what is your purpose?'

'Firstly, to tell Miss Dewar that it has pleased God to spare her parents. They are quite well, as is the rest of the household.'

'I am sure we are all delighted to hear it.' The Major's tone was polite, but Madeleine knew he was on the alert. 'But you have travelled, what, a hundred miles or more. Quite an undertaking, sir, when surely a letter would have sufficed.'

'Ah, but there is more.' Grant showed no sign of being discomposed. He merely smiled and bowed towards Madeleine. 'I am come to escort Miss Dewar back to Perth. We shall leave in the morning.'

'So soon?' the Colonel spoke up.

'Now the panic has subsided it is clear that the infection has been contained and the danger is far less than anticipated,' came the smooth reply. Grant turned towards Maddie. 'Your father was quite distraught after you left. He is eager for your immediate return.'

'Surely that cannot be wise,' objected the Colonel. 'Smallpox is the very devil, you know. The lady must not put her own health in danger.'

'Oh, I will not be taking Miss Dewar to her own house. That is not possible until the doctor has declared the whole village clear of the infection. No, I am taking her to live with me.' He glanced at the two officers. 'My estate is a few miles away, you see. Quite free from risk, but close enough for me to drive Miss Dewar over to see her parents regularly. She may talk

to them from my carriage. They can assure one another that all is well.'

It was Madeleine's turn to object. So far Grant had
had things all his own way. She fluttered her fan and
feigned a modest hesitation.

'That is all very well, sir, but to stay with you, without even my maid! Such a breach of propriety…'

His eyes glinted appreciatively.

'I have housemaids in abundance—you may choose
any one of them to wait upon you. And my housekeeper
will be there to play chaperon.'

'Perhaps Lady McBinnie could spare a maid to accompany you on the journey,' suggested the Colonel.
'After all, you will be obliged to spend several nights
on the road.'

'But then the poor girl would be obliged to return
alone,' argued Grant. 'And think of the dangers to a
female travelling without protection. What say you,
my dear?'

Maddie swallowed. 'I am sure no one could object
to my making the journey with my *betrothed*.'

'Exactly. Your maidenly honour will be perfectly
safe with me.'

His smooth words hung in the air. Maddie kept her
eyes upon him, smiling all the time. Major Rutter was
listening carefully and she breathed a tiny sigh of relief
when Lady McBinnie fluttered to her feet and released
the tension with a few commonplace words.

'Well, well, that is settled then. Shall we go in to
dinner?'

Madeleine would never remember the food on her
plate that evening. She made a pretence of eating and

joined in the conversation, but all the time she was on edge, waiting for one of the officers to declare that Grant was a fraud. She did not know what to feel when Lady McBinnie declared the betrothed couple must sit together at dinner. She would be able to help disguise the fact that Grant did not yet have full use of his left arm, but it would be sheer torture to be sitting so close and not be free to say what she wanted, to ask him all the questions that were buzzing around in her head.

When they took their places at the table she found Major Rutter was on her left, the Colonel sitting opposite. Maddie and the McBinnies did their best to distract attention from the new guest and kept the conversation flowing with uncontentious topics until it was time for the ladies to withdraw.

As soon as they were alone in the drawing room, Lady McBinnie's smile slipped and she sank, exhausted, on to a chair.

'Thank heaven that is over. I have never been more on edge in my life!'

'But we managed it, Mama,' said Anne, sitting down beside Maddie on the sofa. 'You must admit it was quite ingenious.'

'Ingenious! How dare Edmund and young Rathmore play such a trick and never a word to me! I could cheerfully strangle them both.'

Madeleine had been thinking very much the same, but the lady's uncharacteristic outburst went some way towards soothing her own anger and she responded mildly.

'They clearly thought we could be relied upon not to panic. And Grant means to carry me away tomorrow, so that will be a relief to everyone.'

'It certainly solves the problem of how to get you out of the house,' agreed my lady. 'But my nerves are in *shreds*! I only hope we can maintain this charade for the rest of the evening.'

Anne shrugged. 'Perhaps Grant will plead fatigue after his journey and go directly to bed.'

It had been said with more hope than expectation and Madeleine was not surprised when she saw him come in with the other gentlemen a short while later. Lady McBinnie suggested her daughter should play the harp for their guests and, when Anne moved across to the instrument, Grant took her place on the sofa beside Madeleine.

'No one will be surprised if we put our heads together,' he murmured. 'It would surely be expected of two people very much in love.'

'I have not yet forgiven you for springing this surprise upon me,' she told him, under the cover of a glittering smile.

'Ah, yes. That was unfortunate and I am sorry for it. If Sir Edmund had not been called away unexpectedly today, he would have explained everything.' He reached out for her hand and lifted it to his lips. 'However, I knew you would not let me down.'

'Oh, pray be careful,' she whispered, blushing furiously. 'Major Rutter is watching us.'

Grant glanced across the room.

'He is, but he will think your maidenly confusion perfectly normal, between lovers.'

That made her even more self-conscious and she hissed at him to desist.

Grant laughed gently and sat back, to all appearances his attention fixed upon the music. So far his plan was working admirably. Credit must go to his host for his assistance, and Lady McBinnie, too, had risen splendidly to the challenge. And Madeleine, well, he had never doubted she would play her part.

The last notes of the harp died away and after a burst of applause Anne rose from the stool and invited Madeleine to take a turn.

'I am sure we would all like to hear you play, Cousin.'

Immediately Grant was on the alert, but Maddie did not disappoint him. She moved gracefully to the instrument and as her fingers began to pluck at the strings he relaxed. Naturally, she could play. How could he have doubted that her education would include the learning of any number of musical instruments?

She began with a lively jig, followed by a French air, slow and haunting. His mind wandered back to happier times, sitting in the comfortable drawing room at Ardvarrick while his mother played on the *clàrsach* that had been handed down through her family for generations. He closed his eyes, listening to the soft, poignant melody and remembering the unmistakeable glow of love in his father's eyes as he watched his wife pluck at the silver strings. Father always maintained it was her playing that had saved his life, given him the will to live when he was dangerously ill. Perhaps it was true. Grant had to admit the music had the power to soothe him, to make him forget the horrors of the past months.

Feeling more relaxed, Grant opened his eyes, knowing he must not drop his guard too much. He looked across at Madeleine, admiring the way she continued to play so beautifully. There was no sign of nerves or agitation. She even had time to glance up and smile occasionally.

He had known she could be cool in a crisis, but his admiration for her grew with every passing hour, especially the calm way she dealt with the dangers of sharing a house with two British officers. The Major's blatant admiration could have been a real problem, but she handled the situation with such charm and delicacy that the fellow's pride was not bruised.

He felt his smile growing as he watched her. There was no need to be anxious for Miss Madeleine d'Evremont. He would escort her to France, place her into the care of her father's people and then he could forget her. His job would be done and they need never see one another again. Grant knew it was best for everyone concerned, so why did the thought leave him so dissatisfied? He had convinced himself that that was what he wanted, but now...

The notes of the harp died away and, mechanically, Grant joined in the applause.

'Excellent,' declared Colonel Sowton. 'Capital performances from both the young ladies. And Miss Dewar, I believe you have moved Mr Lauder with that last piece. Why, he looks as solemn as a judge! It was very affecting, was it not, sir?'

'What?' Grant wrenched his thoughts back to the present. 'Yes, yes. It is a long time since anything moved me so much.'

He was relieved of the necessity of saying more by the entrance of servants with refreshments, which they laid out on the sideboard. For a while conversation consisted of only compliments on the cakes and the excellence of the wine until a chance remark by Lady

McBinnie caused Major Rutter to remember that two of the party were leaving in the morning.

'You really should not travel without an escort,' he remarked. 'I cannot like the thought of you riding off alone. I shall order some of my men to accompany you, at least as far as Inverness.'

'Ah, that is so very kind, sir,' replied Madeleine, not missing a beat. 'However, we could not possibly take your Dragoons from their duties. After all, it is your patrols of this area that make it quite safe for everyone to travel.'

'It will be no trouble, Miss Dewar,' replied the Major, in a voice that brooked no dissent. 'I insist upon providing you with an escort. I am sure Sir Edmund would agree with me?'

It was an impasse and one Madeleine could see no way to overcome. She was still trying to decide how best to respond when the Colonel sat forward in his chair.

'I tell you what we can do!' he declared. 'If you will delay your departure but one more day, the Major and I will be going to Fort George for fresh orders. It is barely twenty miles, but it will set you well on your way. I shall also give you a letter of introduction to the next garrison on your way south. That should help to smooth your passage back to Perth.'

'Why Colonel, you are too kind,' she told him. 'But, truly, we must not trouble you.'

'No, no, that is an excellent suggestion,' said Grant, contradicting her. 'We would be delighted to ride with you as far as Fort George, Colonel.'

Not by the flutter of an eyelash did Madeleine betray

her dismay at this change to their plans. She inclined her head and gave Colonel Sowton her brightest smile.

'Then it is all settled. I am sure we shall feel much safer travelling with you.'

The matter being decided, Lady McBinnie gently directed her guests' attention back to the refreshments but Maddie felt drained by the events of the past few hours and soon announced that she would go to bed.

'Allow me to escort you.' Grant jumped to his feet. 'I am about to retire, too.'

'An excellent idea, Mr Lauder,' agreed their hostess, waving them away. 'I am sure you must be quite fatigued after your journey.' She added, before the door had quite closed behind them, 'And it will give them a few moments to speak privately, which I have no doubt they will enjoy…'

'I am not so sure of that,' murmured Grant as they set off up the stairs. 'I have the distinct feeling that you are going to rip up at me.'

'And why should I do that?' she asked him, honey-sweet.

'Because I did not consult you on any of this.'

He was perfectly correct that she was cross with him, but his honesty disarmed her.

'You have been astoundingly high-handed!' she told him, trying to sound angry.

'I have indeed,' came the meek response. 'I beg your pardon. Most humbly.'

'There is nothing humble about you!'

'No, alas. You are correct again.'

Maddie could not help it. She laughed, destroying the effect of her earlier severity.

'Ah, good.' He smiled at her. 'You are not in a rage with me.'

'No, not now, but I confess, when you walked in upon us, all unexpected, I was ready to drop!'

'You rose to the occasion magnificently. As I knew you would.'

'Enough of your flummery, sir, let us be serious. I wish the Colonel had not offered to escort us to Fort George.'

'Yes, it is hours out of our way, but it would look highly suspicious if we were to refuse the offer. But despite that, I shall get you to your rendezvous on time, never fear.

They had reached the door of her room and she stopped, peering up at him through the gloom.

'Do you still intend to cross to France with me?'

'Yes. There is nothing for me here.'

He sounded so bleak that she reached out and put her hand on his chest.

'Oh, Grant, I am so sorry.'

It was an instinctive gesture, but it resulted in a sudden, shocking awareness that they were alone. He was standing so close and she wanted to cling to him, to turn her face up to his and invite him to drive every thought from her mind with his kiss. Moments ago they had been entirely comfortable in each other's company but now his proximity felt extremely dangerous.

Simultaneously they stepped apart, Maddie withdrawing her hand as if he had burnt her, while Grant shifted uncomfortably and cleared his throat.

'Goodnight, Madeleine.'

With the smallest of bows, he was gone.

Maddie went into her room and turned the key in the

lock with trembling fingers. She stood for a moment, staring at the wooden panels, waiting for the tumultuous thudding of her heart to subside. Why did he have this effect upon her? One moment they were friends, talking easily together, teasing one another. The next they were literally panting for each other. It took so little to spark their desire, a look, a touch.

She pressed her forehead against the door. Heavens, if they were to journey so far together, she would have to maintain her guard night and day. She was in danger of losing everything to this man.

Madeleine watched the party of Dragoons ride up to the door of Calder House. Colonel Sowton and Major Rutter were waiting for them and their glossy horses looked magnificent, especially next to the two sturdy little ponies that were to carry Grant and Maddie and their saddlebags.

Madeleine turned to take her leave of Sir Edmund and his wife. She had said her real goodbyes to the family the previous day, before Major Rutter and the Colonel had returned from their duties.

'We may not have an opportunity to speak openly in the morning,' she had told them.

They were gathered in the morning room and Sir Edmund had pressed into her hands his copy of *Robinson Crusoe*, saying he hoped she would find room for it in her saddlebags.

'I know you did not have time to finish reading it and thought it might help you fill the tedium of the sea voyage,' he told her, smiling.

'Oh, how kind you are to me!' She smiled up at him

mistily. 'I owe you such a debt of gratitude and I am fearful that our being here will have put you in danger.'

'Hush now, let us not worry about that,' Sir Edmund told her. 'The officers are moving on and it is unlikely the deception will be discovered, but if it should, Rathmore and I have already come up with a story.'

'You have?'

Any feelings of gratitude faded and she cast an indignant look at Grant, but before he could answer Lady McBinnie stepped in.

'Yes, my dear, and I believe it will answer perfectly! The two of you were having a clandestine affair, unbeknownst to your parents, and your visit here presented an opportunity for you to run away together. But then, having discovered the deceit, we will wash our hands of you! There, is that not ingenious?'

Maddie could not be easy. She said, 'But if they look for us in Perth?'

'That is highly unlikely,' replied Sir Edmund. 'I believe the British Army has more to worry about currently than a pair of young runaways, do not you?'

With that she had to be satisfied and, remembering the conversation as she accompanied Grant and the officers out of the house, Maddie reflected that there was nothing she could do now, except pray that she had not brought ruin upon these good people.

Anne ran out to give her a final hug.

'Goodbye, *Cousin*.' She pulled Maddie closer, whispering, 'Take care of Grant, my dear Madeleine. I am trusting you to make him happy.'

As she stepped back Maddie looked at her in consternation, but Anne only smiled, shook her head and went away into the house.

* * *

The journey to Fort George took the best part of the day, their progress slowed by rain that turned the tracks to rivers of mud and soaked through their thick cloaks. The Major had sent a man ahead to bespeak rooms for them and when they arrived at the inn, Maddie's gratitude to the officer for his efforts was not feigned.

Having dismounted to help her down, Major Rutter took her hand.

'It has been an honour to be of service,' he said, bowing over her fingers. 'I hope you will not think too badly of me.'

'Badly of you?' She gave a little trill of laughter. 'Whatever for, Major?'

'For questioning you so closely, madam. For appearing at all suspicious of you.'

'Good heavens, sir, you were doing your duty. How can anyone blame you for that?'

'You are all goodness, ma'am. I bid you *adieu* and wish you a safe journey.'

He kissed her hand, nodding to Grant before climbing back into the saddle to lead his men away.

'Well, thank goodness that is over,' she muttered as the Dragoons clattered off into the mist. 'I was very much afraid they might be staying here tonight and we would be obliged to dine with them.'

'That was a worry, I admit,' Grant replied. 'As it is, we can relax a little this evening. Shall I order dinner?'

'If you do not object, I should prefer to dine in my room,' she told him. 'The rain has soaked right through to my petticoats and I need to dry them before the fire.'

'But you have no maid. Would you like me to help you undress?' His dark eyes glinted.

'No, I would not. Although I have no doubt you are well practised!'

'Oh, yes.'

She met his laughing glance and realised how improper it was to be bandying such words with a man. Her cheeks flaming, she muttered an excuse and hurried before him into the inn.

Chapter Fourteen

They left at dawn the following morning, praying there was no one to see them heading west rather than east, and neither of them relaxing until at last they turned off the road and headed up into the hills.

Occasionally they met groups of ragged people, mainly women, children and the elderly who had been driven from their homes. Grant and Maddie would share their camp for a night before moving on, but mostly they were obliged to sleep in the open, wrapped in thick cloaks that felt inadequate for cold nights on the high mountains. Madeleine made no complaint, but Grant guessed she was feeling the discomfort of travelling in such conditions.

At last the weather improved. Clear blue skies replaced lowering cloud and Grant halted, staring out at the familiar landscape. He turned to Maddie and gave her an encouraging smile.

'We have four, maybe five more days to travel, but the going will be easier,' he told her. 'I know my way much better from here.'

'I am heartily glad to hear it.'

'There is a small village a few miles further on. That is where we are heading.' He glanced at the sun. 'We should be there by nightfall.'

'Really? Does that mean a bed for the night?' She exhaled dramatically. 'That would be so comfortable! However, we have been disappointed before so I shall not build up my hopes.'

Her response was spirited, even though he knew she must be exhausted.

'No, very wise.' He smiled at her. 'Come along, let us see what we can find.'

When they reached the little village, it was very quiet, but there was no military presence and he managed to secure accommodation for them at the small tavern. Their arrival was the subject of much speculation, several pairs of eyes following them as they made their way through the taproom and up the stairs to two adjoining chambers secreted in the eaves.

Madeleine stood quietly as Grant inspected the rooms.

'I do not believe these locks would keep anyone out,' he said at last. 'I suggest you push the washstand across the door when you retire tonight. And do not leave the room without me to escort you.'

'Do you not trust our host?'

'I trust no one.'

They spent an uneasy hour dining in the public room before retiring to their beds, where sheer exhaustion overcame Maddie's anxiety and she fell into a deep sleep.

* * *

By the time she awoke the following morning Grant had already gone out, leaving a note pushed under her door telling her to keep to her room until he returned.

She knew him too well by now to be affronted at his heavy-handed manner and she pottered about her room until he returned and escorted her downstairs to breakfast. When she enquired where he had been, he merely replied that she would know soon enough.

'You are infuriatingly secretive,' she told him crossly.

'I beg a thousand pardons, but it is best we discuss it elsewhere.'

His eyes were glinting with mischief, but she knew he would tell her nothing more and she held her tongue. She would not give him the satisfaction of begging for more information.

They left the inn shortly after. Grant chose to follow a little-used track through the trees that covered the hillside. When they reached a small clearing, he drew rein.

'This will do.'

'For what?'

He dismounted, signalling that Madeleine should follow suit. He asked her to tether the ponies to a tree branch while he rummaged in his saddlebags and pulled out two packages.

'Here.' He held one out to her. 'I think it is time for you to become a young man again. Anyone looking for the young couple who recently left the McBinnies' house will find the trail grows cold after Fort George.'

She looked down at the package. 'Am I to be your younger brother again?'

'No, that will not do. It is much more likely that I will be recognised from here on and everyone knows I am my father's only son.'

His disgraced and disowned son!

The thought came unbidden and Grant was swamped with regret for what he had done. His mother might forgive him, but Father? His fighting for the rebels had put at risk Ardvarrick and everything his father had worked so hard to achieve, including the prosperity of his people. Any hint of Jacobite sympathies and the army would put everything to the torch. They might still lose Ardvarrick because of his rash, impetuous actions.

Better that I had died on Drumossie Moor with my comrades.

'Well, what do you think?'

Madeleine's voice interrupted his reverie. He looked up to see she had emerged from the screen of bushes and was strutting up and down the clearing.

'I make a very convincing young man, do I not?'

The sight of her drove away his dark thoughts.

'An amazing transformation!'

She wore the coat and breeches with assurance and the silk stockings with their embroidered clocks that he had chosen for her displayed her shapely ankles well. Far too well, in his opinion. Thank heaven he had brought with him the spatterdashes to wear with her boots.

He smiled. 'I judged your size very well.'

'Indeed you did, I am not at all displeased with the result. Although the breeches are a little too big at the waist.'

'Come here and I will try to lace them a little tighter for you.'

Obediently she stood with her back to him, holding the tails of her coat out of the way while he grappled with the laces in the waistband.

'There, I have tied them as tight as I can, but I'm afraid they will never fit snugly around you.'

To demonstrate his point, he spanned her waist with his hands, resting them lightly on her hips. Immediately he realised his mistake. Madeleine tensed and he felt the change in the air—everything was suddenly hushed, expectant. He should release her, but for the life of him he could not do it.

Madeleine held her breath. One wrong word, one false move and her self-control would crumble. She wanted so much to turn to Grant and throw herself into his arms, to let him kiss away her worries and her fears. But it would not do. She might want him, desperately, and he might succumb to his desires and live with her for a while. He might even want to marry her, but when the time came for him to return to his homeland, he needed to be free, unfettered. Britain and France were old enemies. Any ties to a Frenchwoman would only hinder his attempts to rebuild his life and take his rightful place as the future Laird of Ardvarrick.

She passed her tongue over her dry lips and forced herself to speak in a matter-of-fact way.

'Well, they will have to do.' She put her hands over his and gently removed them. 'What about yourself, have you no new clothes?'

'My riding dress is shabby and unremarkable. It will not attract attention. The only thing I have purchased is a plaid to add to our comfort if we need to sleep out of doors again.'

Once again her unruly thoughts ran riot. She could not prevent her insides from turning to water at the thought of lying with Grant, wrapped together snugly in the plaid, bodies touching, limbs tangling...

She turned away, jamming her hat over her curls. Damn the man. How dare he have such an effect upon her!

She said, roughly, 'We should be moving, there are many miles yet to travel. Come along.'

They rode on, keeping to the hills above deserted valleys, where Madeleine saw farms and bothies that were no more than smoking ruins. The long summer day was giving way to the twilight that passed for night in these northern lands when Grant suggested they look for somewhere to stop for the night. They found a shallow cave to give them a little protection and sat down on the folded plaid to eat the last of their meagre supply of food.

Their silence was companionable, but Madeleine could not forget the devastation she had seen. Even the land had been laid waste. She had noted Grant's growing anger at such wanton destruction, but had not known what to say to him. She drank from her water bottle and offered it to Grant. He declined and reached into his pocket for his whisky flask.

'Tonight I need something stronger than water.'

'You are angry at what the soldiers are doing.'

'It pains me to see it.' He turned to look at her. 'Is it so obvious?'

'Yes. I am very sorry for what is happening.'

'My homeland is being ravaged and I am powerless to help.'

She could find no words and remained silent. After a moment he gave a long, bitter sigh.

'I had not long left Fort Augustus when I saw what the British are capable of. I came upon a party of soldiers. They were supposedly searching for Jacobite soldiers and, failing to find them, they took out their anger and frustration on the poor. No one was spared. I could do nothing, one man against so many. I chose to hide in the heather and watch.'

'You cannot blame yourself for that.'

'Can I not? By dawn the village was nothing more than a charred ruin. I shall never forget the sight or the smell of it.'

'It haunts your dreams?' she asked, remembering his nightmare.

He nodded. Silently she tucked her arm in his and rested her head on his shoulder, trying to convey some comfort. After a few moments he continued.

'On the far side of the village, upwind, the soldiers were sleeping. They had gorged themselves on the villagers' food and whisky from an illegal still. I thought I might attack them then, but they were not so undisciplined that they had not posted guards and there was little chance of catching them unawares.' He took another drink. 'I might have killed, what…three, four of them before I was despatched. Instead I slunk away. I told myself I would come back one day and have my revenge. Perhaps when the Prince gathers another army, but in truth I have had a bellyful of killing. I want only to go home.'

'To Ardvarrick?'

'Aye.' A shadow of pain crossed his face. 'The one place I cannot go.'

'Perhaps not yet,' she said, wanting so much to comfort him. 'But later, when this has passed—'

'How can it pass? How can I ever return, knowing that my friends are dead, that my family will lose everything, because of me?'

She turned to him 'Oh, Grant, you cannot be sure that will happen.'

'You are wrong,' he said bitterly. 'You have seen for yourself how the army is moving through the Highlands, systematically destroying everything.'

She could not deny it and, as they settled down to sleep, her heart ached for him.

As they moved westwards the land grew more mountainous. Their route took them through high passes where clouds shrouded them in mist, coating their outer clothes in droplets that sparkled like diamonds whenever the sun broke through. At last they crested a hill and reached a pass Grant knew well. A place he had never thought to see again.

Regret twisted his gut as he thought of his family. How wrong he had been to disobey his father and leave Ardvarrick. But even that would not have mattered if he could have persuaded Jamie and the others to return home. He had failed them. He had failed everyone.

'Why have we stopped, where are we?' Madeleine's voice broke through his gloomy thoughts and he tried to be cheerful, for her sake.

'The end of our journey is very nearly in sight. We are not much more than twenty miles from our destination.'

The information was welcome, but Madeleine was too tired to do more than nod. She could see nothing but the enveloping mist. She followed Grant, guiding her pony down the winding track until at last they descended out of the cloud. Before them, away to the west, the sky was almost unbroken blue and the landscape was bathed in the golden glow of the late-afternoon sun. A meandering pass descended like a ribbon through the glen to the very edge of a huge body of water that stretched to the western horizon, bordered on each side by rugged hills covered by woodland.

'Oh, how beautiful!' She spoke without thinking.

'That is Loch Òrail,' he told her. 'The golden loch.'

She nodded, unable to take her eyes from the dazzling waters. 'That is where Papa instructed me to go, is it not? I remember the name from his letter. He said there is an inn at the head of the loch where I will find someone to take me on the final leg of my journey to the coast.'

Grant nodded, keeping his eyes fixed on the view before him. She reached across and touched his arm.

'You have told me how much it pains you to see what is happening here, so near your home.' He looked at her blankly, as if her words had not registered. She continued, 'You have kept your promise to me. You do not need to come further.'

He smiled, although she could see it cost him an effort.

'Of course I am coming with you. Have I not said I have no home in this land now? Come along, we should reach Kinloch before dark.'

Chapter Fifteen

Kinloch was a small village at the eastern end of Loch Òrail. The farmland surrounding it showed no signs of being ravaged, which gave Madeleine hope that the army had not reached this remote place. By the time Grant led the way to the inn the hour was late, although the summer sun was still visible over the distant hills.

They found the tavern and tethered their ponies outside. Grant, she noted, checked his sword, a sign that he was ready for trouble, and she had to fight down the temptation to cling to his coat-tails as they strolled into the building. The small windows of the tavern made it gloomy inside, but she kept her hat pulled low over her eyes, shielding her face from all but the closest scrutiny. They sat down at a table and a jovial figure strode up to them, wiping his hands on a cloth.

'Welcome, sirs, what would be your…' He trailed off. 'Well as I live and breathe, 'tis Grant Rathmore!'

'Aye, but I'd be glad if you didn't broadcast it to the world,' Grant muttered, placing a silver coin on the table.

'Och, no, I will not be doing that.' The man glanced about him before scooping up the coin. 'You may be easy; I'll keep quiet and I doubt anyone here knows your face. I only do so because I kept an inn at Ardvarrick for a few years and used to see ye riding by with the Laird. What can I get for you?'

'A flagon of your finest ale, landlord, and I believe someone might have left a message here for my young companion? A letter, perhaps, addressed to a traveller from Glen Muick.'

The landlord grunted. 'It's not wise to commit anything to paper these days, but I believe I know who you'll be wantin'. Donald Roy. He stays not far from here. I'll send the tap boy to fetch him.'

With that he went off, coming back a few moments later with a jug of ale and two tankards. Grant pulled out a couple of coins for the ale and handed them over.

'Contullach land is not far from here,' he remarked casually. 'Do you have any news from there?'

'Och, very little.' He glanced at Grant. 'Cowie makes no secret he blames you for his son's death, do ye know that?'

'I can believe it.'

'Aye, but no one here puts much store by that.'

Grant's hands gripped his tankard until the knuckles shone white.

'He was a friend, even though we often disagreed. I should have stopped him leaving Contullach. I should have stopped them all from joining the rebels.'

The landlord waved a hand. 'Everyone knows Jamie Cowie was a bad lot, I doubt many will miss him, still less will they blame you for the loss of their menfolk. It is a bad business.'

'Have any of the others returned?'

The reply was grim. 'I have heard of only two.'

Grant felt as if he had been punched in the gut. 'So few? But 'tis early days. More may be hiding out in the hills.'

'Then they'd be wise not to come this way.' The landlord wiped a small spill of ale from the table. 'Fraser Reid and Tom Graham returned, but they had not been with their families a day before Ewan Cowie had them marched back to Inverness and turned over to the army. He wants everyone to think he's a loyal subject of the Crown.' He turned and spat on the floor, making his feelings on this quite clear. A movement near the door caught their attention. 'Here is Donald now. I will send him over.'

Madeleine waited until the landlord had moved away, then she spoke.

'I know you blame yourself for the death of your comrades, but from what I have heard—'

'It does not matter one jot what he or anyone else says,' Grant hissed, shaking off her hand. 'I *am* responsible. If I had not been so weak, if I had not got drunk on that last night, I might still have persuaded them to turn back. As it is, I was too sodden even to help myself. By the time I woke up we were all enrolled in the Prince's army!' Madeleine recoiled and he continued savagely, 'Now do you see why I cannot go home? I have too many deaths on my conscience.' He rubbed a hand across his eyes. 'I beg your pardon, I should not be angry with you, but the guilt is still so raw.'

'Yes.' She took a sip from her own tankard. 'Yes, I see that. I am so sorry.'

'Enough now,' he muttered, sitting up. 'Here is your contact coming over.'

A burly man in rough clothing was approaching their table. He stared hard at Madeleine before addressing her directly, but as he spoke in Gaelic, she was obliged to look to Grant to translate for her.

'This is Donald Roy. He says he was told to expect a lady.'

Maddie pushed back her hat and looked up into the man's fierce eyes. She said, making no attempt to disguise her voice, 'Tell him I *am* a lady!'

There was no need for Grant to translate, she saw the gleam of understanding in Donald Roy's eyes, the slight nod of satisfaction before he turned and spoke again to Grant.

'He asks if you have the money to pay him.'

She pulled out a small purse. 'I have the sum agreed with my father.'

As the man stretched out his hand, she snatched the purse back out of reach. 'Does he understand that you are coming with me?'

She watched the exchange of words, saw the stranger shrug and shake his head.

'If he is asking for more money, tell him I have none,' she said, guessing the gist of their conversation. 'And tell him I will not go without you, since I cannot speak his language.'

Grant raised his brows at her, then repeated what she had said. Another flurry of words before Grant turned back to her, the faintest hint of a smile playing about his mouth.

'He agrees, but says you drive a hard bargain.'

She raised her chin and looked the man in the eye. 'My father was a good teacher.'

She handed over the purse, giving the man a smile as she did so, and she did not miss the slight softening of his features and what might have been reluctant admiration.

The man drew up a chair, the landlord supplied them with another jug of ale and an extra tankard. Madeleine sipped at her drink and waited patiently while Grant and Donald Roy spoke in low tones. At last the man picked up his tankard and sat back while Grant explained to her.

'The French ship is to drop anchor in Loch Tonnan, some five-and-twenty miles from here. But he says there is a problem. Soldiers have been seen riding that way. They are even now encamped somewhere on the road. And there *is* only one road,' he told her. 'It would be impossible for us to avoid them.'

'Then what do we do? They could be in the area for weeks. I cannot delay so long.'

'Roy has arranged for a small skiff to take us to the far end of Loch Òrail.'

'A boat!' She sat back, surprised. 'What about the ponies?'

Grant shrugged. 'We leave them here. They will form part of his payment. We will go as far as we can by water, then it is but a half-mile or so across the narrow bridge of land to Loch Tonnan, where we must make our way to the inn. We are to wait there until we can board the ship.'

'And when do we set off?'

'Tonight. An hour after sunset. The summer twilight

is as dark as it will get then and the trees will screen us from the track for most of the way. We must hope we escape notice.'

Two hours later they were sitting together in the bow of a large wooden boat manned by eight oarsmen. A covering of cloud made the summer night darker, but there was still sufficient light to show them the hills rising steeply on each side, the wooded slopes black against the night sky. Madeleine imagined for a moment that the soldiers Donald Roy had mentioned were watching them from the trees and she shuddered.

'Cold? Come here.' Grant pulled her against him and wrapped the plaid around them both.

She tensed, but only for a moment, then she relaxed back against him. The oarsmen were into their rhythm now and the oars dipped almost silently into the water, keeping them gliding steadily over the loch.

She felt Grant's chest heave in a sigh and, sensitive to his mood, said quietly, 'You will be sad to leave this land, I think.'

'I will. I did not know how much I loved it until I went off to fight. Och, it can be fearful cold in winter, and deadly when 'tis stormy, sending the ships scuttling to find a sheltered bay. And even in summer the wind and rain will cut through a body, chilling one to the skin.'

'As I know to my cost,' she retorted, with feeling.

He laughed. 'Aye. You have put up with it without a murmur, my lady.'

'What would complaining have achieved, save to make us both more miserable?' Sitting here so cosily within his arms, she found it so easy to forget the hardships. She settled more comfortably back against him. 'Tell me about your home.'

'Why, it is not so very different from this, only we are bordered by the sea to the west. On a fine day there is nothing better than to be out of doors with the sun hot on your back and the larks singing high over the moor. And in the distance, encircling Ardvarrick, are the mountains. Snow-capped in winter, but just as magnificent when the grey clouds shroud the tops and spill down the slopes like maiden tresses.'

'You make it sound idyllic.'

'It is by no means that. 'Tis a hard life, but my father has been working to improve it for everyone. There is more trade now coming into the harbour and he has invested in his land, too, trying to improve the breeds, rebuilding the tenant houses.' He paused. 'Everything was prospering when I left.'

He did not need to say more.

'You must not blame yourself, Grant.'

'But I do. What if I am the cause of everything being destroyed? That is why I cannot go back. My father may stand a chance of keeping Ardvarrick if he disowns me. If he says I am no longer his son. That is the best I can hope for.'

'Ardvarrick is so remote. Perhaps the army will not venture so far.'

Grant was not attending. He said bitterly, 'I went about it all the wrong way. I should have enlisted under a false name, but when it came to the sticking point I could not do it. I thought, if anything happened to me, they will want to know.'

She twisted round and gripped his coat.

'Of course they would want to know! And they will

want to see you! Grant, they love you, it must surely be torture for them not to know your fate.'

Grant shook his head. 'I am dead to them. As are those who went with me. There were no men from Ardvarrick, to be sure. When any of them suggested joining the rebels, I ordered them to stay home, that much I did manage to do. But the guilt is no less because it was Contullach's men who died. Jamie persuaded at least two dozen men to march with him.'

'But the landlord said no one will blame you for that.'

'Ewan Cowie will. He will never forgive me for the death of his son.' He looked down at her, his eyes bleak. 'There has been bad blood between the Cowies and the Rathmores for generations. This will bring it all back again. Ewan Cowie will want vengeance and the blame can be laid squarely at my door.'

She wanted to comfort him, but did not have the words. Instead all she could do was hope that the rhythmic swish of the oars and the gentle movement of the boat would alleviate his sadness, as it soothed hers.

'What an adventure this has been,' she murmured at last. 'I have almost lost count of the days.'

'I haven't.'

Grant spoke with sincerity. He could recall every hour spent in Madeleine's company. Every smile, every look. This summer night would give him one of his most pleasant memories since leaving Ardvarrick, sitting here with Maddie safe within his arms, her curls tickling his chin. But he knew that much as he would like to keep her with him for ever, it could not last.

He said, 'You will be glad to see your father again, Maddie.'

'Yes.'

By this time he knew her well enough to be alive to every nuance of her voice and he did not miss the doubtful tone of that single syllable.

'What's this?' he muttered, in mock horror. 'You do not sound very sure of yourself.'

'Truth be told, I am not,' she confessed. 'I think I have had enough of the nomadic life, following Papa from one intrigue to another, never knowing if tomorrow we will be living in a chateau or a stable. Or even a prison. I need to see him, of course, to talk to him, but then I shall go to Tante Élisabeth and throw myself on her mercy.'

'As I recall, you described your aunt's house to me as dreary.'

'I did, but I need not remain there long. I have some of Maman's jewels that I might sell, if I am desperate, but I think I might try to earn my living, while I am able. I am sure my aunt will find me a post as a lady's companion, or a governess.'

'I cannot think such a life would suit you.'

'It is a case of necessity,' she told him. 'Papa may talk of his connections, but I have never known his existence to be anything but precarious. I am tired of wondering if he is going to get himself hanged and would prefer to fend for myself.'

'And your father's plans for you to make a great marriage?'

She looked up at him, her eyes full of disdain.

'Another of his grandiose dreams that will never be realised. But even if he did have such plans, they would be for his benefit, not mine. I think now I would prefer to earn my own living.'

'You would prefer the life of a drudge, little more than a servant, to marriage?' He shook his head. 'You cannot mean that.'

'I do!' she retorted, vehemently. 'I do mean it. I will not sign over my life, my body, to a stranger, be he never so rich. How could I put myself into the power of a man I do not know, do not love? Someone I do not trust.'

And me, Maddie—you know me now; could you trust me? Could you love me?

The words came unbidden and he closed his lips firmly to prevent himself from speaking them aloud. What was he thinking? He had no money, no prospects. He would soon be a stranger in a foreign land. Perhaps, if fortune favoured him and he was able to maintain himself, he would be able to rescue her from a life of drudgery.

No. He should not even think of it. And it was madness to think that Maddie would be reduced to earning her living. From everything she had told him, her father would never allow it. She was a very desirable woman. Yves d'Evremont should have no trouble finding a suitable match for her. A wealthy, handsome honourable suitor to whom Madeleine could safely give her heart. He must not stand between her and the chance of such happiness.

'Ah well, who knows what the future may hold for you.'

He spoke lightly and moved away from her to speak to one of the oarsmen.

Madeleine turned up her collar and huddled into her coat. It was not the warm plaid she missed as much as

Grant's protective presence. His questions had made her face the uncertain future that lay ahead. It would not be so very different from the previous years she had spent with Papa, but *she* felt different and it frightened her.

'We are about halfway through the loch now,' said Grant, coming back. 'Another hour should see us at the jetty.'

She nodded, hoping he would wrap himself around her again, but instead he placed the plaid over her shoulders and sat down beside her.

'What will you do in France?' she asked him.

'I shall deliver you safely to your father, as we agreed.'

He was being flippant, avoiding her question. She said impatiently, 'And after that?'

'I have no idea.'

'You could seek out the Prince and join his entourage.'

His mouth twisted. 'I think not. I never had any real heart for his cause and to survive by hanging on to the Stuart's coat-tails would be to live a lie. I have had my fill of intrigue. I have seen its consequences.'

'Perhaps in time you will be able return to Ardvarrick.'

'No, that cannot happen. Even if my father manages to keep his estates, I have spoiled the peace between him and his neighbour, Ewan Cowie.'

'He would understand. He would forgive you.'

'He might, but I can never forgive myself.' He gave a long, weary sigh. 'No. Ardvarrick is lost to me. I must bear that and make a new life.'

The sadness in his voice tore at Maddie's heart.

'Then come with me. As my husband.'

She spoke on impulse and her shock at hearing the words was almost as great as Grant's. He stared at her.

'What? No. No, your father will want a great marriage for you.'

'My father would sell me to the highest bidder!'

'I think you malign him, Madeleine. He will want you to be happy as well as secure. He will find you a man you can love—'

She turned to him, reaching out to clutch at his coat.

'I thought that might be possible once, but not now. Not since meeting you. I want to be with *you*, Grant.'

'And how would we live?' he asked her, gently removing her hands from his jacket.

'We will have nothing but our talents, but we will survive. We might set up a gaming house in Paris.'

'No!' He was clearly in no mood for her teasing. 'How can you imagine I would ever let you sink so low?'

She shrugged. 'I have been following my father these four years or more, keeping house for him while he schemed his way around Europe. There have been enough lies and deceits to fill a lifetime. Do you think earning a living at games of chance is any more disreputable?'

She regarded him steadily until finally he looked away, shaking his head.

'I am sorry, Maddie. It cannot be. I have nothing to offer you. Less than nothing, I am an outcast.'

'I am not so different—my father is a gambler, always seeking the big prize. I must go to him first and make sure he is safe, but then I intend to make my own way in the world.'

'You are young and beautiful. You will find a man to love.'

She flushed, but kept her eyes fixed on his.

'Have I not already told you? That cannot happen now.'

Grant froze as he began to understand what she was telling him. Breathing suddenly became difficult. Could it be true?

She said, as if he had spoken aloud, 'I love you, Grant Rathmore. There can be no one else for me now.'

His heart soared, but he must be cautious. He dared not give way to this happiness just yet. He chose his next words with care.

'I have little save the clothes on my back, but I have a strong right arm. I can work, I can fight if necessary. I could become a mercenary—'

'No. You have seen enough bloodshed. I will not allow you to do that. We will find another way to survive.'

She was smiling at him and the glow in her eyes set hope burgeoning within him. Suddenly the world was full of possibilities.

'I might find work as a steward for some nobleman! That is something I can do and well. I have spent my life learning how to run my father's lands.'

'Or we could travel,' she told him, smiling. 'I have a little money; we need not stay in France.'

'No, indeed, we might roam the world.' He laughed and reached for her hands. 'It would not be easy. We would have to work together, stand shoulder to shoulder against the world, but we would survive.'

'Oh, Grant, I would ask no more than that, if I could be with you.'

'Would you not?' His eyes searched her face. 'I can offer you no prospect of riches.'

'I have had riches,' she told him. 'Papa and I have lived the life of the very rich, but we have also had times when there has not been a sou for bread. As long as we have each other, and enough to eat, I shall not complain.'

'Then you will marry me.'

She blinked, her eyes misty with unshed tears.

'Yes, my dearest, I will marry you, if you are sure it is what you want, too.'

Grant could wait no longer. He dragged her into his arms.

'It is,' he muttered. 'I have never been surer of anything in my life!'

He captured her mouth, kissing her hard. She responded immediately and he deepened the kiss, teasing open her lips and tangling his tongue with hers as the blood raced through his veins.

There was a muttering from the oarsmen and a few lewd jokes about the lady's unconventional dress, but neither of them paid any heed, until at last the closest man cleared his throat loudly.

'We are approaching the jetty, sir. Ye'll need to budge so we can tie up.'

Grant raised his head, smiling as Maddie hid her face in his shoulder.

'Yes, of course,' he said. 'Come along, my dear.'

They shifted out of the way, but Grant kept his arm about Madeleine. Together they watched the oarsmen guide the skiff through a narrow stretch of water to a small wooden jetty. Minutes later they were clambering out of the boat. Following the sailors' instructions, they made their way past the buildings clustered around the dock and were soon climbing into the low, ancient hills that separated the Golden Loch from Loch Tonnan. The track was difficult to see, but Grant knew the general direction and judged the walk should take them little more than an hour. Because of his injured arm, Madeleine had refused to allow him to carry her saddlebags and she was walking stoically ahead of him, her silent fortitude making his heart swell.

By heaven, how I love this woman!

His step faltered. He hadn't actually told her yet. Not in so many words. He wanted to do so now, but although the land was shadowed with the gloom of the short, summer night, he knew as well as anyone how sound carried on the still air. He had no idea who might be in these hills and any noise could bring them dangerous and unwanted attention. Silence would serve them best now; the words would keep until a more suitable moment.

Maddie could see the faint gleam of water ahead. She felt as if she had been walking all night, but it could only have been an hour or so.

'Loch Tonnan,' murmured Grant. 'Not long now.'

They soon found the small tavern and scratched upon the door. A thin, stooping figure appeared and ushered them inside. Maddie listened while Grant and the man conducted a hushed conversation in Gaelic. When they had finished, Grant explained to her that the French ship had been seen but had withdrawn, out of sight, for safety and would not return until evening. The exchange continued and she listened anxiously.

'What is it?' she asked Grant. 'What is he saying now, is anything wrong?'

'Not at all. You are expected. There is a room here for you until the French agent comes to take you to the ship.'

Somehow that did not tally with the length and tone of the interchange she had heard.

'And what about you?'

He hesitated. 'Only one room was bespoke, because that was the instruction received from your father. The landlord has no other rooms free. There is no need to fret, I shall find lodgings elsewhere.'

Madeleine heard his calm assurance, but did not believe it.

'I doubt there is another hostelry in such a small place and, even if there is, we do not want to announce our presence here.'

She stopped and drew in a breath, summoning up her courage for her next words.

'One room is all we would require. If we were man and wife.'

Grant was watching her closely. She went on with outward calm.

'A simple handfasting or exchange of vows before witnesses is all that is required for a legal marriage in Scotland, is it not?'

'Why, yes.' Grant raked a hand through his hair. 'But I—'

'Then if we can find witnesses to hear our vows we can be wed. We will find a priest when we get to France, for a more conventional ceremony.'

He looked down at her, his eyes searching her face. 'Are you sure about this, Madeleine?'

She nodded, saying frankly, 'I have wanted it almost since the day I met you.'

'Think, madam.' He placed his hands on her shoulders. 'There is no going back. The vows taken and signed before witnesses are binding for life.'

'I am surer of this than anything I have done before,' she told him, echoing his own earlier declaration. 'But only if you are determined to leave Scotland. And only if you want to marry me,' she ended shyly.

'*Want* to marry you!' A smile of pure delight lit up his face. 'Madam, it is the dearest wish of my heart!'

Chapter Sixteen

It took a few moments to explain to the landlord what was required and he immediately summoned his wife to join them. That good lady was at first shocked at the idea of a bride dressed in men's clothes and although she was at last persuaded of the necessity, she insisted upon carrying Madeleine away to tidy herself before the ceremony, while their host went off in search of paper and ink to record the marriage.

Through the taproom window, Grant saw that the summer sun was already lightening the eastern sky, painting it a rich pink, shot with gold. Soon the world would be awake. Another hour or so and customers might start to arrive at the inn. The landlord came back carrying pens and an old broadsheet, which he apologetically explained was the only spare piece of paper he could put his hands on. Grant was about to send him off to hurry the womenfolk when they returned.

Madeleine came up to him. She had removed her tricorne and brushed out her hair so that the curls hung down her back in a lustrous black wave.

'Well, sir,' she said, smiling shyly, 'shall we begin?'

* * *

They made their vows as the low morning sun filled the taproom with a golden light. The atmosphere was as hushed and reverent as any church, but when Madeleine thought they had finished the landlady spoke up.

'And ye'll be needin' a ring for the bride,' she declared, holding one out to Grant. 'I am sorry 'tis such a poor wee thing, just a pewter posy ring that belonged to my mother, God rest her soul, but ye can have it, with my blessing, until ye can buy a finer one for your lady.'

Grant thanked her and offered to pay for it, but the landlady resolutely refused, saying she would be glad to see it put to good use.

'You are very kind,' exclaimed Madeleine. 'I assure you this means more to me than anything money can buy.'

'With this ring, I thee wed.'

Grant murmured the words as he slipped the small pewter band on to her finger and she blinked rapidly as he carried her hand to his lips.

The landlord produced a sheet of paper, which Maddie noticed contained the words to a ribald ballad on the other side. This caused no little amusement, but they all duly signed their names and the landlord declared the marriage legal.

He then insisted they drink a glass of *uisge beatha* to toast the new bride before commanding his wife to mop up her tears and show the wedded couple to their room.

Alone at last with his bride, Grant glanced about at the sparsely furnished room.

'Not quite what I would have wished for our wedding night,' he remarked, hoping to ease the tension that was palpable in the stillness. He waved towards the canopied bed in the corner. 'But at least we have somewhere to sleep.'

Madeleine was still standing just inside the door, nervously twisting the wedding band round and round on her finger. He went over and took her hands.

'You are nervous, Maddie, but it is not too late, if you have changed your mind. I had never thought to aspire to your hand and even now I cannot let you make that sacrifice without asking you again if you are sure.'

'I am, Grant. I am sure. I have always known that my only real value to Papa is as a bride, once he can find someone to pay his price. I am no longer willing to let that happen. I want to make my own choice.' She slipped her hands around his neck. 'I have *made* my choice.'

Grant's breath caught in his throat as she pulled his head down towards her. Their lips met and she melted against him. It felt so natural, so *right*. Her fingers tangled in his hair as she responded to him, returning his kiss with a passion that sent the blood pounding around his body.

Madeleine was shy, but not coy, and Grant was determined not to rush her. They undressed each other, slowly, between long, languorous kisses, then he swept her up and carried her to the bed.

He measured his length against her, his hands caressing, exploring, revelling in her soft, smooth skin and luscious curves.

Maddie followed his lead, quickly learning that her touch could make him gasp or groan with pleasure. Growing bolder, she pushed him on to his back and sat up, gazing at his body, naked save for the bandage about his arm. She touched it gently and glanced towards him.

He smiled and shook his head. 'It doesn't hurt much now,' he said, answering her unspoken question.

'I am glad.' Her eyes moved on, taking in the faint scars of older wounds, the toned muscles. He was strong, but sleek as a panther. And most evidently aroused. Her throat dried.

I have caused this, she thought, excitement pooling low in her body. *I am his wife and he* wants *me*.

She reached out and began to explore his naked skin, cautiously at first, her hands skimming over the hard contours of his chest, pushing her fingers through the shield of dark hair. She heard the hiss of his breath as her hand travelled lower.

'Easy!' He grabbed her wrist. 'Too much of that and it will be over before I have even started!'

She gave a low laugh, revelling in her power over him. With a sudden twist he flipped her over and trapped her beneath him.

'My turn,' he murmured.

He trailed kisses over her face, her eyelids, cheeks, his lips moving along the line of her jaw and down her neck. Maddie closed her eyes, enjoying every sensation. Her skin tingled where his mouth had been, she felt on fire, her bones molten. His head moved down to her breasts which suddenly felt full and taut, aching for his kiss. He obliged, suckling first one hard nub and then the other, drawing a response from deep within her. She yearned for him, her insides felt as if they were unfurling as his roving fingers slipped between her thighs and the dual onslaught was almost more than she could bear. She groaned, her body shifting restlessly against his fingers. Then, suddenly, he was inside her, moving slowly, relentlessly and her body responded. Waves of pure pleasure rippled through her, building slowly. She began to move against him, tilting her hips as he plunged into her, faster, deeper. She arched her back and writhed beneath him as feelings so intense shuddered through her and she feared she would faint. She was out of control and even as he shouted aloud and made his final, hard thrust into her she was rocked by wave after wave of feelings so strong that her mind splintered. She was flying, soaring, falling, all conscious thought suspended.

They were both breathing hard. Grant held her close until she had stopped trembling, then he rolled off to lie beside her.

'I am sorry if I hurt you,' he said, reaching for her hand. 'I know, the first time, it can be painful.'

'I barely felt it.'

She smiled up into the shadowed bed canopy above them. It was true. Pleasure had quite eclipsed any slight discomfort. She felt sated, peaceful. They slipped between the covers and when she woke some time later she found his body curled around hers. She closed her eyes again, smiling. Surely, there could be no greater pleasure on this earth.

It was shortly after noon when they were woken by a sharp knocking on the door of their bedchamber. Grant slipped out of bed and threw on his shirt. Maddie heard the innkeeper's voice, low and urgent. She sat up, pulling the sheets up to her chin and waiting nervously for Grant to explain.

'What is it?' she asked him, as he closed the door upon their host. 'What has happened?'

'Dragoons, approaching through the glen. They are searching the houses and farms as they go. It will not be long before they reach here. We must move quickly.'

They dressed hurriedly and were soon ready to leave. The innkeeper hustled them out of the door, pointing out their route.

'Quickly now,' he said. 'Follow the loch for about a mile until you come to a small bothy close to the shore. Your man will be waiting there for ye. He will row you out to the French ship as soon as she arrives. Go now. If anyone asks me, I have never seen ye!'

He waved them away and they hurried off along a rough track, the hot sun shining down upon them from a cloudless blue sky. The inn was soon lost to sight, but Maddie kept glancing back, fearing at any moment to see the colourful uniforms of soldiers behind them.

At last they came upon a small stone-built hut with a turf roof and two shuttered windows, one each side of a wooden door. Grant approached cautiously and knocked softly on the door. They heard the click of a latch being lifted and a deep, gruff voice sounded from the darkness within.

'Get in quickly, both of ye, and shut the door.'

Grant went first, but as he stepped into the shuttered room some presentiment of danger made him reach for his sword. It was already too late, the light from the doorway was glinting off the barrels of two deadly pistols, both pointing at his chest. He reached back to push Maddie behind him, shielding her with his body, then he looked at the stocky figure holding the weapons and his lip curled.

'Ewan Cowie. I thought I recognised that voice.'

Chapter Seventeen

Ewan Cowie waved them away from the door and locked it, imprisoning them in a murky twilight. Grant kept his hand on the hilt of his sword, even though it would be little use against the pistols aimed at him.

'My dear,' he drawled, 'allow me to present to you my neighbour, Ewan Cowie of Contullach.' He added, his tone dripping with derision, 'By heaven, the Prince's cause is desperate if he must employ the likes of you.'

'Be damned to you, Grant Rathmore!'

Cowie's bearded face had contorted with hatred. He controlled himself, but the smile that succeeded the snarl was even more chilling. 'When I heard who was escorting the Frenchwoman, I knew my prayers had been answered. Now I shall be avenged for my Jamie's death.'

'He died in battle, not by my hand.'

'Aye, but who encouraged him to go, eh, Rathmore? Who persuaded him to skulk away in the night, with never a word to me?'

'Jamie was the one who persuaded *me*,' snapped

Grant. 'I wanted no part in the business and thought I could turn him back. Did his friends not tell you when they returned?' He lip curled even more. 'No, they would be too afraid to defend a Rathmore against you, Ewan Cowie, isn't that so?'

'Not that I should have believed them, whatever they said. Damned traitors.'

'Yes, you handed them over to the army, I hear. They were not only Jacobite soldiers, but your own people. How will that sit with your French paymasters?'

'That need not worry you, Rathmore. Your fate was sealed when you persuaded Jamie to fight.'

'That's a lie and you know it, Cowie. Deep down you know Jamie was the headstrong one, not I.'

'You were too frightened to go alone! Pshaw! You have too much of your father's cowardly Sassenach blood in you to make a soldier!'

Grant held on to his temper by a thread.

'I stayed and fought,' he bit out. 'Even after bloody Culloden, I stayed until word came that it was every man for himself.'

'But why should *you* live,' Cowie shouted at him, 'why should you live when my Jamie is dead?'

'He was my *friend*. Do you not think I grieve for him, too?' Grant added bitterly, 'Is it not enough for you that I can never go back to Ardvarrick?'

'But your father will know you are alive in the world whereas I—' For a brief moment Grant saw something akin to real grief flicker across Ewan Cowie's bewhiskered face. 'No, Grant Rathmore. You shall die, then your damned father will feel the same pain I do. He will feel it even more, once he knows how you disgraced his name.'

'No!' Madeleine had listened in shocked silence to the exchange, but now she moved out from behind Grant and addressed Ewan Cowie. 'My father is paying you for your services and he has promised you much more, has he not, once we are safely aboard the French ship?'

'Once *you* are safely aboard, *mam'selle*. Nothing was said about Rathmore.'

She moved closer to Grant. 'But I will not go without him.'

'Oh, yes, you will. There's a king's ransom on that ship, for the Prince's cause, and it will not be released until you are safely on board.' He scowled. 'This is the very ship that delivered you and your father to Scotland last year and the Captain remembers you. I cannot fob him off with any other woman.'

Grant snorted in derision. 'What an honourable man you are to even think of that, Ewan Cowie.'

'Shut your mouth, Rathmore!' He turned again to Madeleine. 'There's twine for mending the fishing nets on that hook in the wall, *mam'selle*. You'll use it to tie Rathmore's wrists behind his back.'

'I shall do no such thing.'

'Well, that is a pity, because the alternative is for me to put a bullet through his black heart. You wouldn't want me to do that, now would you? And you…' He turned to snarl again at Grant. 'Don't think I wouldn't shoot the woman. If you want her unharmed, then you'll make no attempt to resist me.'

Madeleine was looking mutinous.

Grant said quietly, 'You had best do as he says.'

Reluctantly, she fetched the twine. Cowie insisted

they both turn so that what light there was filtering through the cracks in the shutters fell upon Grant's wrists and he watched as she bound them, ordering her to pull the cord tighter, until he could see that it was biting into the flesh. Then, with a grunt of satisfaction Cowie moved towards the inner door. Madeleine's nerves were already at breaking point and she felt sick with fear as Ewan Cowie opened the door and stepped back, brandishing the pistols menacingly.

'Through here, Rathmore, and you follow him, *mam'selle.*'

The second room was also shuttered. Two bound and dishevelled figures were sitting on the floor against the wall, each one gagged with their own neckcloth. Maddie gasped.

'Colonel Sowton! Major!' She stopped and turned to glare at Ewan Cowie. 'What is the meaning of this?'

'Don't waste your pity on them, *mam'selle*, they are the enemy and would prevent you sailing for France, if they could.'

He motioned to Grant to sit down beside the officers and ordered Madeleine to strap his ankles together.

'There are Dragoons searching the village now,' she said when she had finished. 'When they come here—'

Cowie shrugged and tucked one of the pistols into his belt. 'It will take them a while to cover all the buildings there and along the shore before they come this way. By then we shall be long gone.'

'And how did you snare these two?' Grant inclined his head towards the officers.

'The army had learned of the shipment of gold and sent a troop here to intercept it. Fortunately, the Captain got wind of it and stood off, out of sight. These two strayed a little too far from their camp and I took them prisoner.'

Behind his gag, the Major made a muffled growling protest and shifted angrily.

Grant gave a snort of derision. 'If I know you, Cowie, 'twas you who was their informant. Playing both sides.'

He saw the Major nod, confirming his suspicions.

'And why not?' Cowie jeered.

'Why not indeed. I'd even wager that you have no intention of sending the gold on to the Prince or his supporters.'

'His cause is lost. And the Jacobites owe me something for my son's life. Enough now, time is going on. Come, madam, I have two horses waiting. Collect your bag and I will escort you to the rendezvous.'

'No.' Maddie jumped to her feet and placed her hand on Grant's shoulder. 'I'll not leave until I know what you intend to do here.'

Grant saw Cowie's eyes fall to Madeleine's fingers, watched him walk forward and grab her hand, staring at the ring.

'Unhand my wife, sir!'

In response Cowie laughed, tugged Maddie to him and kissed her. With a cry she pushed him off and struck him hard across the cheek, regardless of the pistol her attacker was still holding.

Grant's blood ran cold. He strained against the cords at his wrists but could do no more than watch, helpless as Cowie threw Madeleine away from him, sending her sprawling against the pile of netting stacked in the corner.

'Your wife, is it, Rathmore? Does Ardvarrick know how low his heir has sunk, to marry a traitorous French slut!'

Inwardly Grant raged, but he would not let it show. Instead he said coldly, 'Have a care, Cowie. Your French Captain might take exception if the lady's not delivered to him safely. He might well withhold the gold.'

Thankfully, his words struck home.

'You are right.' Cowie grunted. 'There is no time to teach her manners. Come, madam. We are leaving. Now.'

Madeleine glared at him. 'I have told you, I want to know what will happen to these men.'

'Och, ye need not fret. The soldiers will find them and release them, in due course.'

Grant knew his old neighbour too well to believe that. Cowie would ensure there were no witnesses to his perfidy.

'No.' Madeleine scrambled over to Grant and clung to him. 'I'll not leave you here!'

Grant closed his eyes, beating down the frustration that he could not take her in his arms. The only way he could save her was to make her leave.

'You must go, Madeleine. Your father has organised your safe passage, you must go to him.'

She clung even tighter and whispered against him, 'Grant, I love you.'

The words were like a knife in his heart. He turned his head and nuzzled her neck, speaking quickly into her ear.

'You can do no good here. If you want to help me,

you must get safely to France. Then you can write to my father, tell him what happened here.'

If there is anyone left alive by then to care about me. If the army has not arrested my father, turned everyone out of doors and torched the houses.

'Enough of this maudlin stuff,' snapped Cowie. 'Do not delay me any longer, madam. The Captain should be even now waiting on the shore for us, ready to hand over the gold to me once I have delivered you. Mark me, woman, if you won't ride with me willingly, I will strap you unconscious to the saddle!'

Grant saw the stormy look in Madeleine's eyes and spoke sharply, afraid she might resist.

'Get thee gone, madam. I have told you, you can do no good here.'

Madeleine climbed slowly to her feet. Grant did not struggle when Cowie stuffed a cloth into his mouth and gagged him. For Madeleine's sake he must not falter now. If she thought he would not survive he knew she would refuse to leave and he could not bear to have her death on his conscience, too.

Cowie grabbed Maddie's arm. 'Quickly now, collect your bag and let us get you to your French friends.'

Reluctantly she went with him, stopping at the door for a last look back at Grant. He closed his eyes, but her face was engraved upon his eyelids. It would be his last view of Madeleine and he would take her wounded, anguished gaze with him to his grave.

The door closed between them, he heard the rattle of the outer door, the rustle of departing footsteps and then silence. He sat still in the gloomy half-light, listening to the grunts and snuffles from the two officers, but their gags made it impossible for any of them to speak. All they could do was make themselves as comfortable as possible and await their fate.

Grant had no idea how long it was before Ewan Cowie returned, but he thought it could be no more than a couple of hours. Cowie would not have risked leaving them all alive if there was any danger that they might be discovered. The Major stirred as the outer door opened. He turned his head to stare at Grant, but, gagged as they were, communication was impossible. The inner door swung open and Cowie came in. He walked over to Grant and pulled the cloth from his mouth.

'You knew I'd be back to finish this,' he snarled.

Grant regarded him with contempt. 'The only reason you are doing this alone is to have no witnesses to murder. Let me see, knowing you so well, I would say that you are going to keep the French gold for yourself and somehow put the blame for everything on to me.'

'There now, you have the right of it, Grant Rathmore. It is pleasing to think your arrival has made my plan so much more plausible. Originally, I should have had to hand the French gold over to the army and make do with the pittance the Frenchie was prepared to pay me for saving his daughter, but now I can have it all. I shall tell everyone that you shot the officers before I managed to kill you.'

There was a grunt of protest from the Colonel, but it was ignored. Grant kept his eyes fixed on Cowie.

He said, 'That will not explain the gold.'

'Och, your men escaped to the hills with it. Desperate rogues every one. I couldna' stop them.'

'And you think anyone will believe that?'

'Of course they will. I have been unswerving in my loyalty to King George during the uprising, even disowning my own son.'

'So, you turned against your own to save your skin!'

'Jamie is dead, thanks to you,' Cowie spat. 'I couldn't help him, nor any of them.'

'Tom Graham and young Fraser Reid? Poor wretches. They are nothing but boys and you have given them up to the army.'

'I couldn't risk them staying at Contullach.'

'You always were a rogue, Ewan Cowie. My mother and yours tried to bring our families closer, but Mother was always wary of you, even if you are her kinsman.'

'What care I for her opinion? I was content to be a peaceful neighbour to Ardvarrick while it was in my interests to do so, but I never liked Jamie's friendship with you. I might hate the British for killing him, but not as much as I hate your family and all you stand for, Grant Rathmore.' That hatred now blazed out from his eyes. 'Why Jamie took such a fancy to you I never knew. He was the better fighter. He could always beat you in a wrestling match. And he was a better shot, too.'

'I don't deny it,' murmured Grant. Jamie had always hated to lose.

Cowie gave a sudden howl of rage. 'It should have been *you* killed in battle, Rathmore. It should have been your body lying at Culloden, not his! You were the one meant to die, cut down by the English.'

Grant almost pitied him. 'Anyone would think you had planned it.'

'I did.' Cowie dragged his hand across his mouth to wipe away the spittle. 'I did plan it. I saw a way to get back at your father after all these years, to rob him of his only son and disgrace his name. I knew you'd never disobey your father and join the rebels. Jamie told me you were reluctant to go, that's why I gave him the poppy juice and told him to play along with ye, to make ye think they'd all turn back before the sticking point. I wanted to see your father's face when I told him—'

'Wait!' Grant sat up straighter. 'What was that about poppy juice? What did you mean?'

'If strong ale didn't give ye the courage to sign up as a soldier, I told Jamie to put it in your drink. One way or another I wanted you in the Prince's army.'

'So that was your design all along,' muttered Grant. 'I never had any chance of dissuading Jamie and the others. You *wanted* him to fight.'

Cowie sneered at him. 'Of course he had to fight. I ordered him to go. I had to make sure Contullach and all my lands were safe, if the Stuart won the day. As it is, the Prince is fleeing for his life and the British see me as a most loyal supporter of King George.'

'When in fact you are a traitor to both sides.'

Cowie bared his teeth. 'But the only people who know that are in this room, Rathmore. And you will all soon be dead.'

He drew the pistols from his belt. Grant sat back, feigning interest, putting off the inevitable.

'Tell me, just how do you mean to carry this off?'

'One shot each to despatch these English vermin, then I shall run you through with your own sword. Once I have removed all the ropes, I shall press the spent pistols into your hands and when the soldiers arrive, they will see immediately what has happened here—' He broke off, throwing back his head and listening intently. 'What was that?'

A faint knocking on the outer door, and a whining voice begging entry.

'It is a beggar,' hissed Grant. 'If we keep quiet, they will soon go away.'

At least, he prayed they would, for he knew Cowie would not hesitate to add another murder to his tally.

The knocking sounded again. Stronger this time and it elicited a muttered curse from Ewan Cowie. He pushed the pistols back into his belt, drew out his dirk and left the room. The Major grunted against his gag and drummed his heels. Grant appreciated the effort, but the floor was nothing more than packed earth and he knew the sound would not carry far enough to warn the vagrant of his fate.

The three bound men kept very still, listening hard. Grant heard the metallic rattle of the latch followed by an angry voice, a grunt, then silence. The little room suddenly seemed airless, the shadows thick with menace as the inner door swung open.

'Madeleine!' Grant watched her come in, Cowie's dirk in her hand. 'Where is he?'

'Outside. I hit him as hard as I could on the back of his head. He is unconscious, but I do not think I have killed him.'

Maddie was aware that her voice was shaking, almost as much as her hand as she quickly sawed through the cord on Grant's wrists.

'Why aren't you on that ship?' he demanded, watching her work. 'How did you get here?'

'When I saw that rogue ride off, I begged the Captain to row me back to the shore and then I walked. It was not so far; Cowie only really needed the horses to carry the gold. I saw how he looked at you, the hatred in his eyes. I knew he would kill you.'

The knife cut through the last threads and she risked a tremulous smile. 'I am not ready to be a widow just yet.'

She started to untie his ankles, but he stopped her.

'No, no, I can do that. Cut the others loose. Hurry, before Cowie comes round.'

Maddie had only managed to free the Major's hands before they heard a roaring bellow. Cowie burst in, waving his pistols, but Grant was already on his feet. He threw himself at Ewan Cowie, knocking his arms so one weapon discharged harmlessly into a wooden shutter. The other was soon wrestled from his hand and slid into a corner. As soon as Major Rutter was free he piled in, helping Grant to overpower Ewan Cowie and tie him up.

'Well, well, you tricked us finely, madam, and no mistake,' declared Colonel Sowton, when Madeleine removed his gag. 'When we learned there were rebels at work here, I did not think it would be our fellow guests from Calder House.'

'*We* are not rebels,' she retorted, cutting him free and helping him to his feet. 'I am merely trying to make my way to France to join my father, and I paid Mr Rathmore to help me.' She picked up Cowie's pistol from the floor before turning to Grant. 'The Captain has agreed to wait another hour before setting sail.'

'You cannot let them escape,' shrieked Cowie, struggling against his bonds. 'The whore is a French woman, an enemy!'

'Insulting the lady will not help you, Cowie!' barked the Major.

'And he is Grant Rathmore, a Jacobite. He fought with the rebels.'

'And he has just saved your lives!' Madeleine came to stand beside Grant, levelling her pistol at the two officers. 'Ewan Cowie planned to murder you, not us, and you have him safe now. Also, his horses are outside with the French gold stowed in his saddlebags. Surely that is enough to buy our freedom?'

She glanced at Grant, who nodded. 'We ask only that you allow us time to board the ship.'

'And if we do not agree, you will kill us,' said Major Rutter.

'I am no murderer,' Grant retorted. 'We will leave you here as prisoners, until your soldiers arrive.'

'Now, now, I do not see there is any need for such measures,' put in Colonel Sowton, who appeared to have regained most of his customary bonhomie. 'As *mademoiselle* has said, we have the traitor and the gold. A very satisfactory result, wouldn't you say, Major Rutter?'

The Major considered for a moment. 'From everything I have just heard, I admit I am more inclined to trust Grant Rathmore than the other one.'

Cowie gave a howl of rage.

'You would reward him for being a traitor!' His manner changed and he added in a wheedling tone, 'Ardvarrick is a prosperous estate. Think how pleased King George would be with you for adding such a jewel to his wealth.'

Madeleine saw the flicker of distaste on the Major's face, but it was the Colonel who responded.

'His Majesty might well be pleased,' he said sharply, 'but he will be even happier to know he has supporters he can depend upon in the Highlands. You have proved yourself to be a rogue, sir. I would rather trust Grant Rathmore to uphold the future peace in this country than you.' He gave Cowie one final, contemptuous glance and turned to smile at Grant.

'We will make out our report in your favour, Mr Rathmore. I believe I have sufficient influence in the right quarters to guarantee you a full pardon. And furthermore, before we part today, I shall make sure you are granted safe passage back to Ardvarrick.'

Glancing up at Grant, Madeleine saw the relief and delight in his countenance.

He bowed. 'You are very good Colonel.'

'But, mind you, we shall expect you to play your part as the Laird's son. Uphold the law and keep your people out of trouble.'

'I will do my utmost, you have my word on that.'

'Capital! The Crown needs reliable, trustworthy people in these parts, ain't that so, Rutter? I might see my way to inviting you to London, too. Put in a word for you at Court, you know. There could even be honours in it.'

Madeleine listened in growing dismay. What might Grant not achieve if he found favour at the English Court? But not with a penniless wife beside him. What had Ewan Cowie called her? A French slut. She was not quite that, but she was the daughter of a schemer, an itinerant gambler. When London society discovered her background and her birth, they would turn their backs on her. And on Grant. He did not deserve that.

Grant stared at the Colonel, hardly able to believe what he was hearing. He questioned him closely and looked to the Major for his confirmation that a pardon was almost guaranteed. Ardvarrick was safe and no blame for his actions would taint his family. He could not have dreamed of such an outcome.

Ewan Cowie interrupted several times, trying to throw suspicion upon him with ever more false and preposterous claims, but neither officer paid any heed to his rantings.

'It is settled,' concluded Major Rutter. 'As soon as our men arrive, we can arrange an escort for you to Ardvarrick. The gold will be taken to Edinburgh, as will Ewan Cowie. He will stand trial there.'

'Then it is only left for me to beg your pardon for our deceiving you at Calder House,' said Grant.

'As to that, I can understand why you considered it necessary,' replied the Colonel, all genial rationality. 'And there is no denying the presence of the young lady added considerably to the pleasure of our stay, eh, Rutter?'

'She was a delightful house guest with a well-informed mind,' agreed the Major, smiling slightly.

'Aye. 'Tis a pity she ain't here now to hear our...'

Grant swung around. He remembered Madeleine murmuring to him, excusing herself, saying she was going to find the privy. But surely that was some time ago? A cold chill ran down his spine and he hurried to the outer room.

Madeleine's red leather purse was on the window sill and from beneath it peeped a fold of paper. It was the frontispiece from *Robinson Crusoe* and his foreboding increased as he snatched it up. There was a single line, hastily written in pencil.

I release you from your vows.

Chapter Eighteen

Madeleine sat on the bunk of the small cabin, huddled inside her cloak and shivering, not so much from cold as misery.

She had reached the shore just as the sailors were putting barrels of fresh water into the last of the boats and sent up a prayer of thanks that she was not too late to board the French ship. Grant could not follow her here. She was safe to return to her homeland and her father.

The thought did not fill her with joy, but she had to go somewhere. She would not stay. She had already decided that she would return to Tante Élisabeth until she could sell the sapphires and what was left of her mother's jewels and set up her own establishment.

But you will inevitably dwindle into an old maid, like your aunt.

No! Whatever happened she would not do that. She would not become a dowdy spinster to be pitied and ridiculed by those younger and wealthier. She might travel the world. If she did not marry, then she would be considered an eccentric, but would that be so very bad? She might even be fêted in society for her peculiar ways.

That would be bearable, perhaps, but it would never make up for losing Grant.

Grant. The very thought of him was like a knife twisting in her stomach, but it was for the best that she had left him. If the Jacobites had won the day, then the war between France and Britain would have ended, but for now at least that dream was over. Grant was heir to Ardvarrick and the last thing he needed was a French wife to hold him back and throw any doubt upon his loyalty to the Crown.

Maddie had heard him talk of his home, seen the way his face softened when he spoke of it. At such times he looked so much younger and she glimpsed the boy he had once been. He loved Ardvarrick and would soon take up his old life there. He would forget her and find a good, eligible woman to be his bride. Someone other than her to stand with him, shoulder to shoulder against the world.

It was too much. Tears welled up and with a cry she threw herself down upon the hard bunk, but even now she was not allowed to indulge in her misery. There was a knock upon the door and a tentative voice called to her.

'Mademoiselle d'Evremont, the Captain wishes you to join him on deck. *Immédiatement, s'il vous plaît.*'

'*Oui. Je viendrai.*' She scrabbled for her handkerchief and wiped her eyes.

Papa was an adventurer, a gambler and a soldier of fortune, she reminded herself, buttoning her coat. He never cowered away, wallowing in self-pity. It was time to show she was her father's daughter.

She straightened her shoulders and left the cabin.

The Captain was waiting to help her up the final few steps to the deck.

'A thousand pardons, *mademoiselle*, but there is a man…'

Grant! She shrank away, looking about her nervously.

'No, no, he is not on board,' the Captain assured her. 'He is on the water. In a boat very small and he is alone.'

'I will not speak to him. I am going back to my cabin. Pray tell him to leave this instant.'

'Alas, he is a man most determined, *mademoiselle*. He insists upon speaking with you.'

'And I have said I shall not see him.' She almost stamped her foot. 'Pray set sail, Captain, as you had planned.'

'*C'est impossible.*'

'I do not see why. He cannot follow us in a little boat.'

The Captain gazed at her for a moment, then spread his hands. 'Come, *mademoiselle*, you must see for yourself my dilemma.'

He led her to the side rail and she was obliged to stand on tiptoe to peer over. There below her was Grant, the painter of his rowing boat secured to the anchor cable of the great ship.

'He refuses to come aboard,' explained the Captain. '*Mais*, if we raise the anchor, then his *petit bateau* will come with it.'

At that moment Grant looked up at her, his hat tipped back on his head at a rakish angle, and Maddie's heart turned over.

'Please go,' she called down to him. 'I left you a note.'

'I know. And defaced a perfectly good book in the process.'

She had no time for his foolery.

'I am going to France,' she told him. 'I am going to join my father.'

'You cannot leave. You are my wife.'

'I told you, I release you from your vows.'

'Ah, but I do not release you from *yours*. I explained to you most carefully the vows are binding.'

The Captain had retired to a discreet distance, but she was very much aware that a number of officers were on deck and several sailors were in the rigging, watching and listening to their exchange. She had no idea how many of them spoke English, but she thought it must be pretty clear what was going on. Her cheeks burned with mortification.

'Things have changed,' she said.

'We promised to be husband and wife, for better or worse.' He looked up at her. 'I would have thought my being pardoned and heir to Ardvarrick would be considered by most to be for the better.'

'You do not understand. I am a Frenchwoman. Our countries are at war.'

'*That* has not changed from when you married me.'

'But then you were a vagabond,' she said desperately. 'You had no home, no prospects. We were going to roam the world together.'

'And we can still, if that is what you want.'

'You are the heir to Ardvarrick. Go home, Grant. Your family needs you.'

She heard a few mutters of approval from the rigging, but Grant made no move.

'That may be so,' he agreed. The light died from his face—he suddenly looked very serious. 'But I need *you*, Madeleine. I need you to be part of that family, to stand with me, to help me rebuild my life at Ardvarrick.'

Tears welled up, misting her eyes.

'Go away, Grant,' she said brokenly. 'Untie your boat and leave here.'

'I cannot do that.'

'Ooh, you—you stupid, *obstinate* man!' she cried. 'Go now or I swear I will order the Captain to set sail and leave you to your fate!'

'I mean I cannot row back,' he called up to her. 'My injured arm, you see. It is too weak, I am too tired to row back alone.'

She did not believe him for one moment and closed her lips firmly against any reply.

'Very well, madam, if you will not come back with me, then I must climb aboard and come to France with you.'

From the muttering around her Maddie knew at least some of the crew understood what he was saying and her consternation grew.

'You cannot! You would be an exile.'

'I would rather be an exile with you than live here without my heart.'

There was a shout of 'Bravo!' from the rigging and she felt her cheeks burn even hotter.

Grant continued, 'I cannot remember if I ever told you how much I love you, Madeleine, but I am telling you now.' Even at the distance between them she could feel the power of his eyes upon her, the tug of a bond so strong she thought it might drag her heart from her chest. 'I love you with all my heart and all my soul, dearest. I cannot live without you.'

Grant stood up and the little boat rocked dangerously. He caught hold of the anchor cable.

'Well, Wife, what is it to be? Do I come to you, or will you come back with me to Ardvarrick?'

She heard a gentle cough from the Captain, who had moved up to stand beside her.

'I regret that I must hurry you, madam, but we must go now. The tide, you see…'

Madeleine stared at him for a long moment, then she raised her chin.

'Then if your men would be good enough to lower me over the side, Captain, I will join my husband.'

Madeleine's male attire made the manoeuvre much simpler than if she had been wearing hooped skirts, but it was accomplished amid much laughter and cheering and any number of ribald comments that Madeleine refused to acknowledge. Once she was seated in the little boat the Captain dropped her saddlebags down to her.

'I have taken the liberty of putting in there a letter from your father, madam. He instructed me to give it to you once we were under sail, but in the circumstances…' He spread his hands and shrugged before turning to address Grant. 'And you, *m'sieur*. I wish you and your lady *bonne chance*.'

Grant showed no signs of fatigue or distress as he rowed to the shore and once they had dragged the small boat up on to the beach Madeleine turned to glare at him, a martial light in her eye.

'Your arm is not troubling you at all! I should have ordered the Captain to weigh anchor and left you to your fate!'

'Why did you not do so?'

'I was afraid you would drown.'

He smiled. 'Devil a bit. I learned to swim almost as soon as I could walk.'

Maddie gave a little hiss of frustration. She was torn between indignation and laughter and, unable to look him in the eye without giving herself away, she pulled her saddlebags to her and marched off, leaving Grant to secure the boat.

She made her way to a small rocky shelf and sat down to wait for him. Remembering her father's letter, she pulled it out of her bag and began to read it.

'Maddie?' Grant ran the last few yards to her, alarmed by her pallor. 'What is it, my love, what is wrong?'

'Papa.' She held out the letter with a shaking hand. Grant took it and quickly scanned the contents.

'I thought it was lies,' she whispered, her eyes wide and unfocused. 'I thought it was all part of his bluff and bluster, but he really is a *comte* now.'

'It would appear so,' murmured Grant, frowning over the elaborate script.

'I was wrong about him, I thought him nothing but a fraud.'

'From what you have told me, his behaviour gave you no reason to think anything else.'

'True, but I should have trusted him. I should have

believed in him more.' She sucked in a breath. 'A *comte*. A nobleman. *Papa!*'

Maddie was still staring into space and Grant sat down beside her.

'Does it make a difference?' he asked, reaching for her hand. 'Would you rather have gone to France?' He glanced up to see the ship was already moving out of the loch. 'It is too late to recall the longboat, but French merchantmen often dock at Ardvarrick. I have no doubt we can arrange a passage for you, if that is what you want.'

'No. No, I do not want that at all.'

She clung to him and the profound sense of relief he felt at her words made him realise how much he had been dreading her answer.

She clung to his hands. 'You have read his letter, you see Papa also says that he has taken a wife.' She laughed, albeit shakily. 'It appears he has won his widowed *Comtesse* after all.'

'So, everything ends happily.'

'Happily!' She tore the letter from his grasp and stuffed it back into her bag, then she jumped up and began to stride back and forth.

'Happily?' she repeated. 'He tells me *nothing*, rides off, leaves me in a war-torn country to fend for myself, to face innumerable dangers and to make myself *sick* with worry, thinking him in all sorts of danger, and all the while he is in France, winning for himself a title and a very rich wife!'

Grant was relieved to see her spirit returning. He walked over to her.

'To be fair, my love, it is most likely this new-found

fortune that allowed him to arrange your passage back to France.'

'What?' She spun round, staring at him.

'He did try to save you, when all is said and done.'

He watched the colour ebb and flow from her cheeks, saw her glorious eyes flash dangerously.

'Oh, yes, I should have known you would defend him, Grant Rathmore. Ha! Men are the same the world over. You go off to war, plan your schemes without a *thought* for the defenceless women you leave behind to worry for you—'

He gave a shout of laughter.

'Defenceless? That I will not allow. Who was it duped those Dragoons out of their ill-gotten gains, battered I don't know how many soldiers over the head and ended by turning up sweet an English colonel?'

He caught her hands, twisting them behind her back and holding her close against him.

'Now lower those hackles and tell me you love me.'

'I don't,' she lashed out, her eyes sparkling. 'I hate you.'

'Do you?' His grip tightened. 'Tell me truthfully now.'

He was looking down at her with such a glow in his eyes that her breath caught in her throat and her heart was no longer thudding with rage, but desire.

'Say it.' He pulled her closer. 'Tell me what you really think of me.'

'You're heartless,' she accused him. 'Ruthless! Shameless…'

Her defences were crumbling. The quirk of his lips told her he did not believe a word of it. She stopped struggling.

'Well, dear heart, have you quite finished?'

The tender amusement in his voice whipped up her flagging spirit. She raised her head and gave him a haughty look.

'No, I have not, Grant Rathmore! You are the most arrogant, infuriating Highlander I have ever met. But you are *my* Highlander and, since you have seen fit to hold me to my vows, I will tell you now that I shall hold you to yours, whatever the future holds.'

His smile sent her heart skittering. He brought his head down, capturing her lips in a kiss that left them both breathless.

'Whatever the future holds,' he repeated, trailing kisses across her face. 'I think we can be sure that it will be anything but *dull*.'

She held him off a little.

'We will face it together, my love,' she told him, gazing up into his face. 'And that is what matters.'

Epilogue

'There.' Grant raised his arm and pointed 'There is Ardvarrick.'

They had crested a low hill and, by standing up in her stirrups, Madeleine could see below her the shore of a sea loch. Cattle and sheep grazed peacefully on sloping fields and a collection of dwellings were clustered around a natural harbour, where a tall ship was tied up at the jetty. She followed Grant's outstretched hand to see a large gabled house, the creamy lime-harled walls standing out against the dark green of the wooded hillside behind it.

'Oh, it is beautiful,' she exclaimed. 'I had been expecting something austere and more...grey.'

'A stone castle, perhaps? I am sorry to disappoint you.'

She reached across and caught his arm. 'I am not disappointed. Not at all. Quite the contrary!'

With a laugh Grant pulled her closer, leaning over to kiss her on the mouth.

'Very well. Shall we go on?'

Madeleine looked again at the house, basking in the summer sun. This was Grant's world, his family. She was the stranger, a Frenchwoman arriving in her man's raiment. How would she go on, what would they think of her? Part of her wanted to turn and run but, glancing up at Grant's face, she saw the love shining from his eyes and it warmed her.

She smiled. 'Yes. If you please.'

It did not take them long to reach the house and as they stopped on the drive a servant came bounding out, a beaming smile on his face.

'Master Grant, 'tis yourself returned at last! Welcome home, sir.'

'Thank you, Leith.' Grant dismounted. 'Where are my parents?'

'They are presently in the garden, the south front. I'll away and—'

'No. No need. We will go to them.'

Giving the reins to the butler, he took Madeleine's hand and led her around the side of the house to where a series of terraces led down to a lawn surrounded by colourful flower borders. A dark-haired gentleman was sitting on the lawn, a book in his hand, while a lady in a green gown and a straw bonnet was collecting flowers in a basket.

As they started down the second set of shallow steps the lady turned and saw them. She hesitated for a moment then, with a cry of delight, scissors and basket were cast aside. She picked up her skirts and flew across the lawn.

Her bonnet slipped off as she ran and from the abundance of red hair now displayed Madeleine knew this must be Ailsa, Grant's mother. She released his hand

and watched as he ran forward to catch the lady as she threw herself into his arms.

'Oh, Grant… Grant, is it really you?'

There was no mistaking the love between the two, but Madeleine was watching the gentleman, who had risen from his chair and was walking slowly towards them. His lean face was so like his son's there could be no mistaking that this was Logan Rathmore, but there was no reading the expression in his dark eyes.

'So you have returned.'

Grant gave his mother another kiss and gently released her.

'Aye, Father. I am returned.'

The Laird's serious features relaxed and in a single step he crossed the distance between them and hugged his son.

'Thank God.'

They clung to each other for a long moment. No words were spoken, but none were needed.

'And you have brought a companion.' Ailsa's soft voice broke the long silence. 'Will ye not introduce the young man, my son?'

'Ah.' Grant realised that Madeleine was still standing on the steps, watching the proceedings with an anxious gaze. 'May I present to you Madeleine, formerly Mademoiselle d'Evremont but now Mrs Grant Rathmore. She is my wife, my friend.' He bent a speaking look upon his mother. 'And she is my heart, Mama.'

Ailsa did not let him down. Her face broke into a smile and she hurried towards Madeleine, her arms outstretched.

'You are most welcome, Madeleine, my dear. Mercy, what a lot we will have to talk about!' She caught Maddie's hands and gently led her towards the two men. 'Logan, my love, we have a daughter at last! Are we not blessed?'

Allowing herself to be pulled into the family group, Madeleine glanced nervously at the Laird. Standing so close, she could see faint traces of grey in the dark hair and the lines about his eyes and mouth were more pronounced, but there was only kindness in his smile as he leaned in to kiss her cheek.

'We are indeed. Welcome to Ardvarrick, my dear. Let us go in. We shall tell Leith to fetch up a bottle of our finest French wine. We have a great deal to celebrate!'

Any fears Madeleine had about her reception at Ardvarrick were soon put to flight. Ailsa and Logan were too relieved to see their son to stand on ceremony, so the four of them retired directly to the morning room, where wine and cakes were brought in while Grant and Madeleine told their story.

They were not finished by dinner time, so Ailsa ordered the meal to be delayed while they all went upstairs to change. She carried Madeleine off to her room to find her a gown, showing her so much kindness that Maddie was moved to express her gratitude.

'Away with you,' declared Ailsa, waving aside her thanks. 'From everything I have heard so far, you deserve so much more for bringing our son back to us.'

'No, no, ma'am, he saved *me*!'

Ailsa hugged her. 'You are both very much in love,' she said, smiling mistily. 'You have saved one another, which is how it should be.'

* * *

They dined in style, amid much laughter and chatter, and by the time the ladies withdrew, Grant was in no doubt that the welcome he and Maddie had received was wholehearted and genuine. He refused his father's offer of French brandy and chose instead to take a glass of whisky.

'I believe I will join you,' said Logan, pouring the amber liquid into two glasses. 'And I will raise the glass in thanks that you are safe returned.'

'And I give thanks for your warm welcome.' They savoured the pungent spirit in silence, then Grant spoke again. 'I cannot tell you how sorry I am, Father, for the way I left Ardvarrick...'

'You have explained it all, my son. I do not hold it against you that you tried to protect your friends. I am only sorry for the people of Contullach.'

'So, too, am I,' replied Grant, frowning. 'They do not deserve the retribution that will surely follow.'

'We will do what we can for them, naturally,' said Logan. 'If this Colonel Sowton is as good as his word regarding your pardon and the assurance that Ardvarrick is safe, I shall be in a position to do something for young Reid and Graham. And to speak up for Cowie, too. Perhaps we might avoid a death sentence for him, although God knows he has done little to deserve any mercy.'

He drained his glass and set it down and Grant, wondering how Maddie was getting on without him, refused another drink, saying, 'Shall we join the ladies?'

They walked arm in arm to the drawing room,

where they found Ailsa and Madeleine sitting close together on the sofa, talking quietly.

Logan chuckled. 'You see, my son, we need not have hurried. They have not missed us in the least. They appear to be getting along famously.'

'We are,' declared Ailsa, looking up at them. 'We have discovered we have a great deal in common, including music and a love of books and...oh, a hundred little things. I vow I am delighted with my new daughter.'

Madeleine blushed and thanked her, laughing.

'Well, my son,' remarked Logan. 'Do they not make a delightful picture? I believe we are very fortunate to have made such good marriages.'

Grant looked at the two ladies smiling across at them, his mother a dainty redhead, Maddie no less petite but enchantingly dark, and he nodded.

'Indeed we are, Father,' he said, his heart swelling with love and happiness. 'The luckiest men in the world!'

* * * * *

If you enjoyed this story, be sure to
read the first book in Sarah Mallory's
Lairds of Ardvarrick miniseries

Forbidden to the Highland Laird

And whilst you're waiting for the next book,
why not check out her other great reads

Pursued for the Viscount's Vengeance
His Countess for a Week
The Mysterious Miss Fairchild